# INEVITABLE

## JENNA HARTLEY

D1565672

**ISBN:** 9798729803965

Editing: Lisa A. Hollett
Cover: LJ with Mayhem Cover Creations

*For Dua Lipa.*

*Your music inspires and uplifts me. It makes me smile and want to sing. It makes me dance, even when life gets hard.*

*Your songs (plus a few others by other badass female artists) played in my head as the soundtrack for Jonathan and Sumner's story.*

# PLAYLIST

"Break My Heart" by Dua Lipa
"Fever" by Dua Lipa
"Hallucinate" by Dua Lipa
"Prisoner" (feat. Dua Lipa) by Miley Cyrus
"Hotter Than Hell" by Dua Lipa
"Pretty Please" by Dua Lipa
"Cool" by Dua Lipa
"Boys Will Be Boys" by Dua Lipa
"Just the Same" by Charlotte Lawrence
"Physical" by Dua Lipa
"Lost In Your Light" (Feat. Miguel) by Dua Lipa
"Love Again" by Dua Lipa
"If It Ain't Me" by Dua Lipa
"All the Time" by Zara Larsson
"No Goodbyes" by Dua Lipa
"Don't Start Now" by Dua Lipa
"Never Really Over" by Katy Perry
"Genesis" by Dua Lipa
"Begging" by Dua Lipa
"Be the One" by Dua Lipa

You can find this playlist and more at
https://www.authorjennahartley.com/playlists

# CHAPTER ONE

## Summer

The front door opened then shut, letting in a burst of cold air with it. "Did you finish grading those papers?" Nico asked from the other room, stomping out of his boots.

Not "Hi." Not "How was your day, babe?" But "Did you finish grading those papers?" What he'd failed to add was *for me.* He should really be asking, "Did you finish grading those papers for me?" Because that's what he actually wanted to know.

"Not yet." I gnashed my teeth as he came into the kitchen, lifting the blue books I'd placed neatly on the table. "Can you just—" I huffed, straightening them once more and making sure they covered the stack of mail I'd taken pains to hide.

"Geez. Someone's touchy," he said, hands lifted as if in surrender. "What's for dinner?"

*Are you freaking kidding me?* I glared at him from behind my laptop, ready to pull out my hair at some of the awful answers his students had provided. Now *this?*

"You were supposed to pick something up for us," I said, thinking he was more than capable. He was thirteen years

1

older than me. He'd been living on his own when I was still learning to read.

He tilted his head in confusion, and I let out a deep sigh. Nico took the whole absent-minded professor thing to a new level. At first, it had seemed adorable. Charming, even. But over the past few months, it had started to grate on me.

I had a full load of classes and managed to maintain a 4.0 GPA, all while volunteering at the local women's shelter, applying to grad schools for my MBA, and slowly working on my business plan. And he couldn't even seem to do the bare minimum, like grade his own damn papers.

When he continued to stare at me with a blank expression, I added, "My flight leaves in the morning, and I haven't packed." I was supposed to fly out to LA first, and he'd join me in a few days to spend the holidays with my family.

"Oh." He waved a hand through the air. "Right. I, um, there's something I've been meaning to tell you. I might have forgotten to buy a ticket."

"*Forgot?*" I sputtered, shaking my head in disbelief. "You forgot?"

I felt as if I'd just woken up from a bad dream, grogginess making way for confusion. Disbelief. Why was I even here? Why was I doing this, grading his papers, putting off packing to help him, when he couldn't even do the simplest things in return? Let alone the fact that he'd "forgotten" to buy a plane ticket. No. I didn't buy it.

He wasn't absent-minded; he was self-centered.

He wasn't disorganized; he was a disaster.

And I was enabling him. Oh my god, how had I not seen this before now?

"You'll only be gone a few days, right?" His eye caught on something on the table, and he slid several letters out from beneath the stack of blue books. "What's this?"

2

I gaped at him. "I can't show up by myself. You said you were ready to meet my family. And it's Christmas."

"I just don't think it's the best time. I'm up for tenure, and even though you're no longer my student, it wouldn't be good for optics."

I swayed on my chair. *Optics?* I shook my head. Nico hadn't cared about optics when he'd fucked me in his office.

He held up the envelopes, ignoring my anger and smiling when he saw the one from Wharton. "You got in? Why didn't you tell me, babe?"

Because I was still deciding what *I* wanted to do. Not what Nico thought I should do. Not where my dad thought I should go. But *me*.

In a few months, I was graduating from MIT with honors and a degree in brain and cognitive sciences, yet Nico treated me as if I were incapable of making my own decisions. As if he somehow knew better. Was more intelligent just because he had a few extra letters behind his name.

I stood there, feeling as if I were watching from above. This wasn't me. This wasn't the woman I wanted to be—attached to a guy. Letting him make decisions for both of us. Doing whatever he wanted, while I tagged along.

"Sumner." He stepped closer with a smile, pulling me into his arms. "I'm so proud of you." I stood there awkwardly for a moment before pushing against him. "We should go out to celebrate. How about the Italian place down the street?"

Had he not been listening at all? I was beginning to suspect the answer was no. For instance, how many times had I hinted at my dislike for the Italian place down the street? Their food was flavorless, and the service was awful. The only reason he liked it was because it was cheap. Oh, that, and we weren't likely to run into anyone we knew.

Where had he taken me for my birthday?

*The Italian place.*

Our one-year anniversary?

*The Italian place.*

I could feel my blood pressure rising. He'd taken me to a restaurant I didn't even like. And it hadn't been until days after my birthday, a week after our anniversary. At the time, I'd brushed it off. Made excuses for his behavior. But now...*now*, I was finally seeing things clearly. And I didn't like what I saw.

"I need to pack." I enunciated the words slowly.

"How long can it take? Just throw a few things in your bag. Come on." He grabbed my shoulder, ushering me toward the door.

"No. Stop!" I shouted, surprising both of us with my sudden outburst. I never yelled, rarely even voiced my opinion. "Just *stop*."

I backed away from him. We stared at each other—me panting, him confused.

"You seem stressed, babe."

*You think?* My eyes nearly bugged out of my head. I'd barely slept or eaten, and he couldn't take a moment to think about what I needed? Let alone wanted?

"I'm not going," I finally said.

"We can pick somewhere else if you don't want Italian."

"No." I steeled myself. "I'm not going to Wharton."

As soon as I said the words aloud, I knew they were the right ones. I'd barely admitted it to myself, but I felt calmer. More at peace. And with the admission came a clarity that had been lacking until now.

"Don't be ridiculous," Nico snapped. "Of course, you're going to Wharton. You'd be a fool not to." He stepped closer, tempering his condescension as he always did. "It's all part of our plan." He rubbed my shoulders.

I scoffed, even as my confidence faltered. "No. It's part of *your* plan. Not mine."

He jerked his head back, unaccustomed to that answer from my lips. It felt good. Freeing, and it spurred me on despite my doubts, despite my fears.

"Okay. Okay. Let's talk about this," he said, softening his tone. I could tell he was beginning to realize just how serious I was. "Is this because I shot down your idea for a coaching business? Because I'm just trying to save you from embarrassment and failure. I'm sorry, babe. I don't care how mature you are—no one wants advice from a twenty-three-year-old."

I pressed my lips together, wishing I'd never told him about my dream to start a life coaching business. I was passionate about helping others. And after volunteering at the women's shelter, I wanted to use my skills to empower other women to take charge of their own futures.

It wasn't worth getting into. Not again. "No. It's not about that."

At least not entirely. I couldn't deny that his casual dismissal of my idea hurt. I'd been brainstorming for months, and he'd shut me down without even hearing me out.

"Are you sure? Because I know how you hate—"

"Nico. Stop." I clenched my jaw. The fact that he needed me to explain this to him, meant it was even worse than I'd realized. "I'm done."

"You finished grading?" He smiled. "Great."

"No." I shook my head, clenching my fists as I prepared to say the words that would change everything. "I'm done with this—*us*."

"Now, Sumner..." He reached out, but his expression was patronizing and completely contradicted his words. "Don't be like that. I've just been—"

"Busy at work? Distracted?" I threw all his previous

excuses back in his face, each one spoken with more venom than the last. "Yeah. I've heard all that before."

"Take a few deep breaths," he said, though he was the one who seemed stressed. "You're...overwhelmed. It's the end of the semester. It's the holidays. But there's no need to act crazy."

"Crazy?" I scoffed.

I turned and headed for the bedroom, throwing my things in a suitcase. Nico hovered behind me, pacing the floor as he wrung his hands. Yeah. Maybe I was a bit crazy, thinking that I meant something to him. That he loved me.

"Okay. Okay. I'll get a ticket to LA. It'll cost a small fortune, but I'll do it if that's what will make you happy."

I ignored him and continued on. What had I ever seen in him?

He was older. Handsome. Brilliant. Prestigious.

At least, that's what I'd thought.

Looking at him now and the apartment we shared, it was as if the spell had been broken. He wasn't any of those things. He was lazy. Condescending. And I was over it.

"Sumner, please," he pleaded, grabbing my biceps and forcing me to stop.

"Let. Go. Of. Me," I seethed. He dropped my arm and stepped back.

I grabbed everything I could, shoving it into my bag, ignoring Nico's pleas as he tried to convince me to stay. Tried to persuade me that he would change. He *could* change. I'd heard it all before, but this time, it went in one ear and out the other. Tears pricked my eyes. How could I have been so stupid?

"Where will you go?" he called as I walked out of the bedroom, grabbing my laptop and the acceptance letters from the kitchen before heading for the front door.

I didn't answer, shutting the door behind me. A moment later, his footsteps scuffed against the ground.

"Sumner, wait." He lowered his voice, catching up to me. He clutched his coat to his neck, his breath filling the air. "Sumner," he hissed, glancing around.

I ignored him, lugging my bags behind me as I marched ahead. I'd already requested an Uber, and I was relieved to find it idling at the curb, exhaust billowing from the tail pipe, the lights from the dashboard aglow.

I opened the door and tossed my bags inside. Nico grabbed my arm, and I turned to face him. "I don't think this would look good for *optics*, Professor Cunningham. Do you?"

With that, he released me, hanging back as I climbed in and shut the door. I didn't glance his way, the tears already falling as the driver pulled away from the curb. How could I have been so blind? So naïve?

I headed for the airport, determined to catch an earlier flight home to California. There was no point waiting around in Boston. There was nothing for me here. And I realized with sudden clarity that there hadn't been for a while.

While I waited in the terminal, hoping to make it on standby, I sent a quick text to Piper. We'd been best friends since kindergarten, and despite living across the country, we were still as close as ever.

*Me: I might be flying in tonight. Can I crash at your place?*

My phone rang almost immediately, her image flashing on the screen. "Hey," I said, accepting the FaceTime request and watching as my name inched up on the standby screen. *So close.*

"Is everything okay? I thought you weren't coming home till tomorrow."

"Change in plans," I said, with one ear tuned in to the announcements. The flight was boarding soon, and my name had just moved to the top of the list. "Can I stay with you tonight?" I didn't feel like explaining everything to my dad and Lea. My dad had never been a fan of Nico.

"Yeah. Of course." She held the phone closer to her face. "Have you been crying?"

I forced a smile. "I'm fine. Or at least, I will be."

"What about Professor Dick?" she asked. For once, I didn't roll my eyes at her nickname for Nico.

"I broke up with him."

She let out a sigh of relief. "It's about damn time. You always were too good for him," Piper said. It was something I'd heard often from her the past few months.

"And I'm moving home. Well, home-ish." I joined the line at the desk for the gate agent. "I'm going to Stanford."

She cheered and did a little happy dance that made me smile. "That's awesome news. We're totally celebrating when you get here."

"I could definitely use a drink," I said, more to myself.

"What about the book tour? Have you talked to your mom?"

My mom was a best-selling author known for her memoirs, and we'd agreed that I'd join her on her latest book tour this summer. Well, she'd suggested it in a way that sounded more like a demand, and I'd conceded, as always.

"Geez, Piper. Give me a second to catch my breath."

"No way. You're on a roll. Don't stop now!"

"Yeah, but would it really be that big of a deal to go with her? It's just for the summer. I can work on my business plan in my spare time."

"Right. Spare time." Piper barked out a laugh. "I thought we talked about this, Sum."

"It's a good compromise," I said, even knowing it wasn't true.

"You mean *sacrifice*."

"Whatever." I stepped to the front of the line and asked Piper to hold. I got the ticket sorted out and then returned my attention to her. "We're about to board. I'll see you later."

"I can't wait!" she squealed and blew me a kiss before disconnecting the call.

I boarded the plane and checked my phone. There were a few missed calls from Nico, a few texts too. I ignored them all and navigated to my inbox. I selected a recent email from Stanford and logged in to my portal, my thumb hovering over the button to indicate my acceptance.

This was it. There was no going back.

Finally, I pressed the button, knowing that I was finally making the right choice. Because it was one I'd made for me.

With that done, I settled back into my seat with a smile. I had no idea what came next, but I knew I'd taken the correct next step. I'd finally listened to my inner voice, and I hoped it wouldn't lead me astray.

## CHAPTER TWO

# Jonathan

Alexis waved when I stepped out of my truck, holding up a finger as she finished a call. "Just a minute," she mouthed.

I held my hand to my forehead to shield my eyes from the sun. The house was...interesting. Definitely different from our usual project. But I could see why she'd been drawn to it. The style was unique, the neighborhood had potential, and I could feel my blood pumping as ideas coursed through me. It was the first time I'd felt alive in weeks.

"Hey. Sorry about that." She grinned, coming to join me. "I probably shouldn't keep LA's Businessperson of the Year waiting."

I rolled my eyes, even though I knew she was teasing. "Oh please." I wrapped my arm around her shoulder. "How have you been?"

"Good. Closing a few last-minute deals before the end of the year. You know how it is. Anyway... I know you're short on time."

It felt like I was always short on time, running from one

thing to the next in an attempt to do more, be more. I often wondered when—or if—it would ever be enough. I could remember thinking I'd be set when I made my first million. Then I did it, and I was focused on making ten. And then the goalpost moved again. I'd passed so many milestones now, they'd begun to blur together. Yet, it never seemed like enough. The excitement of my earlier days faded beyond recognition, and with each new accomplishment, I seemed to care less.

I nodded. "I've got an interview after this." Followed by a dinner meeting, an evening run, and looking over figures until I fell asleep in bed.

"And I've got a ballet recital to attend." She beamed. "Sophia is so excited to be the Sugar Plum Fairy." She headed up the drive, her heels clicking against the concrete. "Let me show you around."

I marveled at the difference in Alexis. She'd always been professional, polished, an astute businesswoman. But she'd changed over the past few years. She used to be all about work—much like I was. Then she'd met Preston, and there'd been a shift. She now prioritized family and downtime over work, and she seemed a lot happier. But surely it had come at a cost, I consoled myself. Though her company seemed as successful as ever. It made no sense.

I listened as she told me about the home's price and features, surveying the work that needed to be done. I nodded, agreeing with her assessment.

"Let's do it," I finally said when we returned to the front entry. The tile was crumbling, the walls likely had water damage, but I relished a good challenge. I needed it. It was the only thing that made me feel…well, *something*.

"Awesome. I thought you'd see the potential."

I nodded, sliding my hands into my pockets. "The view alone—" I shook my head, glancing toward the dark living room and peering through the grimy windows. Everything was already taking shape in my mind "—is worth the price."

"Agreed. I'll get the ball rolling. Are you going to want to do some of the work on this one or...?"

"Absolutely." I didn't hesitate. "Yeah. Let me know when you're ready for demo."

"You sure?" she asked, head tilted. "I know you're crazy busy, and it's the holidays."

"Did I miss any deadlines on the last house?" I asked, cutting her off before she could inquire about my holiday plans or lack thereof.

"No, but—"

"Then trust me to make it work."

"Okay." She ran her fingers through her hair. "Yeah. Absolutely." Her phone chimed. "I've got to head out if I'm going to make it to Sophia's recital on time."

"Of course." I followed her to the door, waiting while she locked up.

"Wolfe," she said as I walked her to her car. "Can I give you some advice?"

"Sure."

"I know you're killing it. Rocking the commercial real estate scene. And you've done incredible for yourself. But there's more to life than work."

I barked out a laugh. "What do you think *this* is?" I gestured toward the house.

"An expensive hobby? An outlet?"

I nodded. "Exactly. Flipping houses isn't work. It's fun."

"I get that." She grinned, but then her expression softened. "I do, but have you ever stopped to wonder when it will all be enough? When the money, the accolades, the *stuff* will be enough?"

I lifted a shoulder, unnerved by how eerily accurate her observations were. But I wasn't ready to admit it, wasn't prepared to show a crack in my façade. I had everything. I had every reason to be happy.

*But you're not.*

I'd achieved everything I'd set out to accomplish and more, and yet it felt hollow. I no longer felt the same kind of thrill I used to from closing a deal or scoring a new client.

My parents had worked their asses off to give me opportunities they'd never had. Opportunities they could've never dreamed of. And here I was, whining about my privileged life. If anything, my guilt spurred me to work harder. To seek happiness in my so-called perfect life.

So, instead of facing the truth, I buried it deeper. Because that's what was expected of me. Always strive for more, reach higher. Push. Push. Push. It was in my DNA.

"Is it ever enough?" I asked.

"That." She pointed at me. "That's exactly the kind of attitude I'm talking about. Be careful, Wolfe."

I shook away her concern, wishing I could rid myself of the feelings that accompanied it. "It's fine. *I'm* fine," I ground out.

She held my gaze a moment before finally opening the door to her car and sliding behind the wheel. I got the feeling she didn't believe me, and I couldn't say I blamed her.

❧

THERE WAS A KNOCK AT MY OFFICE DOOR, AND I GLANCED UP from my computer to find Ian standing in the doorway.

"You ready?" He had a basketball tucked beneath his arm, bag slung over his shoulder.

"Oh shit. I totally forgot. Is it Thursday already?"

"Yep. And it's on your schedule, as always. Can't believe I have to schedule an appointment with my best friend," he grumbled, though I knew he was joking. He loved to give me shit for my insane schedule.

I pulled up my calendar, where it was indeed listed. Despite how busy I was, I always made time for my oldest, and best, friend. I hit "Send" on my email and closed my laptop before shoving it in my bag. "All right, then. Let's go."

I waved to my assistant as we passed his desk. "See you tomorrow, Cody."

"Have a good night, Wolfe."

"Thanks. You too."

Ian and I headed for the elevator bank, riding it up to the rooftop gym. Weekly basketball games were a tradition we'd started in high school and one we continued to this day. All these years—*decades*—later.

"You ready to have your ass handed to you?" he teased.

"Are you, old man?" I followed him into the locker room to change.

"Maybe you should take a look in the mirror." He smirked, but then his expression turned serious. "Seriously, though. Are you feeling okay? You look like shit."

I waved off his concern. "I'm fine. Speaking of old, what's the plan for your forty-fifth?" I tied my laces, knowing Ian's wife, Lea, would have something planned, even if it was still months away.

Where I preferred to ignore my birthday, Ian liked to celebrate. Or at least, he indulged his wife's desire to celebrate. For his fortieth, a small group of us had gone to Monaco. I'd taken Rachel, and we'd... I gnashed my teeth. Let's just say, that trip had made us realize just how incompatible we were.

"Not sure, but I think I convinced Lea to do something smaller this year."

"Really?" I chuckled. I'd believe it when I saw it.

"Yeah, really. So, what's new with you?"

"My New York team is growing. I'm heading out there soon for a week, and then I'll go back again sometime this summer."

"Damn." He rubbed a hand over his jaw. "Does that mean you've finally stopped playing *Flip or Flop* with Alexis?"

I shook my head, closing the locker and securing it. "Nope. In fact, we're going to flip another house."

"Another one? I don't know how you find time to run the Wolfe Group and take on the work of flipping houses in the meantime. When do you eat? Sleep? Have sex?"

I barked out a laugh as I followed him onto the court, dribbling the ball.

"I'm serious."

"If you haven't noticed, you're pretty much my entire social life."

"Aw." He stopped bouncing the ball and placed his hand to his chest. "I'm flattered, but also…that's pathetic, man." He shot the ball and sank it.

I retrieved it and started jogging around the court, avoiding his efforts to take it. I feinted; he dodged. And then I ran toward the basket and shot a lay-up. Score.

"What happened with Kristy?" he asked.

"She was getting too clingy. And she called me 'baby.'" I scrunched up my face.

He chuckled. "Celeste, then? She seems normal, nice."

I shook my head, sinking another shot. "I'm not letting Lea fix me up with another one of her friends." Hell, I was still trying to dodge the last one.

We played a while longer before heading to the bench for water. "So…" Ian said.

I'd known him long enough to sense when he was going to ask me for a favor. "What do you want, Ian?"

"I was wondering if you'd give Sumner a job for the summer."

I furrowed my brow. That wasn't what I'd been expecting. It was so out of left field that I blurted, "Why?"

"Honestly?" His shoulders slumped. "I miss her. And I think something's going on with her. She's been...different lately."

"Different how?"

"Ever since Christmas, she seems more impulsive. Erratic, even. She signed up for Semester at Sea at the last minute. She doesn't want to attend graduation. And she was dead set on going to Wharton for her MBA for years, then suddenly, it's Stanford."

I frowned. "That doesn't sound like Sumner." At least, not the Sumner I knew.

Though we talked about Sumner occasionally, I hadn't seen her in years. Not since she'd graduated high school, in fact. She'd come home infrequently for breaks. And I'd often had to travel for business over the holidays. But I'd kept tabs on her through Ian.

"How's the Semester at Sea thing going?" I asked.

"Good, I guess." He shrugged. "She's sent a few emails and postcards, but I haven't really gotten to talk to her since she left. Anyway," he sighed, and I could see that the situation with his daughter was wearing on him. "I'm really hoping to spend some more time with her before she moves to Stanford in the fall. Maybe figure out what's really going on."

"I'm surprised she doesn't already have a job lined up."

"She did, but it was in Boston. But, like with everything else lately, she changed her mind. Which obviously didn't go over well with the firm." He rubbed a hand over his face. "This whole mess wouldn't have happened if she'd listened to me in the first place and chosen Stanford for her MBA."

That piqued my interest. "So why the shift?"

He lifted a shoulder. "I wish I knew. She's been somewhat

cagey about all of it. Though my guess is that it has some-thing to do with this guy she was dating."

*Huh.* Stanford and Wharton had two of the top MBA programs in the US. Neither was a bad choice, just different.

"And I *know* she doesn't want to go on Helena's book tour, even if she won't admit it."

I frowned. "Why won't she admit it?"

"You know Sum. She's got a big heart, and she hates to disappoint people."

I nodded. I remembered that about her. Even as a child, she'd been a people pleaser.

"I hate to ask this of you, but I just thought…" He paused. "I don't know. I thought maybe spending the summer with you would be good for her. Help her toughen up a little."

I chuckled. "So, you want me to be a jerk?"

"I didn't say that, though we both know you can't help yourself."

"Hey!" I shoved the ball at him, but he caught it.

"I just think she could use someone like you in her life. Someone who can guide her, mentor her. And you two always seemed to get along so well."

*True, but…* "Have you talked to her about this? Is she even interested in commercial real estate?" I asked.

"Does it matter?" he asked. "Her resume is stellar, and she's a hard worker. Besides, it's only for the summer."

Did I really have the time to take on another thing? I was already swamped as it was. And if she had no interest in commercial real estate, this summer would be nothing more than a big waste of time. That wouldn't be good for either of us, let alone my relationship with Ian. It all sounded a bit too…messy. Complicated.

I must have taken too long to answer because Ian stood, tossing his towel aside and picking up the ball. "Never mind.

Forget I asked. I know you're too busy. I'm just—" He tugged on his hair. "I'm not sure what's going on with her."

"No. Wait." I held up a hand. "I'll do it."

He paused midstep. "Are you sure?"

"Of course." As much as I cared about Sumner, I wasn't sure I wanted to mentor someone who wasn't all in. That said, Ian was my best friend, and I'd do anything for him.

"Thank you." He smiled. "That's such a relief. I think this will be really good for her."

I sensed there was more he wasn't telling me, but I let it slide. "Send Cody her contact info, and I'll have him reach out to her with the details."

Ian smiled. "Great. You won't regret this."

I hoped he was right. If nothing else, babysitting Sumner might be a welcome change from the monotony that had become my life.

# CHAPTER THREE

*Summer*

"Hey, kiddo." Dad pulled me into his arms the moment I climbed out of the car. My fellow Semester at Sea students and I had disembarked in San Diego, and while most students had flown home, I'd driven to LA in a rental car, and I was looking forward to being back in my Jeep Wrangler.

He squeezed me tightly. "I missed you."

"Missed you too," I mumbled into his chest, my eyes stinging. I'd missed him, perhaps even more than I'd realized. "But I kinda. Can't. Breathe."

"Oh, sorry." He released me with a chuckle.

My visit at Christmas felt like a lifetime ago, though it had just been five months. That trip had only cemented my desire to move home to California. I'd had zero interest in returning to the East Coast, but with one semester left, I'd had little choice. But then a spot had opened up in the Semester at Sea program, and I'd jumped on it. I'd spent my last semester traveling the world, meeting new people, and discovering who I was and what I wanted.

"We can't wait to hear all about your adventure!" Lea said,

giving me a hug before ushering me inside the house. "Oh, and your storage pod arrived last week."

"Awesome," I said, though I hadn't missed most of the stuff in it.

"Now, I know you don't want to attend graduation," Lea said, leaning against the kitchen counter while Dad carried in my bags. "But what about a small party here?"

I shook my head, grateful she wasn't trying to change my mind about graduation. If my parents thought it odd that I didn't want to attend, they'd since given up on trying to convince me otherwise.

"I'm good. Really. Why don't we wait and throw an even bigger one when I graduate with my MBA?"

"Are you sure?" she asked.

I nodded. "Definitely."

"Well, we should do something to commemorate you finishing college. It's a big deal!" She considered it a moment, then said, "I know. How about a spa day? Just the two of us."

I smiled. "That sounds perfect."

Dad and Lea cooked, dancing around each other in the kitchen with grace and ease. While they prepared dinner, I told them all about Semester at Sea. Communication during the trip had been limited, so I'd only been able to send them postcards or emails occasionally. I'd mentioned the flight from hell briefly, but I'd downplayed the severity of the situation. There was no need to worry them; I was fine.

I told myself I was fine, but the flight to join my classmates for Semester at Sea had been one of the most terrifying experiences of my life to date. Terrifying and eye-opening. It had made two things abundantly clear—I was done living my life for anyone else, and I didn't plan on flying again anytime soon.

"Sounds like quite the experience," Lea said as we sat

down to eat. "Have you made any decisions about this summer?"

My dad had mentioned the possibility of interning with his best friend. While it was a great opportunity, I hesitated, knowing commercial real estate wasn't where my heart lay.

I sipped my water. "Not yet, but I have an interview later this week."

I didn't mention it was with a potential client. I was working to build my client base for the coaching business. The one Nico thought was stupid and destined to fail, though I didn't want to believe him. I'd put together a solid business plan, and I'd been reading everything I could get my hands on about life coaching, productivity, motivation, and more. I'd also devoured any podcast I could find that related to those topics, and I was planning to start my own one day.

Dad and Lea shared a hopeful glance, then Dad said, "So, you're still available?"

"Yes, but..."

"Great. I know Jonathan's really hoping you'll intern with him."

"I don't know, Dad. I'm not sure I'm interested in commercial real estate." I cut into the chicken, swirling it in the lemon-butter sauce.

"What better way to find out?" He spread his arms wide. "Besides, it could be good for you. You've had a lot of change lately, and this might give you some stability."

I frowned but said nothing, taking a moment to focus on my dinner as I digested his words. "Are you sure this is what he wants?"

"Yes." Dad nodded, swallowing his food. "There's always been an open invitation for you to intern with him—you know that."

I furrowed my brow. Perhaps that was true, but I got the

sense there was something more at play. My dad was just a little *too* eager. Lea, too, now that I thought about it.

"Okay. What's really going on?"

They glanced at each other, silently communicating something in couple-speak, then turned back to me. Bright smiles. Wide eyes. *Totally* guilty.

"Nothing," Lea chirped.

"Oh please." I rolled my eyes, settling back into my chair. "You're both lying."

"Fine," Dad huffed, and Lea's shoulders immediately relaxed. "The truth is, you'd really be doing me a favor."

I tilted my head to the side, not sure I followed. "Huh?"

Lea placed her hand on my dad's. "We're worried about Jonathan, aren't we?" They shared a sad smile.

A hole opened in the pit of my stomach. "Worried?"

"He's been...different lately," Lea said. "Withdrawn. He—well, we think he's having a midlife crisis or something. But every time your dad tries to mention it, Jonathan shuts down."

I nodded, hoping what she said wasn't true. Jonathan had always been a fixture in our lives. He was my dad's best friend, more akin to a brother. Which was why my first instinct was to say yes. To do something, anything, to help Jonathan. But I wasn't sure what difference my taking an internship would make. For starters, I hadn't seen the man in years.

"And you think I'm somehow going to be able to help?" I wasn't trying to be flippant; I honestly didn't know what they were thinking.

"Yes," Lea said. "You're so excited and passionate about your future. I—*we*—" she smiled "—think that seeing you, someone on the cusp of their career, will remind him of his own excitement, his passion."

"For work." I wasn't sure whether I was questioning it or confirming it.

"Please, Sum?" Dad asked. "He means a lot to this family —to me."

I knew this was important to him. So, despite my hesitation, despite the fact that I'd intended to work on a business plan and start developing my client base, I rushed to say, "Of course. I'll help in any way I can." And then I immediately kicked myself for falling back into my old habits.

"Thank you." Dad smiled.

"If nothing else, seeing you will be a good distraction," Lea said. "He was always so fond of you, always so sweet to you when you were younger."

I nodded, remembering it well. Every look, every touch was firmly embedded in my memory. But that was years ago. I'd been young and naïve, crushing on a man nearly double my age. I doubted I'd be as enamored as before.

"Sumner," Dad said, interrupting my thoughts. "You okay, kiddo?"

"Yeah." I laughed, shaking away the memories. "Just reminiscing."

"*See?*" Lea straightened. "This is why you're perfect for the job. It's a win-win. You get experience that looks amazing on your resume. Jonathan gets an incredible intern for the summer, and he'll be out of his funk in no time."

My dad smiled and stood, carrying our dishes over to the sink. When he was out of earshot, Lea leaned in. "Thank you, Sumner. Your dad's been all out of sorts. It's like the balance of his universe is off if Jonathan's upset."

I laughed but quickly sobered when I saw how serious she was. Despite my desire to help my dad and Jonathan, I had reservations. "I really don't know—"

"Sweetie." She patted my hand. "Just by saying yes, you've taken a load off your dad's shoulders. Mine too."

Lea and I carried the remaining dishes to the kitchen, setting them beside the sink for Dad to rinse. Why couldn't I just say no? Why was I so afraid to share my plans for my coaching business? I'd promised myself to trust my instincts. And yet here I was, doing the exact thing I'd promised myself not to do anymore—allowing others to make plans for me.

"Now, on to my next question," Dad said, handing me the rinsed plates to stack in the dishwasher.

*Here it comes*, I thought, but I bit my tongue.

"We want you to move home for the summer."

"I am," I said, intentionally misinterpreting his question.

"No." He shook his head. "*Here*. We want you to live here —with Lea and me. We've really missed you while you were off having fun at MIT and then gallivanting around the world."

I narrowed my eyes at him. "I think you mean working my ass off."

"That too." He grinned. "And you'll be moving to Palo Alto in the fall."

"Yeah, but…"

"You know how busy your mom is," he said, already anticipating my next argument.

"She's already disappointed that I'm not going on the tour with her."

"True, but she's also in the middle of writing her next memoir, and she's leaving soon to promote her latest release. You'd be alone most of the time."

"Or giving her more material." Lea arched her eyebrow.

*Good point.*

I'd never liked the fact that my mom included personal anecdotes about her family, me especially, in her books. But I'd never felt comfortable telling her that. Which was why I often found it easier to avoid her.

"I'll consider it," I said, ready to end discussion on the

matter. I'd barely returned, and already it felt as if I were being pulled in a million different directions. I couldn't win. I couldn't please everyone. And I was sick of trying.

Dad dried his hands on the towel and patted me on the shoulder. "Good. And if you want me to talk to your mom, just say the word."

I was about to tell him I could handle it when my phone buzzed. I pulled it out of my pocket to see a new text message from Piper.

"Let me guess," Dad teased. "Your fellow troublemaker?"

I laughed, not surprised he'd guessed who it was from. "Yeah. She wants to meet up."

I debated deferring to another night. I'd just gotten back in town, and I knew my dad wanted to spend time with me.

"You should go." Dad pushed off the counter. "Apart from family, there's nothing more important than your friends." He padded through to the living room.

I shot off a quick text, promising to meet her in an hour. I showered and got dressed, picking through my suitcase before selecting an olive dress that clung to my curves. I curled my black hair in loose waves, swiping some mascara over my lashes before finishing off with a coat of lip gloss.

Lea was in the kitchen when I headed out, letting out a loud wolf-whistle. "Lookin' good."

I laughed with a shake of my head, thinking she often felt more like a friend or a big sister than a stepmom. It was one of the things I loved about her.

"I'm glad you're getting back out there." She gave me a hug.

I'd long stopped being sad about what had happened with Nico, that feeling quickly replaced by regret and embarrassment. The fact that I'd been so blind when it came to him made me second-guess my ability to coach others. As well as doubt my competence to run a business. And while I didn't want to admit it, that was a big part of the reason I hadn't fought my dad harder when he'd pushed me to intern with Jonathan.

"Be safe," Lea said. "And call if you need a ride."

I smiled. "Thanks, Lea."

"Now, go." She shooed me toward the door. "Before your dad sees you and has a heart attack."

I rolled my eyes. My dress wasn't *that* scandalous. But sometimes my dad—cool as he was—struggled to see me as an adult.

When I arrived at the rooftop bar, Piper was waiting, drink in hand. Half the men stared at her as she snapped a few selfies and then typed on her phone.

"Hey!" She hopped up from her stool, giving me a hug. "You're here!" she squealed.

"I am!" I squeezed her.

"Mm, girl. Lookin' good."

"You too. Love that dress. And your new haircut is gorgeous."

"Thanks. And thanks for your latest tips for batching my tasks. It's been huge."

"Right?" I was pleased that she'd not only taken my advice, but it was helping. "It's so much more efficient." I ordered a lemon drop, thanking the bartender when he delivered it.

"Yes, and I've noticed an improvement in my focus too."

"That's great!" I swiveled on the stool to face her, and she mirrored my movements.

"So...how does it feel—being home?"

"Fine." I lifted a shoulder. "Good. Dad wants me to stay with him and Lea."

"Surprise. Surprise." She grinned. "What do *you* want to do?"

"What do you think?" I took a sip, the sweet and sour flavors lingering on my tongue.

"Yeah. I figured. I'd stay with them too. Not that your mom's not awesome," she added. "Wherever you end up staying, this summer is going to be epic. I've already got a party and a sailing trip lined up for us."

"That sounds great, but I'm not sure how much partying I'll get to do. I have a lot going on."

"Yeah, but it's flexible, right? I mean, you're working on building your clientele, and these are all great opportunities to network."

Piper had built a popular vlogging channel on YouTube and was an Instagram influencer. She had glossy brown hair that flowed down her back like water, though she no longer used it to hide her hearing aids. Expressive hazel eyes that changed color depending on the makeup she wore, or the colored contacts she'd put in that day. Cupid's-bow lips that she tried a rainbow of lipsticks on.

While her job looked fun and easy from the outside, I knew how much time and effort went into her makeup and hair tutorials. How much pressure she put on herself to continue to produce quality original content. She was beautiful, but it was the way she encouraged her followers to embrace what made them unique that made her so popular. She wasn't about covering up the "flaws"; she wanted people to be themselves. And we all adored her for it.

"True, but I sort of agreed to work at the Wolfe Group." It was said in a rush, and I quickly braced for her reaction.

I hadn't told Piper about the internship because I hadn't been considering it seriously. At least, not until my dad and Lea had voiced their concerns about Jonathan.

She coughed a few times before setting her glass down on the bar. "Wolfe? As in *Jonathan Wolfe*? The man you've been crushing on since middle school? The man—"

"Okay. Okay." I rolled my eyes, wanting to put this embarrassing crush behind me. "I think that's enough. That was years ago."

"Yeah. And have you seen him since?" she asked, and I shook my head. "Let's just say, the man has only improved with age."

"Well, good for him, I guess." What did she expect me to say? He *was* my childhood crush, and he was going to be my new boss. Not to mention the fact that he was my dad's best friend.

"I don't understand. You aren't interested in real estate, so how does this fit in with your coaching business?"

"It's an amazing opportunity. I could really learn a lot," I said, not willing to reveal what my dad and Lea had told me about Jonathan.

"I bet you could." Her mischievous grin had me shaking my head. "In fact, I bet the big, bad Wolfe would be a very good teacher."

I rolled my eyes. "You did not just go there."

She snort-laughed then quickly covered her mouth. "Oh, hell yes, I did. If you're intent on taking this job, you should seize this opportunity, and not just for what it could do for your resume."

"This is a professional opportunity. Nothing more. Besides..."

She turned to me, her eyes homed in on me with a laser-like focus. "Yes..."

I shook my head. "Nothing."

"You really haven't seen him since high school?"

"I rarely came home, and he was often traveling for business." Though sometimes I found it hard to believe myself. He'd been such a part of my life growing up, and then *"poof!"* no more. I'd missed him but figured it was for the best.

"A lot has changed. *You* have changed." She assessed my

curves before flashing me a wicked grin. "Besides, wasn't he engaged or something back then?"

I swallowed hard but kept my mouth shut. "Mm-hmm."

"Okay. Okay. I can tell you don't want to talk about this, so I'll move on." She leaned in. "*For now.*"

"For *good.*"

She grinned but didn't otherwise acknowledge my statement. I thought we were finally moving on when she said, "Wait. You never answered my question. How does this fit in with your coaching business?"

I stared at my glass, wishing I had an answer.

"Sumner," she chided, and I could hear the disappointment in her tone.

"Yeah. Yeah. I know." I waved a hand through the air. "Can we please just drop it?"

"Is this because of what Professor Dick said?"

I didn't want to admit it, but a small part of me doubted my business idea. Doubted that I could help other women when I couldn't even speak up for myself. But something deep inside me, in my gut, told me to persist.

"Why are we even still talking about him?" I laughed, no longer annoyed by the nickname. It was fitting, even if it had taken me longer than it should've to see it.

"Has he tried calling again?"

I lifted a shoulder. "I don't know. I blocked his number."

"Good girl." She sipped her drink, smiling at a man at the end of the bar.

"Just go," I said with a laugh, giving her a gentle push in his direction.

"Only if you'll go with me," she said. "His friend is cute."

I shook my head. "Nah. I'm good."

"Gah. I had high hopes for us this summer, and you're ruining everything." She pouted.

"And you're always so dramatic," I teased. "You should be applauding me for standing my ground."

"You always stand your ground with me. It's everyone else that's an issue, especially men. Now, why is that?" she teased.

"Hm." I tapped a finger to my lips, which twitched with the promise of a grin. "I don't know."

She stared into her glass in a rare pensive moment. "I've missed my bestie. And I'm sorry if I'm pushing too hard about this internship. I was really looking forward to spending time with you this summer."

"I've missed you too." I wrapped my arm around her shoulder, pulling her close. "And I promise we'll hang out."

Less than twenty-four hours back, and already my new boundaries were being tested. I'd made so many promises, I didn't know how I could possibly fulfill them all, but I was going to try. I hated the idea of disappointing any one of them—my parents, Lea, Piper, even Jonathan.

# CHAPTER FOUR

*Jonathan*

"**S**umner Gray is here," Cody said through the intercom.

I glanced at my computer and stood. I wasn't sure where the past few months had gone. It seemed like just yesterday Ian was asking me to bring her on as an intern. Take her under my wing. And now it was time to make good on my promise, even if I sensed it was a waste of time.

As much as I'd always enjoyed Sumner, I hadn't seen her in years. And while I was curious about the woman she'd become, I wasn't looking forward to having to "mentor" her if it meant explaining everything. I had a feeling this was going to be a long summer.

"Send her in, please," I replied.

There hadn't been a formal interview, not that it was necessary. She'd had the job by virtue of her resume and Ian's request. Even so, I wanted her to feel welcome here. Which was why I'd had Cody block off some time on her first day for us to get reacquainted and discuss a framework for the summer.

The door to my office swung open, and I smiled,

expecting to see the same little girl I'd known since she was born. My best friend's daughter. A shy girl with a sweet smile and pigtails. Later, a teen blossoming before my eyes. But in walked a woman with confidence and curves. A woman who made my mouth water and my eyes bulge.

Surely this wasn't the same girl. I hadn't seen her since she was nearly seventeen. But it couldn't be…

"Sumner?" I asked.

My mouth went dry as I scanned her figure. Her black hair fell in waves that caressed the tops of her breasts. Full and perky, they made me want to peel off her shirt and bury my head in them. Her suit nipped in at her waist before flaring out over a pair of luscious hips. I continued my perusal until I met her eyes and realized she was scanning me too, likely cataloguing the changes to my appearance.

"It's good to see you, Jonathan," she said, stepping into me and wrapping her arms around me. Even though she'd been shy with others as a child, she'd always been very affectionate with me. We'd always had an easy familiarity, and I'd assumed we'd slip back into it.

But nothing about this felt easy or familiar. It was as if my entire world had tipped on its axis. Sumner wasn't the girl I'd watched grow up; she was all woman. And holy fucking shit, she smelled amazing. The feel of her in my arms… There was no way to describe it other than to say it felt right, like coming home.

*Like coming home? What the hell is wrong with you?* I cleared my throat and put some space between us.

"Please, take a seat." I gestured to the two empty chairs in front of my desk, while I rested my hip against the edge. "So…" I cleared my throat. "Your dad tells me you enjoyed your time at MIT."

She smiled. "I did, though I was ready for a change. Ready to return to California. I missed the beach."

I nodded, laughing to myself as I rubbed a hand over my chin. How many summers had we spent together on the beach? Her parents and her. My flavor of the month and me. And who would've guessed she'd grow up to be such a bombshell.

She'd always been pretty as a little girl—raven hair, jade eyes that appeared gray in certain lights, kindhearted. But the woman before me was fucking stunning. If she were anyone else—and we were anywhere else—I wouldn't have hesitated to make a move. But she was my best friend's daughter and my new intern.

Even so, a memory came to me unbidden. She tilted her head to the side, a smile playing at her lips. "Something amusing?"

"You know... I can remember days at the beach, you flinging off your swimsuit and wiggling your cute little butt around. Then you'd march down to the water's edge buck naked."

Her cheeks reddened, turning the most beautiful hue, and I wondered what she'd look like now—naked on the beach. Naked in my bed.

"I don't remember that," she said in a soft voice.

"It was years ago. Hell, I'm sure you barely remember me."

"Barely remember you?" It was said softly, her head dipped as if to conceal her expression from me. "How could I ever forget someone like you?"

I arched a brow, intrigued by her response. I couldn't help but feel gratified by her reaction.

She cleared her throat. "I mean, you always were part of the family."

I groaned inwardly. *Of course she remembers you...like she would a lovable uncle.*

I stood, turning toward the window so I wouldn't stare at her delicate neck or study the flutter of her eyelashes. This was Sumner Gray. She was my best friend's daughter. I'd always promised to protect her, watch out for her, not *lust* after her.

I squeezed my eyes shut briefly. If Ian knew I was thinking about his baby girl this way... I cringed. He'd kill me —and rightfully so. Let alone the head of my HR department. Talk about a sexual harassment nightmare.

I turned back to her, forcing myself to focus as I sank down in the chair beside her. *Get a fucking grip.*

Sumner was here to learn, gain experience. Not be ogled by a man nearly twice her age. A man old enough to be her father.

"So, brain and cognitive sciences for undergrad. MBA in the fall. How does this summer fit in with your plans? What are you hoping to learn during your time at the Wolfe Group?" Standard question. A safe question, putting us back on solid footing.

Her legs were crossed at the ankles, both her demeanor and dress poised and professional. If only I could keep my thoughts on a more professional plane. But every time I looked at her, I found something new and intriguing to study. It was like rereading a favorite book and discovering even more things to love. More hidden gems and favorite passages to underline.

"I hope to gain from your insight and expertise so I can one day leverage my business degree to create a business of my own."

I leaned back, crossing my arms over my chest. As far as elevator pitches went, it wasn't half bad. But it lacked heat, passion. I sensed she was capable of so much more. That she wanted so much more. Or maybe I was projecting my own yearning onto her.

"Let's try that again."

She furrowed her brows, and it was fucking adorable. "Was there something wrong with what I said?"

"It was…" I debated my word choice briefly. "A bit too rehearsed. Too stiff. Where's your passion? Whether you want to work in this field or be an entrepreneur—if you're serious about being successful, you're going to need to have some fire."

She flattened her lips, and I wondered if I'd pushed too far. Still, I kept going, sensing I was getting somewhere. I wanted to see that spark. The passion.

"Come on." I uncrossed my arms, leaning in. "Why are you really here?"

"To learn from the best." It was a shit answer, intended to appease my vanity without offering anything of substance. And judging from the expression on her face, she knew it.

"I agreed to do this as a favor to your father, but I'm not willing to waste both our time. If you can't give me some insight into your motivations, then—" I lifted my hand "—there's the door."

I held my employees to high standards—some might have said impossible ones. But it was part of the reason I'd been so successful. I hired the best and expected the best from them. And I paid them handsomely.

With Sumner, I felt the need to hold her to an even higher level. She'd been smart and well-spoken; she still was. I'd always seen the potential in her, and I wanted her to achieve her wildest dreams.

"I don't need you to do me a favor." Her voice was strong, resolute. "I graduated top of my class. I was on the dean's list every semester. I—"

"Yes. You're brilliant and have the credentials to prove it. But there are others who are just as smart. Just as capable. What sets you apart? What makes you special?"

I knew, or at least sensed I did. But I wanted her to know it. To say it. To fucking own it.

Her head dropped, shoulders sagging. "Because..." Her lips parted, and then she shook her head and grabbed her purse. "You know what? Never mind. I didn't even want this job, and I never should've agreed to it."

I grabbed her elbow before she reached the door, my grip gentle yet firm. She could leave any time, but I got the feeling she didn't want to. She stared at my hand on her skin before slowly lifting her head to meet my eyes. Her breathing was labored, the tension growing thick between us. I didn't have any right to pry, to push her like I was, but I couldn't seem to help myself when it came to this woman.

"What are you talking about, agreed to this job? Your dad asked me to bring you on as a favor."

She laughed, though it lacked mirth. "That's funny. He told me the same thing."

I jerked my head back. This didn't make any sense. "Sumner, why did you take this job if you don't want to be here?"

She straightened. "It's not that I don't want to be here." She blew out a breath, still not meeting my eyes. "It's just— I..." she stammered.

"What is it?" This close, her eyes were almost gray, the light hitting them in such a way that they became a pale green like jade. She blinked rapidly, and I could remember her doing that as a child. A million memories came flooding back in that instant, and I knew she was lying. It was her tell. "You can trust me. You know that. I've always said you can tell me anything."

"I know." She smiled, and I suspected she'd joined me for her own stroll down memory lane.

But then she shook her head, raven-colored waves curtaining her face from view. "I-I shouldn't have said anything. Please just drop it."

*Drop it?* Was she kidding? I was alarmed by her tone and her words, so I guided her over to the chair, taking a seat next to her. "You're lying to me. I want to know why."

She twisted her hands in her lap. Blew out a breath. "My dad and Lea are worried about you."

A muscle twitched in my jaw even as I attempted to maintain a calm façade. "And what were you going to do? Come to work, keep an eye on me, then report back to them?"

She scowled. "No. I guess I—" She glanced toward the windows briefly then back at me. "It's not like I didn't have other plans this summer, but maybe I wanted to know you were okay. Maybe I missed you."

I scoffed, but then the way she leaned forward, her expression so earnest, made me realize she was serious.

We'd always had a connection, and though it had been years since I'd seen her, it burned just as strong, even if it was different now. I still wanted to protect her, sure. Wanted to make her laugh. But now there was another layer—attraction, burning hot and bright like a poker.

This was going to be a long summer. But not for the reasons I'd expected.

# CHAPTER FIVE

*Summer*

I crossed my legs, electricity arcing between our bodies. "So...am I fired?"

I couldn't believe some of the things I'd said to Jonathan. They were so bold. So...not like me. At least, not like the old me. But I'd made a promise to myself to speak my mind, to speak up. I figured this internship was as good a place as any to start. How would I feel confident to advise other women—ones who were likely older than me—if I couldn't even say what I thought?

Besides, what did I have to lose? I didn't even want this job anyway.

He chuckled, leaning back in his chair as if he didn't have a care in the world. "It's your first day. Do you want me to fire you?"

I lifted a shoulder, trying to portray more confidence than I felt. I didn't want to be fired, but this wasn't exactly part of my summer plan either. "I made a promise to my dad."

He nodded, rubbing a hand over his chin. "Are you even interested in commercial real estate?"

I scrunched up my nose, knowing I couldn't lie to him. He'd always seen right through me; this morning had only proven that. "Honestly?" I asked, and he nodded. "No."

"What are you interested in?"

"I, um—" I glanced toward the door then stood. "It's not important. Besides, I'm sure you have meetings to attend, and I've wasted enough of your time." There was no way I was telling Jonathan about my coaching business. He'd probably mock me for it, just like Nico had.

He grasped my wrist, his fingers lingering a moment before he released me. "You could never be a waste of time. And it is important."

I swallowed hard, the sight of him peering up at me almost more than I could handle. Piper was right. Jonathan had improved with age. His blue eyes were the color of the sky, his jawline like glass, even beneath his salt-and-pepper beard. His hair was longer on the top than the sides, with flecks of silver at the temples.

And while I'd hoped my childhood crush had been stamped out, it was turning into a raging inferno. My attraction to this man was off the charts. And he was completely off-limits.

*Breathe in. Out. In. Out.* I chanted the words in my head like a mantra as I tried to steady my heart rate. I needed out. I needed space. In the past, Jonathan had always been a safe place to land. And I hadn't realized how much I'd missed that —*him*—until I'd seen him again.

"I haven't seen you in years, Sumner. I want to know what's going on with you. Come on." He stood, slipping a hand into his pocket. "I'd like to take my new intern to lunch."

"It's three o'clock in the afternoon."

"I haven't eaten since breakfast. Is it too early for dinner?" he asked.

I laughed, some of the earlier tension between us easing. "A little."

"Drinks?"

I arched an eyebrow, surprised by his suggestion. Surprised by his insistence. He was different than I remembered. Or maybe he was treating me differently now that I was an adult.

"Don't you have work to do?"

"It's called the *Wolfe* Group for a reason," he teased. "I'm the boss."

"Yes, but I'm not sure it would look so great for you to be skipping out with your new intern in the middle of the day."

"Oh. So, you're staying now?" He typed a few things on his laptop and then flashed me a cheeky smile as he picked up the phone on his desk.

"Cody, please cancel my appointments for the rest of the day." Jonathan was silent for a moment, then said, "It's fine. Just do it," before hanging up the phone.

His commanding tone had me clenching my thighs together, and he peered up at me as if he'd noticed. His nostrils flared, palms pressed against the top of his desk. He was glorious. Like a captain in control of his ship. A man certain of himself and his destiny.

He rounded the desk, and I stood as he pocketed his keys. "Let's go."

He placed his hand on the small of my back, and a bolt of lightning raced up my spine. How could such a simple, singular touch affect me so profoundly?

"Sumner?"

I shook my head as if to clear it. "Yes?"

"I asked if you were ready."

"Ready for what?"

"Anything." He grinned, and I liked the sound of that, reading more into his playful tone than I had any right to.

"But your clients and your—"

"It's fine. I'll introduce you to a few people you'll be working with this summer. Then we can go check out a couple properties and grab drinks or dinner."

Our eyes locked, and my breath caught. *Holy shit.* The way he was looking at me... He was looking at me as if he wanted me. Which was absurd, right?

"Deal?"

I nodded, completely under his spell. He could've told me to strip naked and run through the office, and I'd have agreed if it meant he'd keep looking at me that way.

"It's settled, then," he said, opening the door so I could step through.

I felt everyone's eyes on us as we walked down the hall, but I told myself I was just paranoid. We headed toward the elevator, and he greeted every employee by name. For a man who owned one of the biggest full-service commercial real estate firms in Los Angeles, he really was very down-to-earth. I mean, I'd heard the gossip—that he could be demanding, a perfectionist, difficult to work with. But all of it had been said with the utmost respect, bordering on awe. My dad was right; I could definitely learn a thing or two from Jonathan.

"Eric." He rapped his knuckles on the door to an office. "There's someone I want to introduce you to." Jonathan beckoned me over then said, "This is Sumner Gray. She'll be interning with us this summer."

"Great." Eric smiled, and I immediately liked him. He looked like he'd be more at home on a skateboard than in the boardroom, with his long brown hair that he had to brush out of his eyes.

When Eric's phone rang, Jonathan said, "We'll leave you to it."

Eric picked up the phone and said, "Nice to meet you, Sumner," before answering the call.

Jonathan ushered me out of the office and back down the hall. He introduced me to several other employees—Eric's administrative assistant, a woman in her sixties named Isla, who reminded me of one of my favorite professors. An associate named Jack, who was a recent college graduate. Everyone seemed so nice, so welcoming, and I found myself growing more excited about the opportunity.

After the tour, we entered the elevator, and Jonathan's arm brushed against me as he reached across to press the button for the parking garage. I shivered as the doors closed, remaining frozen to the spot. He smelled crisp, clean, and I wanted to inhale him. No, I wanted to taste him. Would he taste masculine and salty or... When he cleared his throat, I snapped my attention to him.

*Get it together!* "What was that?"

"I asked if you need to be home at a certain time. The listing is across town, and with traffic..." He lifted a shoulder. "It could get late."

I shook my head. "I'm yours for the night."

I cringed when I realized the implication in my words. Not that I didn't want to be his for the night—far from it. I could only imagine how amazing a night with a man like Jonathan would be. His beard scratching the delicate skin of my thighs. His hands exploring my body.

It wasn't the first time the thought had crossed my mind, but it had never seemed like a possibility before. When I was an awkward teen, Jonathan had always seemed so out of reach. He still did.

The arch of his eyebrow and upward tilt of his lips told me my slip hadn't gone unnoticed. Guess I hadn't totally lost that awkwardness, at least not around him.

"What I meant—" I rushed to clarify, hoping it hadn't come off as a desperate plea "—is that I'm free. You can do what you want with me."

I covered my face with my hands and shook my head as if that would somehow make me disappear. My cheeks were on fire, flames of embarrassment licking at my skin. I needed to stop talking; I was only making this worse.

His deep chuckle threaded its way through my belly, making me weak at the knees. His touch was gentle when he placed his hands over mine. "Sumner." He tugged, but I refused to uncover my face. "Come on. It wasn't that bad." Even so, I could hear the laughter in his voice.

And when I finally lowered my hands, there was no escaping the teasing glint in his eyes. It wasn't even an hour into my new job, and I'd just implied that my boss could sleep with me. *Awesome.*

I'd nearly screwed up my future by getting involved with a guy who was wrong for me. As much as I was attracted to Jonathan, I wouldn't make the same mistake twice. I took a deep, calming breath, avoiding his gaze.

The elevator chimed and the doors slid open, saving me from further embarrassment. *Thank god.*

Jonathan reached out, holding back the door. "After you."

"Thank you." I smiled and walked past, feeling his eyes on me the entire time. What did he see when he looked at me? A little girl? The teenager he'd known? Or the me I was now—the woman I'd become?

The lights on a silver pickup truck blinked, and I tried to hide my surprise. I'd expected Jonathan to drive a sports car, something sleek and fast. And the closer we got, the more intimidating his truck seemed. I wondered how on earth I was going to climb up into the cab without exposing, well, everything.

Again, Jonathan placed his hand on my lower back. He pressed a button on the key fob, and a running board slid out, providing the perfect step.

I peered up at him. "Fancy."

"Yeah." He chuckled, running a hand through his hair. "Your dad calls it my 'old man step.'"

"You're not old," I said, preferring not to dwell on the fact that he was practically the same age as my father.

Age didn't matter—at least not to me. I wasn't sure Jonathan would agree, and I knew my dad sure as hell wouldn't. He'd never liked Nico, and I knew a lot of it had to do with our age difference.

But it wasn't like anything would ever happen. Jonathan was my boss, my father's best friend. He... Well, to Jonathan, I was like a niece. It didn't matter how many times I'd fantasized about him; it would never happen.

He opened the passenger door for me, and I climbed into the cab. He grinned, shutting the door before rounding the hood to the driver's side. Though the cab was large, it seemed to shrink the moment he entered. The scent of his body wash was everywhere, and if I'd closed my eyes, I could've imagined I was walking through a forest. Crisp. Earthy. Primal. *Oh god.* If I'd thought being in the office alone with him was difficult, this was going to be impossible.

"What are we looking at today?" I asked as he handed me a tablet, where several properties were displayed on the screen.

"Medical offices, law firms, the like," he said, and I swiped through the images, evaluating.

"And what are we looking for as far as square footage and specs?"

He glanced over at me quickly, surprise and something like admiration shining through. "For someone who's not interested in commercial real estate, you sure speak the lingo like a pro."

"Just because I'm not interested doesn't mean I don't like to learn. I did *try* to prepare for this internship. It's a good opportunity, and I don't do things half-assed."

He shook his head with a smile, accelerating as he drove us onto the highway. The radio played softly in the background, some country song about hot days and warm nights. His taste in music hadn't changed.

"So, Sumner, tell me what you've been up to. Catch me up on the past few years."

"You act like you're offended that I didn't call or something," I teased, feeling more comfortable now that we were away from the office. If I closed my eyes, I was fifteen again.

"We used to be close. At least, I thought we were. I haven't seen you since you graduated high school. A lot has changed."

"Yeah. The last time I saw you, you didn't have a New York office, and you were engaged."

He stared straight ahead, and I immediately regretted mentioning his ex. I placed my hand over his and said, "I'm sorry," in a soft voice.

"That was a long time ago." He shook his head, and I quickly removed my hand. But then he said, "And you were headed to MIT, ready to take over the world of online marketing. Yet you graduated with a degree in brain and cognitive sciences."

I stared at the passing scenery. "Things change. People change."

"Well, I'm glad you're back." He smiled, and I took the hint and changed the subject.

I told him about living in Boston and how cold the winters were. We discussed some of my classes and our favorite podcasts. It was *nice*.

I stared at the road, watching as the asphalt faded beneath

us while trying to ignore the heat emanating from him. I'd told myself he was a childhood crush, nothing more. But seeing Jonathan again had brought all these feelings rushing back. I pushed them away just as quickly. I was focused on my future. I'd been distracted by a man before, and I wouldn't let it happen again.

# CHAPTER SIX

## Jonathan

"**H**ey, man," Ian said when I opened the front door. "Lea's grabbing a few things out of the car. I hope it's okay—I invited Sumner."

"Of course." I opened the door wider, welcoming him in. "It's always nice to see her."

Ian, Lea, and I often got together for a weekend meal. I provided the groceries, Ian brought the booze, Lea cooked. It suited me just fine.

Once the door closed, he asked, "So, how's it going with Sumner?"

"Great." I took one of wine from him and carrying it through to the kitchen.

"Good." He sighed. "Good. She seems to be enjoying herself, and I'm glad this is working out so well."

I studied my friend as he glanced around, wondering why he'd felt the need to lie to both Sumner and me, setting us up to "help each other." It seemed more like something Lea would do, and I wondered if she was the true architect of this plan. I was positive it wasn't another one of her match-making schemes, but still…it made me wonder.

The front door opened, the alarm chiming with it. "Hello," Lea called out, interrupting my thoughts.

"In here." Ian opened a drawer, grabbing the corkscrew before opening the bottle.

"Hey, Jonathan," Lea said, giving me a hug.

"Hey." I smiled but faltered when I saw Sumner standing behind her.

I'd grown accustomed to seeing her at the office this past week. We'd gone to lunch a few times, and it felt as if no time had passed at all. And while she was the same girl I'd known, she wasn't a girl anymore. Even so, working together hadn't prepared me for this version of Sumner. She was relaxed. Happy. The sun kissing her shoulders and cheeks, her dress revealing large expanses of skin that had remained covered up at the office. Forget dinner; I wanted to swipe my tongue along her collarbone, sink my teeth into her neck.

I quickly pushed away the thought, my eyes darting toward Ian and Lea. Neither seemed to have noticed my reaction to Sumner, even though I felt as if it were displayed above my head in neon lights. Warning: Dangerous Attraction.

"Hey." Sumner waved, flashing me a sheepish grin. "Sorry for crashing the party."

"Oh please," I teased, pulling her into my side and telling myself to act normal. All the while, the contact with her skin made me feel like a live wire. "It's nice not to be the third wheel for once."

She laughed. "I feel you. Try living with these two." She hooked her thumb in the direction of Ian and Lea. He had his hands on her waist, his lips hovering near her ear. We didn't exist for all they cared.

"You could've stayed with your mom," Ian said, never taking his eyes off his wife.

Sumner coughed. "Um. Excuse me, Mr. I-want-you-to-move-home-with-us?"

I laughed, relaxing a little as we settled back into a sense of normalcy. I'd always admired their relationship. And as she'd gotten older, I loved the fact that she called Ian on his shit. She respected him, adored him, but they could tease each other. It made me wonder what my relationship with my parents would've been like.

When I caught Sumner glancing around, it struck me that she'd never visited my house. I'd purchased it a few years ago as an investment, as a testament to my success, but I'd never felt at home here. It was only when Ian and Lea came over and we cooked together and hung out that it felt like more than just the place I rested my head at night.

"Come on." I hooked my arm over Sumner's shoulder before thinking better of it and rubbing the back of my neck instead. "I'll show you around."

I led her down the hall toward the office and guest room, stealing glances at her all the while. I wondered what she was thinking—about the house. About me.

"It's nice," she finally said after I'd given her a tour. We stood on the upstairs landing, music streaming through the built-in speakers. Ian and Lea were likely busy in the kitchen. *Or getting busy*, I thought but quickly pushed it away.

Those two. They couldn't keep their hands off each other. I found it both amusing and, at times, surprising. I enjoyed sex, craved the release. But my relationships—if you could call them that—never lasted. Either they wanted more than I was willing to give, or I simply lost interest. I couldn't imagine ever being that crazy for someone, that insatiable, especially not after ten years.

"Nice?" I asked, sensing Sumner had more to say on the matter.

"Well..." She glanced around before returning her attention to me. "It doesn't really fit you or your personality."

"How so?" I leaned closer, intrigued.

"It seems so cold."

I couldn't help it; my brow arched in surprise. Most people thought I was cold. "What kind of house would you picture me in?"

"Something with more character. Something with history." I found myself nodding with her description. "You used to love poring over old woodworking catalogues. Yet you chose this. Why?"

I felt a sharp pang in my chest but quickly pushed it away. "You remember that?"

"Of course. I still have the jewelry box you made me for my twelfth birthday."

"You do?" I laughed, my insides warming at her admission. "I'm not sure I'd want to see that. My skills have improved a lot since then."

She smiled. "Which merely proves my point. And begs the question—what are you doing with this house? It's impressive, don't get me wrong. But it's not you."

For the first time in years, I felt seen. I blinked a few times, unprepared for the surge of emotion that accompanied that revelation.

I lifted a shoulder. "It was a good investment."

"Can I ask you a personal question?"

I leaned against the wall, crossing my legs at the ankle. "Only if you'll answer one of mine."

Something seemed to pass through her eyes, and she asked, "Do you do anything for yourself?"

"Sure."

"You hesitated." Her lips curled into a smile, and for a minute, it was easy to imagine that it was just the two of us. That we were alone, and she was here because of me.

"What about you?" I asked, turning the question back on her. She was a hard worker—her grades were evidence of that. But it was more than that. I saw how disciplined she was at the office. How diligent and determined. I'd never been so attracted to someone for their brain, their work ethic.

"All you seem to do is work," she said, ignoring my question.

"You're one to talk."

"Yeah, but I'm still in school. I'm trying to establish myself and my business. You're at a point in your career where you can afford to do what you want."

"Business?" I tilted my head to the side. "What business?"

"It's nothing." She blinked several times in quick succession.

"Liar," I teased. She rolled her eyes but didn't deny it. "Now, tell me about this business."

"It's—" She huffed, her skin flushing with color. "You're going to think it's silly."

"Try me." I held her gaze, daring her to tell me. *Trust me.*

"I want to start a coaching business."

"Like a life coach?" I asked.

"Sort of. I mean, that's definitely part of it."

"What else?" I pushed.

She let out a deep sigh, and I wondered why she was so reticent to share. At the office, she rarely held back her opinion.

"Please," I added. "I want to know."

She twisted her hands together, keeping her eyes focused on the floor, the wall, anywhere but at me. "I want to empower women to take charge of their lives and their finances. My goal is to help small business owners reclaim their time so they can live with purpose. So they can work smarter and find more joy." Her eyes lit up, and the longer

51

she spoke, the more confident and excited she seemed to become.

I stared at her a beat, completely captivated. "There it is."

"What?" She furrowed her brow.

"Your passion. Your purpose. That's what I was looking for your first day, and now I see it."

"You don't think I'm naïve?"

"What?" I jerked my head back. "No. I think you're passionate and…" *Beautiful.* Fuck. I couldn't say that. I should never say that. "I'm sure you've done your research."

She nodded. "Yes, but…well, would you want to take advice from a life coach who hadn't really experienced much life?"

"Why not?" I stepped closer, placing my hands on her shoulders. "I think that anyone who spends any amount of time with you will see how wise you are. They'll see your enthusiasm and be sucked into your orbit." I certainly was.

"Thank you." She held my gaze, her eyes shining with something that looked a lot like appreciation and…desire.

"Jonathan, Sumner," Lea called.

I took a step back from Sumner just as Lea reached the top of the stairs. Lea glanced between the two of us, and while Sumner's smile looked natural, mine felt forced. The three of us remained there a moment, my chest tightening as I tried to imagine what Lea was thinking. And worse still, what she might tell Ian.

"Something smells good," I said, rushing to fill the silence.

*Fuck.* I clenched my fists. I had to stop doing this. I had to stop having these thoughts about Sumner. Even just thinking them felt like a betrayal of my friendship with Ian.

Lea smiled. "Dinner's ready."

"Excellent." I gestured for her to lead the way, waiting for Sumner to follow.

I took a moment to compose myself, wondering what it

was about Sumner that knocked me so off-kilter. *And why her?* Why, of all the women I could be attracted to, why did it have to be my best friend's daughter?

I wasn't sure I could pinpoint any one thing. She was gorgeous—with curves that made my mouth water. But it was more than that. She was insightful and wise, passionate and caring. And somehow, despite our age difference, despite our life experience, she got me.

As we ate dinner, I couldn't remember a more pleasurable evening. Candles flickered on the patio table, the sun setting in the distance. The wine, like the conversation, flowed easily. And I wasn't ready for it to end. Wasn't ready to be alone again.

When Sumner volunteered to wash the dishes, I jumped at the chance to help her. I wanted to know more about this coaching business, more about her. I followed her into the kitchen, trying to ignore the sway of her hips, the seductive curve of her ass. She was absolutely beautiful, standing at the sink, her delicate hands graceful as they rinsed the dishes. *And* I was staring.

I opened the dishwasher then grabbed a towel from the drawer. "So, how would you advise me, if I were your coaching client?"

"Seriously?"

"Yeah. I want to hear your suggestions."

She handed me a rinsed dish that was ready to load. Her fingers slid along mine, the soap making our hands and the dish slippery and slick. She almost dropped it, and I grabbed the dish with one hand and her wrist with the other.

"Good catch," she panted, our eyes locked. We remained that way a moment before she reached for the faucet and switched off the water.

She considered my question a moment, then said, "Well,

I'd start by sitting down with you and asking what's working and what's not."

"Everything."

She laughed. "Everything is working?" When I shook my head, she asked, "Nothing is working?"

I nodded, drying the crystal glass she'd handed me. But when she nearly dropped the next one, I said, "All right, switch," and toweled off my hands before placing them on her hips and shifting her to the side. I lingered there a moment, the sight of her bare skin so tantalizing. Her shoulder begging to be kissed. It was so tempting, but I forced myself to let go.

"You can dry." I handed her the towel.

"Okay." Her cheeks were flushed, voice breathless. She shook her head. "Right." She cleared her throat. "I hate that you feel that way. When I look at the Wolfe Group, I only see success. There's always room for improvement, but I'd like to know why you feel nothing is working. Or more specifically, what is no longer serving you."

I glanced outside to where Lea and Ian were laughing, drinking wine. I returned my attention to Sumner, her eyes so open, so gentle. Like a feather bed you could dive into.

"I'm…" Could I really admit this to her? Should I? After a week together, we were as close as we'd ever been. Maybe more so, the professional aspect providing additional depth and dimension to our interactions now that she was an adult. And the fact that she'd trusted me with her business idea made me more willing to share something in return.

"I'm fried," I said, keeping my eyes focused on the sink. "I feel like I can barely keep up, and most days, I wonder why I'm still doing all this. I wonder what I'm trying to prove."

She swallowed, and I would've killed to know what she was thinking. Had I admitted too much? Gone too far?

But when she spoke, I didn't feel judged or pitied like I'd

expected or, rather, feared. I felt understood. Or at least, I got the impression she genuinely wanted to understand me.

"In that case, I think we should start with one of the most basic—and important—questions. What does success mean to you?"

I opened my mouth, ready to answer, but she shook her head, placing her hand on my arm. "No. I want you to spend some time thinking on it. Not the answer you think you should give, but the one you really want to. I'll send you an email with some prompts that might help you reframe this question and your answer."

My initial reaction was to brush off the exercises, but I could see she believed they would help. And I was desperate enough to try. Especially if it gave me an excuse to spend more time with her.

"In the meantime," she continued, giving my arm a squeeze before releasing me. "It may be useful to do a time audit."

I groaned, but she wasn't deterred.

"Now, hear me out," she said and proceeded to explain her reasoning. By the time she'd finished, I was convinced. Though I certainly had questions.

"I already track some of my time at the office, but you want me to track my entire day in fifteen-minute increments?"

"Yes—work, personal, et cetera. Then we'll get a feel for the areas that are dragging you down or ones where you'd rather spend more time. See—" She dried her hands on the towel and grabbed a journal from her bag. It was one I'd often see her pull out at meetings; she never went anywhere without it. "This is an example of one of mine."

I scanned the entries, intrigued by this insight she'd given me into her life. I could see what time she woke up. When she ate lunch. How she'd spent her days—volunteering at a women's shelter on weekends, drinks with friends.

"What's this?" I asked, indicating an entry I'd seen several times before, marked "JJ."

She attempted to snatch the journal from me, but I held it away, continuing to flip through the pages.

She reached around me to grab it, but I kept my back to her. "It's nothing."

Which only fanned the flames of my curiosity. "Really? I noticed it *several* times in your time audit. Must be important."

"It's...personal."

"JJ," I mused. "Could be a guy. Or a girl." I watched her, gauging her reaction.

"If you must know," she let out a puff of air. "It's *me* time."

Oh. *Oh.* My eyes widened as the realization hit me. I kicked myself for pushing.

"But why 'JJ'?" I asked, still trying to make sense of it. Still unable to let it go.

"You know..." She blushed, her cheeks stained with the most beautiful hue. "Just Jillin'."

I couldn't help myself; I laughed. She'd taken the female equivalent of "jacking off" and made it into a clever acronym.

"That's actually pretty cute." Though the image that followed of Sumner, naked and touching herself—preferably while thinking of me—was the furthest thing from "cute." "*Annd*...this conversation just crossed the line from inappropriate to weird."

"Why is it weird?" she asked. When I didn't answer, she said, "I'm not a kid anymore. It's okay to talk about this stuff."

"This *stuff*?" I chuckled. "You can't even say the word."

"What? Sex? Fucking?" She shrugged, each word rolling off her tongue. "And it's only weird if you make it weird."

The air between us thickened, and I swallowed hard

when she licked her lips, slicking them until they were shiny. Without any conscious thought on my part, I stepped closer, lured to her.

"Now, will you please give my journal back?" She grabbed it and tugged, but I wouldn't let go. I couldn't.

"Why even log it at all?" I asked, ignoring her request. "Why not just group it with 'Shower' or 'Sleep'?"

She released her grip on the journal with a huff. "Because that wouldn't be accurate. If you're willing to go to the trouble of logging your day in fifteen-minute increments, you need to be honest about where the time is going. If you log it as 'Sleep' or 'Shower' as you suggested, then looking back on it, you'll think—oh, I can cut some time from my morning routine. Or you'll think you're getting more rest than you are."

"You've clearly given this a lot of thought. I'm impressed."

"Thank you. Now, my journal, please." She held out her hand expectantly.

"One more thing," I said, opening to another page that had drawn my attention. It looked like sketches of logo designs. "Can we talk about this?"

"That's—" She snatched it from my hands and quickly closed it. "I think that's enough digging around in my personal info, thank you very much. Anyway..." She forced a smile. "I'll send you the prompts, and you can work on your time audit, and then we can talk more."

"I can't believe you're the one giving me homework," I teased, leaning my hip against the counter, still amazed by how quickly we'd fallen back into the easy familiarity we'd always had.

"You don't have to do it," she said.

"I know." I pushed off the counter as Ian and Lea slid the back door open. "I want to."

"Want to what?" Ian asked, and Sumner startled.

"Have dessert!" Sumner chirped.

I studied her, and she met my eyes with a slight shake of her head. *Interesting.*

"Dessert?" Ian laughed. "This guy?" He hooked a thumb over his shoulder at me. "No way. Jonathan doesn't eat desserts."

Sumner tilted her head to the side, likely thinking of all the times I'd taken her for ice cream growing up. "Yes, he does."

I grinned. "Only with you."

# CHAPTER SEVEN

*Sumner*

"Hey, Cody." I waved as I approached his desk, noticing that Jonathan's office door was closed. "Is Jonathan available?"

"He should be almost done with his meeting." He paused. "Jonathan, huh?" He arched his brow. "Interesting."

"What?" I asked.

"I think you're the only person who calls him Jonathan besides your dad."

I laughed. "Yeah. What's up with that? Even you call him Wolfe."

"Everyone calls him Wolfe," he deadpanned.

The door opened, and a man walked out, with Jonathan just behind. When Jonathan saw me, he smiled, his face transforming from serious to gorgeous. "Hey. Give me just a minute."

I nodded, scanning his figure hungrily. The gray material emphasizing his broad shoulders and narrow waist. How could a man be so handsome? It should be illegal.

When he returned, he placed his hand on the small of my

back, ushering me into his office and shutting the door behind us.

"You sure you have time for this?" I asked, still in disbelief. I knew coaching could benefit my clients, give them more time in the long run. But I hadn't expected a man like Jonathan—CEO of the Wolfe Group, LA's Businessperson of the Year—to be so eager to work with me.

I briefly wondered if he was just doing it to be nice, but I knew better than that. Jonathan appreciated efficiency and was results-oriented. He wouldn't waste his time with me unless he believed I could actually help him. And having him on my roster of clients would be huge for attracting new ones.

"Absolutely." He took a seat, inviting me to join him. "Where do you want to start?"

I resisted the urge to fidget with my bracelets. Though I'd worked with the women at the shelter, none of my clients had ever seemed so...intimidating. Even so, I pressed on. This was my dream job, and he was giving me an opportunity to hone my skills.

*He's just like any other client.* I took a deep breath and smiled. "Why don't we start by talking about what success means to you."

"Is this how you speak to all your clients?"

I tilted my head to the side, wondering if I'd come across as too formal, unapproachable. I'd been striving for professional, warm, but now I was second-guessing myself. "How's that?"

He leaned forward, resting his elbows on his knees. "In your sexy, I'm-a-badass-boss-bitch voice?"

I laughed, feeling my cheeks warm. "I wasn't aware I had a badass-boss-bitch voice." Though my mind kept coming back to that one word—sexy. Did that mean he thought I was sexy?

"You have no idea how amazing you are," he rasped. "Which makes you all the more attractive. But one day you'll realize...and then you'll be unstoppable."

My insides warmed from his compliment. "Maybe you should be the life coach because, damn, you give good pep talks."

"Thank you." He grinned. "And yes, I completed my homework."

"I'd expect nothing less." I smiled, feeling more relaxed, more confident. "What did you learn, if anything?"

"I spend a lot of time doing tasks I hate."

I nodded. "Good."

"Good?" he scoffed. "How is that good?"

"We can use that data to make better decisions going forward. We can delegate, delete, or keep the task. And then we can free up more of your time to do the stuff that really matters. Can I see your time audit?"

"Sure." He leaned over, grabbing his phone from his desk and opening the notes app before handing it to me.

"Okay." I scrolled through the entries. "I see what you mean." There was definitely room for improvement. There were a number of things he was doing that he could absolutely delegate. "Why do you think you continue to do these tasks you could easily give to someone else?"

He smoothed a hand down his beard. "I started the business, and I used to do *everything* because it was just me. As we've expanded and grown, I've continued to take on more, without necessarily letting go of other things. I want to make sure we continue to meet, and exceed, the standards our clients have come to expect."

I'd guessed as much, but I wanted to get to the heart of the issue. Not the surface reason, but the true one.

"Would you be open to off-loading some of the tasks—at least temporarily—as an experiment?"

He bunched his shoulders, and I could see his internal struggle. He had a difficult time relinquishing control, even when he knew it would benefit him.

"Let's just walk through the steps that would require—hypothetically speaking," I offered. Sometimes it was easier to relax and be open to the possibilities when you were brainstorming solutions without actually committing to them.

He nodded, then detailed the steps necessary to do so. When he finished, he seemed more at peace. So, I said, "Good. Do that."

"Okay, boss." He chuckled.

"You're still the boss," I said. "Just think of me as your running buddy."

"Running buddy?" he asked, and I nearly laughed at his confused expression.

"You still make all the decisions. You're the one actually doing the training and the running." I smiled. "But I'm here to help you achieve your goals. I'll be cheering you on, by your side, as you run the race of life."

"I like that," he said. "I can't tell you how nice it is to be able to talk to someone about this. It can be lonely at the top."

I latched on to that, wondering if he meant that he was lonely in business or in life. Perhaps both? While I didn't want him to be lonely, I hated the idea of him with someone else. I could remember the day he'd announced that he was engaged to Rachel. In that moment, I'd felt my heart shatter and break. Which was ridiculous. I'd been seventeen. I'd known nothing about the world, about love.

I still didn't know why they'd broken up. All my dad had told me was that they'd called off the wedding after his birthday trip to Monaco.

"Do you want to talk about success for a minute, then come back to the time audit?"

"Sure." He grabbed a pair of glasses from his desk and slid them on as he reviewed a piece of paper. They rested on the bridge of his nose, and every thought, every question I'd been poised to ask fled my brain.

I'd thought he couldn't get sexier. But, apparently, I'd been wrong. The dark frames highlighted his dark lashes, making his blue eyes appear even more striking. I attempted to compose myself, though my jagged breath said otherwise. Glasses, beard, suit—I was a goner.

"Did you walk through the ideal life exercise?" I asked, shifting in my chair as if that would ease the ache building.

He nodded, removing his glasses before setting them aside with a sigh. "Though I struggled with it."

"Why?"

"I don't know. I mean, what more can I possibly achieve? I have it all. Financial freedom. The ability to do whatever I want. A fabulous house, expensive cars, a successful company."

"Mm-hmm." I watched him, reading his body as he spoke. He seemed to shrink into himself with every word. "Do you actually want those things?"

"Of course," he answered quickly, almost instinctively.

"Why?" I asked, wanting to dig deeper into his motivations. I crossed my legs and felt his eyes track the movement.

"Isn't that what you want? What everybody wants?"

"This isn't about me," I said, sensing resistance. An attempt to deflect. "This is about you and what you want. Do you know what that is?"

When he didn't answer, I decided to take a different tack. "Have you ever felt torn between what you think you should want and your true desires?"

"I-I..." He hesitated, and I wasn't sure I'd ever seen him at a loss for words. "Yes." He swallowed hard, my eyes tracking the movement of his Adam's apple as it bobbed.

"I can help you audit your time and make all the positive changes in the world. But unless you get to the heart of why you're doing it all, unless you figure out your 'why,' none of it will make a lasting impact." It was easy to forget my nerves when passion took the wheel.

"What if what I want is something I can't have?" His fervor was unnerving, and it made my skin tingle with awareness.

Was he talking about... I shook my head. Surely he couldn't mean me.

"Then you decide whether you can live without it," I said.

"And if I can't?" The rasp in his voice made my temperature rise a million degrees. This wasn't all in my head? Right?

I leaned forward. "Then you find a way. You do whatever it takes to make it yours."

I wasn't sure I could handle his intensity or this conversation, so I decided to switch gears to a safer topic. "Let's get back to your time audit for a minute. What is JO?"

He smirked. "It's the category you wouldn't let me put as 'shower' or 'sleep.'"

It took me a minute, and then it dawned on me. It was Jonathan's "me time." Definitely not a safer topic. Judging from the way he shifted in his chair, we were veering into dangerous territory. But I didn't want to back down.

I rolled my eyes. "Would you stop being such a weirdo about this?"

"I'm sorry, but it is weird. I changed your diapers."

I rolled my eyes. "Yeah. Right."

"Well, I could've. I was there."

I playfully slapped at his chest. "You're being ridiculous."

He caught my hand, holding it in his. "Don't you think it's odd, knowing the sexual habits of your clients?"

"It's data."

He chuckled, releasing my hand. "Right. Data."

Jonathan's phone buzzed on the desk, startling me. He glanced at the screen, and I saw the name "Alexis" there before he said, "Just a sec," and answered it with a smile.

"Hey." His tone was overly familiar, and I wondered if she was a friend? Lover? But why would he be jacking off so frequently if he had a lover? Maybe she'd been out of town? Maybe I shouldn't care so much.

"Sure," he said and then paused. I tried not to listen in. "That's not a problem." Another pause. "Yeah. I'll see you later."

He disconnected the call and then returned his attention to me like a spotlight. I felt the heat of it, the intensity. "Do you dissect the sexual habits of all your clients?" he asked, diving right back into the deep end.

"Just you."

"Because I'm special, right?"

"Or maybe it's because you're my only client at the moment."

"I've been thinking about that. You should talk to Isla on the third floor." How could he switch gears so quickly? I was getting whiplash.

"Yeah." I ran a hand through my hair, feeling his eyes on me. Did he have any idea how turned on I was? How keyed up? If he didn't stop with the sweet compliments and smoldering gazes, I was going to have to add another "JJ" session to my calendar before the day ended.

"She runs a small business making wreaths and T-shirts and various things."

"That doesn't bother you?" I asked, surprised he not only knew about her side hustle but was okay with it.

He lifted a shoulder. "Who am I to say what she does in her spare time? Anyway, you should talk to her. If she's interested, I'll pay you to coach her."

"Really?" I tilted my head to the side.

"I think it'd be good for both of you. And happy employees are more invested in their job."

"Yeah, but...wow. That's really very generous of you."

"Why?" The corner of his lips curved into a smile. "How much do you cost?"

"I'm not sure you can afford me," I teased.

"I know I can't." He leaned back, one leg crossed at the knee. He was so masculine. Sexy. Everything about him projecting an air of dominance. "You're priceless."

I smiled, warmth suffusing my veins. It was so nice to be valued, to be esteemed for my accomplishments. To have someone like Jonathan believe in me and my vision.

But there was more to it. There'd been a shift in our relationship these past few weeks, and I felt the potential of what could be. The easy banter, the friendship, the support, but also the heated way I'd catch him looking at me sometimes. Then he'd say things like that, and I'd melt.

His intercom buzzed, and it reminded me of his phone call with Alexis. Did he say things like that to her? To other women?

He pressed the button to indicate the speaker. "Yes?"

"Sheffield is on the phone," Cody's voice announced through the intercom.

"Thanks. I'll just be a minute," he said to Cody before turning to me. "Thank you, Sumner. Thank you for taking the time to do this with me. I really appreciate it."

"It's my pleasure." I stood, taking that as my cue to leave. "And I'm happy to continue. That is, if you'd like me to."

"Of course. I've already noticed a difference, and I absolutely want to continue working with you."

"I'm glad. And thank you."

I'd been sharing my opinions more at the office. Eric and Jack had both been receptive to my ideas. But seeing Wolfe embrace my coaching suggestions meant even more.

"Look, I have to take this call. I'm seeing this client in New York in a few weeks, and I need to speak with him." He hesitated, then added, "Unless you want to stay and listen in?"

"I've taken up enough of your time," I said. "Besides, I need to check in with Jack and Eric on a few things."

"Sure." He walked me to the door. "And don't forget to talk to Isla. While I'd love to be your only—" he cupped my elbow, his tone laced with meaning "—I also want you to succeed."

I bit back a smile, feeling the sincerity of his words. He had no idea how much it meant to me. "Thank you, Jonathan."

He'd already answered the call before I opened the door, but I heard him say, "Hold on just a second," before calling my name. "You busy this weekend?"

I shook my head, wondering why he'd asked.

"Good. There's something I want to show you. Let's talk later."

I nodded, closing the door behind me with a soft snick. I stood there a moment, dissecting everything that had happened, but then Cody's voice snapped me out of it.

"Uh oh. Don't go getting all moon-eyed over the boss. That never ends well."

I pushed off the door and rolled my eyes, though my face heated as if to broadcast my thoughts. "*Please*. I was just thinking about a solution to a problem. Besides, he's way too old for me."

"Mm-hmm."

I could hear his unspoken words just as clearly as my own thoughts. *Liar, liar, pants on fire.*

CHAPTER EIGHT

*Jonathan*

"Here we are," I said as I pulled up to the curb of a house in Los Feliz. The yard was more weeds than grass, and one of the windows was boarded up. I glanced to Sumner, trying to gauge her expression.

"Are you buying a new house?" she asked.

I shook my head, unbuckling my seat belt as Alexis pulled up behind us. "I've been flipping houses the past few years. It's a passion project of mine. Come on." I grinned. "Let me introduce you to Alexis."

I'd invited Sumner earlier without thinking. For some unknown reason, I wanted to show her this. I wanted her to know this side of me. To *see* me. And even though she knew how many times I'd jacked off last week, somehow sharing this felt more personal than letting her study my time audit.

I climbed out of the truck and greeted Alexis with a hug. "Hey."

"Hey." Alexis smiled, but her attention was directed at Sumner, curiosity written in her features.

"Alexis—" I glanced over my shoulder at Sumner, her smile like a punch to the gut. She was so gorgeous, it stole the air from my lungs. She was also my best friend's daughter and my intern.

I cleared my throat and turned back to Alexis. "This is Sumner. She's working as an associate at the Wolfe Group this summer."

Alexis extended her hand to shake. "Nice to meet you. Are you interested in residential development?"

"I'm here to learn." Sumner and I shared a secret smile, and I knew she was thinking of her time spent coaching me.

"Wolfe's the best. Even if he can be a pain in the ass sometimes." Alexis nudged me with her elbow, grinning as she said it.

I wrapped my arm around Alexis's shoulder. "You know I'm your favorite client."

"Come on." She shook her head with a laugh, and I released her. "Let me show you the house."

The inside of the house wasn't as awful as I'd feared. But it wasn't much better either. Alexis stayed with us until her phone rang.

"I'll just be outside." She slid open the back door and stepped out to the backyard, which was basically a concrete pit. Algae rested on the surface of the pool, trash and debris littering the yard.

"What do you think?" I asked Sumner.

"Honestly?" She scrunched up her nose, and it made me want to kiss her. "It's kind of a dump."

"I know." Excitement churned through my bones, brimming with potential. "It's a diamond in the rough."

"Or it's just…rough."

"Maybe I like it rough." *I shouldn't have said that.*

"Mm." She scanned my body, humming with satisfaction.

I gnashed my teeth. What the fuck was wrong with me? Why couldn't I stop thinking about her? Why did I continue to push these boundaries when I knew I was flirting with disaster?

I cleared my throat. "What I meant to say was that I love a good challenge. And this house has so much potential."

"If you say so…"

I went on to lay out my plan, leading her through each and every room. I loved how she listened with her whole body, as if she were a sponge soaking up my every word. She was passionate, smart, and attentive, but she didn't hold back her opinion either. And it only made me respect her more.

"How do you make this an economical investment? Because everything you described sounds expensive," she finally said when we returned to the living room where we'd started.

"I do a lot of the work myself."

She gawked at me. "You? The man who wears $5,000 suits and owns one of the most successful commercial real estate firms in Los Angeles?"

"Seven, but who's counting?"

She tilted her head to the side. "Seven?"

"The suit. And commercial real estate has become… tedious. Ian says this is a phase, a midlife crisis or whatever, but I need to do something with my hands. I need to make something. Leave a tangible legacy."

"By building other people's homes?"

I straightened and stared ahead, her words like a slap across the face. I shouldn't have brought her here. For all her maturity, she didn't get it. Didn't get me. "I wouldn't expect you to understand."

She placed her hand on my forearm. "I do understand. I was just surprised since you never mentioned it before. Though I guess it explains some of the blocks on your time audit."

When I met her gaze, I saw the apology in her eyes, sincerity there too. And I felt it in her words.

"No one knows, apart from Ian," I said, unable to bring myself to call him "your dad." It felt strange. Wrong, somehow. "Alexis, and now you."

She peered up at me. "Why…"

The back door slid open, and Alexis returned. Sumner jerked her hand away, Alexis's eyes watching, questioning. I mourned the loss of Sumner's touch, while cursing myself for wanting it in the first place.

"Everything okay?" I asked Alexis.

"Oh yeah." She ran a hand through her hair. "It's our anniversary, and the sitter canceled at the last minute. But Lauren and Hunter offered to take care of the girls."

"Congratulations," I said, and Sumner echoed the sentiment. "Wait." I frowned. "I thought you got married in the fall?"

"We, um—wow, you have a good memory," she said, and I smirked. "This is a, um, different anniversary." She dipped her head, cheeks flushing.

*Interesting.* Alexis was always composed, in control, a badass. So, to see her ruffled… I laughed to myself but didn't inquire further.

"Anyway, what do you think of the house?" she asked.

I rubbed a hand over my jaw. "The price needs to come down, but I'm game if you are."

"I wouldn't have shown it to you if I weren't." She grinned. "And I'll see what I can negotiate."

She locked up and we said goodbye, and then I helped Sumner into the truck before climbing in myself. She shifted, her skirt riding higher up her thighs. I gripped the steering wheel, struggling to push away thoughts of them wrapped around my head. Her taste on my tongue. My name on her lips.

"You and Alexis seem close," she finally said. "Are you business partners? Friends?"

"A bit of both. She owns a very successful residential brokerage, and she wanted to get into development. Sometimes, we collaborate. I'm her silent investor, and I do some of the work."

She nodded, though I could tell she still had questions. "Thank you for trusting me with this. It's clear that you love it. That it lights you up inside."

"You asked about my ideal day," I said, twisting the steering wheel beneath my hands. "This is it." I met her eyes, referring more to the time spent with her than anything else.

✧

"Your four o'clock is waiting in the conference room, and Eric's appendix ruptured," Cody said from the doorway to my office.

My head snapped up from my desk. "What?"

"The client is waiting." Cody's calm tone did nothing to relax me.

"Yes. I heard that part," I seethed. "What's up with Eric?"

"His fiancée just called. He's going in for emergency surgery now."

I stared at Cody. "He'll be able to go to New York, right? I mean, it's a fairly straightforward procedure."

"Wolfe, it's major surgery. Even my brief internet search told me he's going to be out for a week, maybe even two or three."

"Three weeks?" I choked. "He's the lead on the Sheffield project. He's spent weeks preparing for this trip. Not to mention all the work he did on Anderson and the other clients we're supposed to meet."

"Perhaps we can have him join you virtually?" Cody

offered. "But considering the painkillers he's going to be on, he'd probably be more of a liability than anything."

"Fuck." I slammed my palm against the desk, needing to expel some energy. It didn't accomplish anything, but it felt good. "Okay." I straightened, smoothing down my tie. "We'll talk about this when I'm done with my meeting. I want options."

"Already on it."

I tried to focus on the client, but my mind was elsewhere. After I'd escorted her to the lobby, Cody met me outside my office. It was nearly six, and I loosened my tie. The office was fairly empty, most of the employees having already left for the day.

"I thought of someone."

"Great. Who?" I pushed open the door to my office and settled behind my desk as I waited for my laptop to wake up.

"Sumner."

I opened my mouth, ready to balk at his suggestion. Eric was a senior member of the team. She was an intern. I didn't have a problem with taking her, but I imagined our clients might see it as a sign of disrespect.

Cody was undeterred. "She's great with clients, and it would be a good learning experience for her. Besides, you don't have many options. Amanda is on maternity leave," Cody said, eliminating my next suggestion. God, he knew me well. "And Layton has that meeting with the Windham Group next week, plus a number of other obligations it would be best not to shift, period, let alone last minute."

I narrowed my eyes at him. "Why are you so keen for me to take Sumner?"

"Because I see her potential, and I know you do too." I continued to stare him down, scrutinizing him until he lifted his hands in mock surrender. "What?"

I could see right through his innocent expression. But I

worried that he could see right through me—see through to the feelings for Sumner I worked so hard to keep at bay.

"Like I said—" he moved around the coffee table, laying out more documents for me to review "—she knows her stuff. She's been working with Eric on this—"

"She has?" I knew she'd bounced between the groups, helping with various projects, but Cody made it sound as if Sumner had put in long hours with Eric. I frowned, not liking the thought of that, even if he was engaged.

"Just last week, he told me that he was impressed."

"*Eric* said that?" Eric was rarely impressed.

Cody nodded. "He also said she's well versed in the accounts. But if you want me to find someone else..."

Even though I knew he was right, I hesitated. This was a bad idea. Not because I didn't think she'd do a good job. But because I knew she'd do an amazing job, and then it would be even more difficult to fight my attraction to her. I already thought she was brilliant. Beautiful, smart, passionate. I didn't need even more reasons to like her. If anything, I needed to stay away from her.

"Plus, I think your trip will be more successful if Sumner's there," he added in a tone laced with unspoken meaning.

"Why's that?" I picked up one of the packets and skimmed the contents. *Where are my...*

"Here." Cody handed me my reading glasses as if he could fucking read my mind. Scary idea considering how inappropriate my thoughts had been lately regarding a certain raven-haired beauty.

"Thanks." I stared at the document while contemplating my options.

"You're more pleasant when she's around."

"I am?" I glanced up from the document.

"Do I really need to answer that?" he deadpanned, as if the reason were obvious.

"Yeah." I glared at him over the rim of my glasses. "I think you fucking do."

He shook his head. "Like I said, she's good for you. Just think about it, but don't wait too long. I'll need to make the necessary arrangements for whoever's going."

He left my office, closing the door softly behind him. But his words continued to reverberate through me.

*New York.*

*Sumner.*

*Good for me.*

A week alone with Sumner. In New York. It sounded like the worst idea ever. It seemed like the best idea ever. Did I really have any other choice? Without giving it too much thought, I swung open the door and marched over to his desk.

"Cody?"

"I already called her," he said, clearly having already anticipated my request. Sometimes he could be so annoying. "She'll be down in a minute."

I didn't even question his uncanny ability to read my mind anymore, simply answering, "Excellent. Thanks," before returning to my office.

I closed the door and crossed the room to my desk. Sat. Clicked on an email. Tossed my glasses on the desk. Stood. Paced the wall of windows. What the hell was wrong with me?

My clammy palms made me feel like a teenager asking a girl to be his date for the prom, not... I shook my head. Dammit. I was a forty-four-year-old man. I was inviting her on a business trip, the operative word being "business."

Then why did my body seem to think otherwise? Why had my heart rate sped up the moment Cody had mentioned Sumner's name in connection with New York? Why did the idea of a week alone with her both thrill and terrify me? Why—

There was a soft knock on the door, halting the train wreck that was my thoughts. I straightened, smoothing down my tie as I strode over to the door with a sense of purpose, of confidence, that I didn't currently feel. As expected, Sumner stood just outside. I hadn't seen her today, but I feasted on her as if it had been a week not a day. Her army-green silk shirt matched her eyes, but mine were following the fabric, admiring the way it flowed over her breasts. Her nipples hardening beneath the...

"Jonathan?"

I snapped my eyes up to meet hers. *What the fuck are you doing?*

I cleared my throat and stood aside so she could enter. "Yes. Come in."

With the door closed, I took a few deep breaths to center myself. *Big fucking mistake.*

Her fruity shampoo lingered in the air, and instead of calming down, I only felt more agitated. I hissed and smoothed down my tie before striding across the room to join her. I considered sitting behind my desk, but it seemed too formal and standing, impersonal. I never debated where to sit or whether or not to stand. This girl was fucking with my head. All I wanted to do was sit beside her, but that was definitely out. Finally, I opted to lean against my desk and hoped I looked more relaxed than I felt.

"You're still here," I said, though it came out as more of a question.

She peered up at me with an angelic expression so full of concern. "Of course. With Eric in the hospital, I wanted to make sure his clients were taken care of. Everyone did."

She continually impressed me. She could've just bided her time this summer as a favor to her dad, but she was busting her ass. Not to mention the fact that she was coaching me on the side. I'd already seen a marked improvement in my productivity and my mood thanks to her tips.

I nodded, rubbing a hand over my chin. "Thank you. How would you feel about accompanying me to New York?"

"New York?" Her eyes went wide. "Seriously?"

I tried to contain my smile and failed. A week alone with Sumner in New York sounded too good to be true. Except, I wanted to work her hard between the sheets, not pore over spreadsheets. "As you've probably already guessed, Eric can't go. I want to take you."

Her eyes darkened, the pupils flaring momentarily before she seemed to recover herself. "You want to take me?"

I nodded, replaying my words and her reaction in my head. It was a slip. A turn of phrase. Nothing more. I didn't want to *take* take her.

*Liar.*

"Just me," she said again, as if she couldn't believe her ears.

"Yes." I chuckled, some of my earlier tension dissipating. This wasn't a big deal. "Is that really so hard to believe?"

"Not to sound ungrateful, and at the risk of you changing your mind—aren't there more qualified employees who would give their right arm to go?"

I crossed my arms over my chest, enjoying the way her eyes darted to my biceps. "Do you not want to go?"

"No," she rushed to answer, though I sensed hesitation. *Why?* "Of course, I want to go."

"Cody tells me you're well versed in the Sheffield project. Is that correct?"

She nodded. "Yes, but—"

"Why don't you grab your laptop and meet me back here in ten. I'll have Cody order us dinner." When she twisted her hands together, I added, "Unless you have other plans."

She shook her head. "No. I'm, uh, yeah. I just need to make a quick call, and then I'm all yours."

I liked the sound of that more than I should.

"We can do this tomorrow night, if that's better," I offered, wondering what her other plans were. A date? I clenched my fists but then reminded myself that she was my employee. I shouldn't care what she did in her free time. Even if the thought of her out with another man made me want to break something.

"It's fine." She smiled and stood, smoothing down her pants. "I'm sure Piper will understand."

"Piper?" I laughed, something in my chest easing. "As in Piper Merrithew? Your best friend growing up?"

"Yeah." She smiled. "One and the same. You remember her?"

"Is she still as wild as she was?"

"Worse." She grinned, and I didn't like the mischievous gleam in her eye.

Maybe it was a good thing she wasn't going out with Piper tonight after all. I had a feeling the two of them could get themselves into some trouble. It was always the quiet ones you had to worry about. If I had to guess, I'd say my girl had a naughty side.

I shook my head. Not my girl. Not now. Not ever.

"I don't mind rescheduling. I know I sprung this on you."

"It's fine, really." She smiled. "I'm sure I won't be missing much. Besides, I wasn't really looking forward to going out with the guy she set me up with. He sounds like a complete tool. So, really, you're doing me a favor."

I gripped the edge of my desk, forcing out a laugh. I had no right to be jealous, but I was. What I wouldn't give to have a chance with Sumner, to be able to ask her out and spend time with her. To enjoy her company. Not as her boss. Not as her dad's best friend. But as a man.

I often wondered if part of the reason she was alluring was the very fact that she was off-limits. I'd grown up poor; I was no stranger to wanting something and not being able to have it. But that was a lifetime ago, and I'd grown accustomed to taking what I wanted. To working for something and accomplishing it.

"So, no boyfriend, then?" I finally asked the question I'd been dying to know for weeks. A question I had no right to ask. It was like some sick part of me had been waiting for this opening.

Again, a shake of her head. "No. I'm not seeing anyone. What would be the point? I'm moving again at the end of the summer."

"Right." I nodded, digesting this new information. "Yeah. I just thought your dad said there was someone—"

"There's no one." Her curt tone had me even more curious about the men from her past. "What about you?" she asked, her voice more tentative.

"Do I have a boyfriend?" I teased, intentionally misinterpreting her question.

She rolled her eyes then headed for the door. "Never mind. It's none of my business."

But I realized I wanted it to be. As the door closed behind her, I said, "There's no one," but she was already too far away to hear.

# CHAPTER NINE

## Summer

"You okay?" Jonathan placed his hand on my shoulder. I glanced away from the screen displaying the latest information on our flight to New York.

The past few days had been a whirlwind of preparations, long hours, and packing. The long hours I didn't mind, especially if I got to spend them with him. And while I'd tried to push my anxiety over the flight from my mind, I hadn't done a very good job. I'd barely slept—keeping myself busy until I'd eventually pass out.

"Yep," I chirped, placing my hand on the small bag of pills buried in my purse. It was so tempting to take one. I was exhausted, on edge, and also excited. It was a dangerous mix.

"I'm great," I said, bouncing on my toes, more to dispel my nervous energy than from any actual excitement.

"Anxious flyer?"

"A little." *Huge understatement.*

I forced a smile, trying to push away memories of my last flight. But my mind immediately went to that moment—the plane plummeting toward the ground. Sweat beaded along my forehead, though a chill came over my skin at the recollection. A certain-death moment, I'd later learned it was called. Nearly crashing had given me clarity, but it was still scary as hell to contemplate flying again.

*I can do this.* I breathed, repeating the words in my head. *I can do this.*

This would be the first flight I'd taken since, and to say I was on edge would be an understatement. We hadn't even boarded, and already, it felt as if the walls were closing in. I could only imagine how trapped I'd feel once I was inside the tin can, but there was no going back now.

I shifted my hand in my purse, feeling around for the little baggie once more. When Piper heard I was flying, she'd insisted on giving me a few of her antianxiety meds. And while I'd been totally opposed at first, I was now rethinking my stance. Five-plus hours confined on the plane was a long time. A *very* long time.

The gate agent made an announcement about boarding, and my chest constricted, spots dancing before my eyes. For a brief moment, I thought I was going to pass out. And that fear of making a fool of myself pushed me over the edge. I slipped a pill from the bag, placing it on my tongue and swallowing it down when Jonathan wasn't looking.

"First class is now welcome to board."

"That's us," Jonathan said, and when he placed his hand on my lower back, I knew I wouldn't go back even if I could.

There was no way I'd miss a trip—an opportunity—like this. Especially not when it meant a week alone with Jonathan. Well, a week alone with him outside work meetings anyway. But I was so desperate for any time with this man that I'd take whatever I could get, pathetic as it was.

I didn't know what I hoped would happen. There were times he seemed attracted to me, but he'd never acted on it.

He'd never been anything but professional, polite, kind. Realistically, I knew nothing would *ever* happen between us.

He continued talking as we walked down the jet bridge, and I wondered if he could tell how nervous I was. I gripped the suitcase handle tighter, my stomach churning with every step. Even so, his voice was calming. His touch—distracting. It was the only thing keeping me sane as I smiled at the flight attendant and stepped onto the plane. I swallowed, reminding myself that I was okay. That we weren't destined to crash-land like my last flight. And I prayed that wouldn't be the case. I also hoped Piper's pill would kick in soon.

Even so, with one look at the strip of lights lining the floor, I was ready to bolt. A gentle nudge on my lower back had my feet moving again. Jonathan smiled, and I tried my best to return it, but the smell of burned coffee, the hiss of the air pumping through the vents, had my body on high alert. I took a seat, my hands shaking as I attempted to buckle the seat belt.

After he'd stowed our carry-on bags in the overhead bin, he peered down at me. "Sumner, are you sure you're okay?"

I gave him a curt nod, hoping he'd drop the matter and leave me the hell alone. He seemed unconvinced, so I smiled and tried to distract both of us by talking about New York. I'd visited a few times while attending MIT, and I'd always longed to attend a Broadway show. I doubted there'd be time for that, but we didn't have any meetings until the morning.

I thought I was doing fine or, at least, giving the appearance of it. But then the pilot asked the flight attendants to prepare for takeoff, and my heart rate ratcheted up. I busied myself with the in-flight magazine, quickly returning it to its place before reaching for my Kindle. I'd read the same sentence twice when the plane started to race down the runway. My stomach was in my throat, and I was holding my breath so I wouldn't be sick.

"Sumner." Jonathan placed his hand on mine, his touch warm, comforting. "Breathe."

My gaze snapped to his. It wasn't the first time we'd touched, but something about it felt more intentional, more electric. That was the only word to describe it. My body hummed, every neuron firing all of a sudden like a generator that kick-started to life. And he was only touching my hand. I couldn't imagine what it would be like to have him touch me...*other places*.

"That's it," he said in a calm, soothing tone. I didn't realize how tightly I'd been gripping the armrests until I shook out my free hand. "There you go."

My heart rate alternated between excitement and calm, though it was no longer solely due to the flight. This man had my heart racing and my stomach in knots. I was so preoccupied, I didn't realize the plane had leveled out and the roar of the engines had become more of a distant hum.

He signaled to the flight attendant, speaking to her briefly before she returned with a tumbler of amber liquid. "Here. Drink this," he said, handing it to me.

I eyed the glass, not sure it was a good idea. Perhaps sensing my hesitation, he nudged it in my direction, "Come on, Sum. Trust me, it'll help."

I nodded, accepting it and downing a large gulp. "Ah." I winced. "That burns."

He studied me, and I continued to evaluate the assault on my senses. Everything felt...fuzzy. Softer, somehow.

"Oh wow. That's—" I shook my head, placing a finger to my mouth as if to stifle my giggles. "My lips are tingling." I giggled some more, feeling as if my head were floating. "Is that normal?"

His deep chuckle warmed my belly like the whiskey heating my insides. It was an odd, but pleasant, sensation. And I wanted more of it—both the whiskey and the man.

"Let me have a taste." He leaned in, and for a moment, I thought he'd sample it from my lips. But then he took the glass and raised it to his mouth. He placed his lips to the exact spot where my lipstick marked the glass.

He watched me over the rim of the glass, taking a sip before setting it back down. "Yep. Maker's Mark." He licked his lips, and I stared at him, my mouth watering at the sight. "You've never had whiskey, have you?"

I laughed. "Is it that obvious?"

He chuckled. "One day, I'll have to give you a proper tasting."

He opened his mouth as if to say something else, but the flight attendant interrupted. "Would you like a refill?"

He held my gaze a moment longer before turning his attention to her. My thoughts felt hazy, and I closed my eyes.

I must have fallen asleep because I awoke with a start, my stomach jolting along with the plane. Fear bubbled up inside me, and I glanced around, surprised to see Jonathan sitting next to me.

*Is this a dream?*

"Hey there." He smiled, placing his hand on my forearm. "You okay?"

*Yep, definitely a dream.*

"No." He chuckled, making me realize I'd said the last part aloud. "You fell asleep."

The plane bounced again, and I clutched at my neck as if my oxygen supply had been cut off. My eyes darted about the space, through the window, at the flight attendants. How could everyone be so calm?

"Is it hot in here?" I reached up and opened the vent with a jerky movement.

Was it even blowing? I started fanning myself with the in-flight magazine, which only made me queasy. Everything was too hot. Too tight. I couldn't breathe. I plucked at the buttons on my shirt, the feeling of being strangled lessening slightly with each one I loosened.

"Sumner?" He tilted his head, his expression one of concern. "What are you doing?" He gently placed his jacket over me like a shield.

"Is everything okay?" the flight attendant asked, false positivity ringing through her voice.

"We're fine." Jonathan's smooth voice conveyed a sense of certainty that put me at ease. "Could you bring us some water and a charcuterie plate?"

"Sure thing," she said, her eyes darting to me.

Jonathan returned his attention to me. "Why don't we get you settled again and then have a snack?"

I closed my eyes, a wave of embarrassment washing over me. A moment of clarity slamming into me. *Oh. My. God.*

I hastily buttoned my shirt, tucking it into my skirt before returning his jacket to him. "I think, um... I think I'll just go to the restroom. Some cold water on my face might help."

"Stay," he pleaded, clearly not trusting me on my own. "I'll see if I can get you a cold compress."

"No." I drew in a sharp breath. "I really... I really think I just need a minute." Unfortunately, he was blocking my exit.

The flight attendant returned with the requested items in the midst of our little stare-off, and after Jonathan thanked her, he said, "Sure. Just have some water and a snack first. Okay?"

Begrudgingly, I accepted the water and ate some cheese and crackers.

"See? I'm fine. I'll just be a minute." I stood, forcing him to do the same. "And if I'm gone more than five, you can come after me. Deal?"

He held my gaze a moment then nodded. "I'm setting a timer. If you're gone too long, I *will* come after you."

I was tempted to stay longer than five minutes just to see

if he'd follow through on his threat. To find out what would happen.

I grinned up at him as I brushed past. "Is that a promise?"

"Sumner," he growled.

I smirked then walked down the aisle, feeling his eyes on me the entire time. But the moment I shut myself in the bathroom and locked the door, my bravado evaporated. I sagged against the sink, wishing I could go back and undo the past hour. What the hell had happened?

Already some of the fog was clearing, only to be replaced by regret. Had I really unbuttoned my shirt and tried to strip on the plane? I didn't consider myself particularly modest, but this was definitely *not* how I'd imagined undressing for Jonathan. I squeezed my eyes shut. What had I been thinking?

I'd been working with Isla on overcoming her fears in business, and I could barely face my own fear of flying. With that reminder, I splashed some water on my face and took a few deep breaths before returning to my seat.

"Hey." I tapped Jonathan on the shoulder, and he immediately stood.

"Glad I didn't have to send out a search party."

I brushed past him, wobbling a little before he placed his hands on my hips. I swallowed hard, gripping the back of the seat in front of me. I froze, as did he. And then he gently guided me to my seat. Even after he released me, the feel of his hands on my skin was burned into me.

"There we are." He sank down next to me. "How are you feeling?"

*My heart's racing, and I feel like I was just electrocuted by your touch.* "I'm good, and I want to apologize for acting so...unprofessionally."

"I couldn't give a fuck about that. I just want to make sure you're okay." Concern swirled in his eyes, and I knew I owed him an explanation.

I took a deep breath. "I took an antianxiety drug, but it obviously had the opposite effect and sent me into freak-out mode."

Jonathan nodded, his expression contemplative. "Have you ever taken that medicine before?"

I shook my head, hanging it between my shoulders. "No. And I should've known better. Again, I'm so sorry. I promise it won't happen again."

"Sumner." He placed his hand on mine. "You're not in trouble. I just want to make sure you're okay. Okay?"

I nodded, though I almost wished the plane would crash so I could avoid the embarrassment of this moment.

"Why didn't you tell me you had a fear of flying?"

I shook my head, my cheeks heating. The plane engine hummed in the distance, the flight attendant continuing about her business as if I hadn't just freaked the fuck out.

"Because I don't." Or at least, I refused to believe I did. I would not let the fear of crashing prevent me from experiencing life. No freaking way.

"Okay." I could feel his eyes on me, and I sensed the skepticism in his tone. "Then what's going on? Talk to me."

I closed my eyes, heart sinking. I knew I couldn't deny him, especially not when he asked in such a gentle tone. Not when he'd been so forthcoming and open with me the past few weeks when we had our coaching sessions. He was still struggling to define what success meant for him, but he'd aced all my other assignments.

"You know how I did the Semester at Sea program?" It was on my resume, and we'd spoken about it in the past but mostly in terms of my sea and land experience, not the flight from hell.

"Yeah." He smoothed his thumb over my hand, and I'd tell him anything if he'd keep doing that.

"Well, I had to join the group late, and my flight..." My throat clogged, my nose stinging. *I will not cry. I will not.* I sniffed and glanced toward the ceiling. Just like that night, the cabin lights were on, the air conditioning vents open.

"Hey," he hushed. "It's okay. You're okay."

I shook my head, a tear slipping out and falling down my cheek. "I—" I took a deep breath and stared at the back of the seat in front of me. "My plane hit some turbulence. We lost an engine, and we had to make an emergency landing." I rushed out the rest of the story, just wanting to be done with it.

He gripped my hand tighter, and I could sense the concern radiating from him. "I had no idea. I mean, Ian mentioned your flight having some trouble, but I didn't realize..."

I nodded. "I know. I didn't want to freak him out, so I downplayed the seriousness of the situation. But if I'm being completely honest, I was certain I was going to die."

"Fuck," he said in a low voice, one I could imagine him using in the bedroom. He dragged his free hand through his hair. "Sumner, why didn't you tell me? I never would've..."

"You never would've what? Invited me to come?" I shook my head. "That's why I didn't say anything. I didn't want to miss out on this opportunity. Besides..." I lifted a shoulder. "What would be the point? I knew I'd have to fly again sooner or later. And with Eric recovering from surgery, I couldn't exactly leave you in the lurch."

"Yeah, but maybe I could've done something. Helped you."

"What? With drugs? We see how well that went," I scoffed. "Besides, you are helping me," I said, and I meant it. His touch, his words, they were like a balm to my soul. His kind smile helped me relax even more.

"So, what can we expect this week?" I asked, feeling a little calmer and needing to change the topic.

"We'll have time to go over all that later," he said, though he released my hand. "You sure you're okay?"

I nodded. "Yes. Thank you. And I'd appreciate it if you kept this between us."

"Of course I won't tell anyone at the office. But—" he rubbed a hand over his chin "—I don't like keeping secrets from Ian."

"You know how he stresses. Especially about me," I said, and he nodded his agreement.

"True, but—"

"What reason is there to tell him?" I asked. "What will it change?"

"Nothing, but don't you think he deserves to know? Maybe he could help you."

I scoffed. "Um. No. I'm a twenty-three-year-old woman who's fully capable of taking care of herself."

"I know, but—"

"Jonathan." I narrowed my eyes at him.

He held up his hands in mock surrender, but his lips twitched at the corners as if he were fighting off a smile. "Okay. Okay. I promise."

"What's so funny?"

"I don't know." He lowered his hands. "I guess sometimes I see glimpses of you as a little girl, and it makes me smile."

"Oh." I tried not to let my disappointment show. Would he ever view me as the woman I was and not the little girl he'd known? Would he ever see me as Sumner and not Ian's daughter?

"It's not a bad thing," he said.

"Mm-hmm."

"I know." He grinned. "You don't like it when I mention how you were as a child. But you forget, I was there for most of your childhood, most of your life, at least until the past few years."

His words burned more going down than the whiskey had. And it only reminded me of our roles and how he viewed me, how he'd always viewed me—as Ian's daughter.

"Did I say something to upset you?"

I shook my head. "No, but can I ask you something? Why did you invite me to New York? Not that I'm complaining. But we both know you're more than capable of handling these clients by yourself."

"Maybe I wanted to spend time with you," he said, as if it were that simple. "And maybe..." He leaned in, his arm brushing against mine. My head was in overdrive, still trying to decipher his last statement, when he added, "It's because I think you're brilliant, and I value your opinion."

"Thank you. I think you're pretty brilliant too."

He settled back in his seat. "Hell, if you weren't going to grad school, I'd offer you a full-time job after this summer."

"That means a lot, especially coming from you."

He narrowed his eyes at me. "What's that supposed to mean?"

I lifted a shoulder, turning to glance out the window. We passed through the clouds, only occasionally catching glimpses of the land below. I didn't feel as unsettled as I had before, the food and water helping quell some of my earlier anxiety.

"Sumner," he growled, though his tone held a teasing note. When I didn't answer, he tickled my side.

"Hey! No fair." I blocked his hands, though I secretly loved it. "It was a compliment."

"You think I don't know what everyone says about me?" he asked. "That I'm a demanding asshole who insists on perfection. And expects the impossible."

"No. I just didn't think you cared."

"You're right." A muscle twitched in his jaw. "But I do care what you think."

Before I could ask why, the flight attendant returned to check on us. I spent the rest of the flight wondering why he cared. And what it meant.

# CHAPTER TEN

## Jonathan

I kept stealing glances at Sumner—on the flight, while we waited for our bags, during the ride to the hotel. I wanted to pull her into my arms and comfort her. And even though she seemed fine, I worried, nevertheless. I worried that I'd put her in a position where she felt the need to do something she wasn't comfortable with. I worried that she was putting on a brave face—again, when she wasn't okay. When she was suffering in silence. Boy, did I know what that was like.

The driver pulled up to our hotel before putting the car in park and coming around to open the door for us. "Here we are, Mr. Wolfe."

"Thank you." I climbed out and placed a tip in his hand before turning to help Sumner.

The driver unloaded the trunk, and Sumner stared up at the hotel, endless glass towering above us. Her black hair swirled about her shoulders, and she looked so powerful standing there. Nothing like the tearful girl on the plane, afraid we were going to die. No. Shoulders back. Chin lifted. She was proud. Confident. Beautiful.

She turned to face me, and a strand of hair fell across her face. She laughed, and I reached up to sweep it aside, both of us stilling as my knuckles brushed against her cheek. She licked her lips, and I tracked the movement of her tongue as I tucked the hair behind her ear, lingering a moment as if to ensure it stayed put. When, really, I couldn't stop touching her.

Car horns honked in the distance, startling us both. And then all the sounds, all the people around us came back in a rush. She turned for the door, and I followed her inside.

People buzzed around, the hotel a hive of activity. In the lobby, banners welcomed the WAP Annual Summit. Sumner covered her mouth to stifle a laugh. Again, I was reminded of her as a little girl. And while her expressions were similar, her mannerisms, everything else, was so different. She was different.

"What's so funny?" I asked.

"The WAP Summit?" She laughed again. "Surely someone realized..."

"Realized?"

"That's right, you're a country boy."

"Country music listener," I corrected. It wasn't the first time we'd had this argument, and it had become sort of a running joke between us.

"Well, 'WAP' was a really popular song this past year. And I'll—" She tapped on her phone, holding the screen up to me. "Here."

I skimmed the lyrics, amused by some of the inventive phrases including "pussy" or "wet-ass pussy" before handing Sumner back her phone. I wanted to laugh at the poor acronym choice, but now all I could think of was Sumner's pussy. Was it bare? A small thatch of hair? Did she come from clit stimulation? Or did she like penetration?

*Stop thinking about her pussy, dickhead.*

Maybe it would be easier if I hadn't seen her tits on the plane. When she'd started undressing, I'd frozen. And the more buttons she'd undone, the more I wanted to see. The more I wanted to touch. That lace bra cupping her breasts, pushing them up so I could think of nothing else.

"Wow," Sumner said, bringing me back to the present. She glanced around, and I followed her gaze. Everyone was dressed in suits, lanyards draped around their necks like Olympic medals. "Looks like a busy weekend for the hotel. The WAP is getting a lot of action."

This time, I really did laugh. "I hope they have a mop."

"Gimme all you got." She did a little dance, popping her hips and her ass. She had some moves, and I groaned, imagining her rolling those hips in bed. She laughed, walking on, completely oblivious to the effect she had on me.

The concierge greeted me as we approached. "Good afternoon, Mr. Wolfe. We're glad to have you staying with us again." I nodded, watching Sumner out of the corner of my eye. "Very good. And I see you have a companion this time."

"A colleague," I corrected, not wanting him to get the wrong impression. Though maybe I was the one who needed the reminder.

After he escorted Sumner and me to our rooms, we agreed to meet up for dinner. I called down to the front desk and asked them to arrange for tickets to *Hamilton*, knowing how much Sumner would enjoy it. I'd done it on impulse, remembering the way she'd spoken about wanting to attend a Broadway show.

And since she was my coach, I had a feeling this was a plan she'd support. She'd been encouraging me to branch out, to try new things and spend less time working now that I'd delegated or deleted more of my tasks in the wake of the time audit. And the more I let go of, the better I felt.

On previous business trips, doing something as spontaneous as taking a night off for a show would've been unthinkable. But any concerns over losing a few hours of work evaporated the moment I told Sumner of our plans. It was all worth it to see her reaction. To feel her body pressed to mine when she wrapped her arms around my neck out of excitement and gratitude.

"Thank you, Jonathan," she whispered in my ear, her breath tickling my skin. My cock stirred, and I gave her a quick squeeze before releasing her.

"My pleasure."

Dinner was filled with talk of the upcoming performance, and her excitement hadn't dissipated, even hours later when we filed out of the theater. Her megawatt smile was bright enough to light up Times Square. It certainly had the circuits in my brain going haywire.

"Oh my god." Sumner hooked her arm through mine, grinning as we walked down the street back to our hotel. I'd offered to call for the car, but she'd insisted on walking. I didn't mind. It meant more time with her. "That was amazing. Thank you."

I chuckled, amused by her pink cheeks and loose smile, her bright eyes. She was gorgeous, and I wasn't the only one who'd noticed. All evening, every man in a five-mile radius had been looking at her. *Us.* Trying to figure out if I was her father, her colleague, or something else. Not for the first time, I wanted us to be something else. Something more.

I'd never experienced this deep longing. This desire for something or someone that was so clearly off-limits. In the past, if I wanted something, I took it. If I was interested in a woman, I pursued her. *But with Sumner...* I shook my head. Sumner was different.

And we could never be anything more.

Even so, I couldn't help imagining it. Especially here, away from LA. Away from everyone. I couldn't remember the last time I'd had so much fun with a woman, and I wasn't ready for the evening to end. Hell, I'd spent more time watching her than the performance.

"That was amazing." She released me and floated down the sidewalk.

"Yes." I chuckled. "You already said that."

"I know, but it's true! And I'm so amped up now, I'm not sure how I'm going to fall asleep." She spun around, her dress twirling with the movement, lifting higher so I could see her thighs. Did she have any idea the effect she had on me?

"We could grab a drink?" I gestured to a bar down the street.

"That sounds nice," she said. "So, what'd you think of the show?"

"The actors were talented, and I loved seeing history come to life in such a visceral way."

"But...?"

"But I guess maybe I'm not a fan of rap."

She laughed, the sound light.

"What?"

"You sound like my dad."

I froze, reality splashing over me like a bucket of ice-cold water.

"You must think I'm so old," I teased, even though she made me feel young. "First, 'WAP.' Now this."

She rolled her eyes. "Hardly. I just know he's never been a fan either."

I nodded, but I didn't want to talk about Ian, let alone think about him. Because every time I did, I felt like a bad friend. I'd kept my relationship with Sumner professional— well, mostly professional—but my thoughts were a different story altogether.

"Here we are," I said as we arrived at a bar.

I pulled open the door and followed her inside, guiding

her over to an empty table with my hand on her lower back. A waiter served us quickly, and when she wrapped her hand around the stem of the glass, I could easily envision her small fingers wrapped around my cock. Her lips sucking, swallowing me down.

*Stop. Just stop.* I breathed through my nose.

It was wrong. She was off-limits for so many reasons, it wasn't even funny. Too bad my body hadn't gotten the memo. Every time we were in a room together, I was attuned to her. I often knew when she entered a space before turning to confirm it. She had this energy, this presence, that called to me, luring me in like a siren. It was almost too powerful to ignore.

I craved her touch. I wanted to protect her. And I knew I should avoid her, but I wasn't even sure if I could.

"Wait." I grabbed her drink, sliding it away from her. "Are you sure you should be drinking?" I was mostly teasing, but still, my concern lingered. It had only been this morning that she'd had a meltdown on our flight, a side effect of the meds she'd taken. Meds that hadn't been prescribed to her. Topped off with the whiskey I'd convinced her to drink.

She glared at me. "You promised we'd never speak of *that*," she ground out, "again."

I had promised never to speak of it, but that didn't mean I'd stopped thinking of it. Far from it. I'd spent most of the afternoon thinking about that moment on the plane. I'd thought about it during the drive. In the shower. *Especially* in the shower, even though I'd been sure to shut down those thoughts quickly.

If I were a younger man...

"Jonathan." She stared at me expectantly.

"What?" I shrugged. "I'm not the one who mentioned it."

She leaned back in her chair. "You alluded to it."

"So, the drink?" I stared at her pointedly.

"I'm sure the pill is out of my system by now. I've felt fine all evening—great, actually."

"Me too," I said, a wistful note to my voice. I couldn't remember the last time I'd felt this light. This carefree.

"So, would you please stop worrying?" She stole the glass back, the liquid sloshing in the process.

"I can't help worrying about you, Sumner. I always have, and I always will."

She dipped her head, and I wondered what she was thinking. How she saw me. As a father figure? A family friend? Her annoying and overprotective boss? Something else?

"Anything else you were hoping to do while we were here?" I bumped her shoulder with mine.

"I haven't given it much thought. I assumed there wouldn't be much time for sight-seeing."

"Probably not," I admitted. Tonight's plans had been outside the norm. Typically, I'd be catching up on emails, preparing for meetings, checking in with the LA office. But I'd pushed all that aside to be with her. I tried not to dwell on my reasons for doing so. "But if you could go anywhere in New York City, where would you go? Would it be the Bow Bridge or the Staten Island Ferry?" I asked, recalling our conversation from the flight.

"I can't believe I forgot about The Met."

"I've heard it's amazing."

Her jaw dropped. "You've never been?"

"Whenever I come to New York, I'm usually too busy working to be a tourist."

"What about vacations? Do you ever take time off?"

I considered it. Frowned. "Honestly, I'm not sure the last time I took a vacation."

She shook her head. "You should change that. Everyone needs time to recharge. I can't believe we haven't covered this before now."

"You're one to talk, Little Miss Workaholic."

"I am not!" She laughed, nudging me with her elbow.

"Hey! Ouch." I grabbed her hand and trapped it in the crook of my arm.

She struggled to break free, her breasts brushing against my arm. "Geez. You're strong. And I'm not. A." She grunted, attempting to free herself as I laughed and tried to ignore the way she writhed against me. "Workaholic."

"You're not?" I teased, finally letting her escape with an exasperated grunt. "All this talk of helping your clients reclaim their time so they can live their purpose. Yet you're working full-time at the Wolfe Group, plus building your coaching business, volunteering, and god knows what else."

"I'm happy. Fulfilled." She smiled, straightening her shirt. "This is the current season of my life, and I'm enjoying it. It won't always be like this. One day, hopefully, I'll get married, have kids. And I'll be juggling work and being a mom. Not now," she added, perhaps noticing my grimace. "Does that surprise you?"

"No. I think you'd be a great mom." I wanted kids, but I always put it off for someday. At the rate I was going, someday would never come.

"I think you'd make a great dad," she said. "You were always so gentle and caring with me."

And now I cared for her for a different reason. My throat tightened, my drink sloshing in my stomach. *Fuck. I'm so messed up.*

"Did I—should I not have said that?" she asked.

"No." I shook my head. "I'm just not sure fatherhood is in the cards for me."

"Not unless you make it a priority. Have you thought any more about your dream life? Was being a dad part of your vision?"

"I—uh—" I tugged at the collar of my shirt. "I never really

thought about it. I was more focused on my professional goals."

"I think that's part of the problem. Correct me if I'm wrong, but you seem to define success only as it relates to things—money, houses, cars—not people or relationships. If you want to be happy, you need to look at the bigger picture."

I sat back in my chair, but she wasn't finished. "Unless you think a family is something you should want but don't actually desire."

I didn't answer, not even sure what I'd say. And she didn't push. We talked a while longer, until she yawned a second time, and I knew it was time to get her home. I texted the driver our location then paid the tab. She slid into the back seat, and I joined her, my thigh pressed against hers. I didn't move even though there was plenty of space.

She was quiet during the drive, and when she started to nod off, I shifted my shoulder lower so she could rest against it. Her body was warm against mine, her scent infiltrating my nose. Her arm fell, her hand landing on my thigh, and my heart sped up as I held my breath. But when she moaned my name softly, I stilled.

Was she dreaming about me?

I almost hoped for more traffic to prolong our time together. But we didn't have far to drive, and when we pulled up to the hotel, she roused. She dragged her feet, exhaustion evident in her features as we made our way to the elevator. Once inside, she sagged against the wall.

"Tonight was nice," she said around a yawn as the elevator ascended to our floor. She smiled, and we stared at each other for a beat before she glanced away, severing the contact.

"It was." I kept my hands tucked behind my back.

I wanted to cross the elevator and kiss her. I wanted to back her into the corner and have her panting in my ear as I made her come. But when the elevator doors opened to our floor and she didn't move, I grabbed her hand and tugged her toward the exit.

"Come on, sleepyhead."

"I'm—" Another yawn. "Not *that* tired."

"You were practically snoring in the car," I teased, though I kept thinking of how she'd moaned my name. I was still wondering if I'd imagined it.

"Was not!" She nudged me with her elbow, but I grabbed it and pulled her into my side.

She let out a little squeak, and I leaned down to whisper in her ear. "You and those damn elbows."

"It wasn't undeserved," she taunted, attempting another jab with her elbow, but it came off as more of a chicken dance.

I wrapped my arms around her, caging her in just as we reached her door. "Sumner," I growled. "You're playing with fire."

She stilled, our bodies aligned, my cock painfully aware of her closeness. "Maybe I like playing with fire."

I shook my head and released her. She turned and stared at me a beat, a million questions passing between us. But in the end, there was only one answer.

I leaned in, settling for a kiss on the cheek. "Good night, Sumner."

"Good night, Jonathan." Her voice was breathless, and I moved an inch, kissing the corner of her mouth. She let out a gasp of shock before leaning into me.

*What are you doing? Stop!*

I closed my eyes. It took every ounce of control I had remaining not to sample her lips, but it was so tempting. It was only us. There was no one here to see.

And yet, I would know. I'd have to live with the fact that I'd betrayed my best friend. So, I released her and took a step back. She reached out as if to stop me, but I merely shook my head, regret swirling through me, finally overpowering my desire and making me see reason.

"It's late. Get some rest." I turned and walked away.

I returned to my room and immediately started pacing the floor of my suite. What the hell had I been thinking? I'd nearly crossed a line. I'd nearly devoured those lips I'd spent so many hours watching. Too many hours obsessing about.

I was restless, my body boiling over with pent-up energy. *A run. Yeah*, I thought, heading over to my suitcase. A run would do me some good, work off some of this feeling of being restrained.

I changed and headed down to the hotel gym. I hopped on a free treadmill and set to work, pushing myself faster and faster. But it still wasn't enough. I couldn't outrun the demons that chased me, the things I craved. Her lips on my skin. The feel of her pussy gripping me as she screamed my name.

Yet I forged on, punishing myself physically as if that would rid me of this all-consuming need. A need for a woman I could not have. Mile after mile, my feet pounded the treadmill. Meanwhile, my mind was stuck on a loop. *Sumner. Ian. Sumner. Ian.*

I ran farther, but it felt as if I were standing still. Sweat dripped down my forehead, and I wiped it away with the hem of my shirt. I stared out at the skyline, the city different from LA. Lights glittered in the darkness—concrete and steel as far as the eye could see.

A glance at the screen told me I was nearing the hour mark. I'd been so absorbed in my thoughts that I'd completely lost track of time. And it was getting late. I slowed to a walk before turning off the machine and wiping it down and heading over to a free area to stretch. Yoga mats and blocks were stacked neatly on the shelves, along with towels and bottles of water with the hotel's logo printed on their label.

"Hey." A woman smiled, sinking down on the mat next to me. Her dark hair was in a ponytail, sports bra pushing up a pretty nice rack. We stretched a moment in silence before she asked, "Are you here for the WAP conference?"

I shook my head. "You?" I gulped down some water then groaned when I attempted to reach toward my foot.

"Yoga conference. I'd be happy to give you a private session." The seductive lilt to her tone told me she wanted to teach me about more than yoga.

I was on the verge of saying no, when I hesitated. Just because I couldn't have Sumner didn't mean I had to be celibate. Hell, maybe this would help relieve some of the pressure I felt around her.

"You know what? That sounds nice." I stood, dusting off my hands. "If you have the time, that is."

"Absolutely. My name's Kelli," She grinned, but it only made my stomach sour.

Even so, I pushed on. The only reason I wanted Sumner was because I couldn't have her. Here was a woman—an attractive, single woman—who was offering herself up to me. Maybe it was the universe's way of telling me to let it go. Let this sick obsession I had with Sumner go.

## CHAPTER ELEVEN

*Sumner*

I lay in bed, replaying everything that had happened in my head. I lingered on the end of the evening. The feel of Jonathan's hands on my skin sending lightning racing through my bones. His gaze had been so intense. And I could remember my chest tightening, constricting around my heart as if to protect it. This was... This man held me captive, and I'd have given him anything. And I did mean *anything*.

"Sumner." My name had been said on a tortured groan, his forehead kissing mine as we stood in the hallway.

My body heated, and I slid my hand over my breasts and down my stomach. Down. Dipping beneath my panties, sliding through my slick folds.

"Yes." It was a whispered plea, a prayer, a demand. I'd wanted whatever he was willing to give. Even if it was only for one night.

I panted, teasing myself as I imagined his lips on mine, his finger inside me, his—

My phone buzzed, and I tensed. *Shit.* I ignored it before resuming my daydream, but when I closed my eyes, I went back to the memory, not the fantasy in my head. Reality and rejection slammed into me instead of the release I craved. It was never going to happen now.

So close. After all this time, he'd come so close to kissing me. So close and then… nothing.

My phone rang from the nightstand, and I grabbed it, feeling as if I'd been caught. Piper's name flashed across the screen with a request to FaceTime, and I let out a deep sigh as I pushed out of bed and switched on the light. I'd tried calling her earlier, but I'd had to leave a voice mail. I connected the call and tried to force myself to act normal. As if I hadn't just been imagining my boss in bed.

"Hey, Piper." I smiled at the screen, though it was forced. "I was getting ready to go to bed. Is everything okay?"

"Hang on." She fiddled with her hearing aid, then said, "Okay. Now I can hear you. I wanted to check in after the flight. I know you were anxious. Did everything go okay?"

"Oh, fine," I sighed. "Apart from the fact that I flashed my boss and most of the passengers in first class."

"What?" she shrieked, eyes going wide. "You're kidding, right?"

"I wish I were." I slumped. "But, yeah. Your 'antianxiety' pills," I said, complete with air quotes. "Not so great."

Her eyes went wide, and she leaned forward as if trying to come through the screen. "Oh shit. How many did you take?"

"One." I held up a finger as if to underscore the point. "I took *one*, and it was awful."

She covered her mouth, but it didn't muffle the sound of her laugh. "At least it sounds like you were distracted from your fear of flying."

I glared at her through the screen. "Piper! That's not the point!"

"I know. I *know*." She held up her hands. "I'm sorry, okay?

I've never had any issues with them. I never would've expected that you'd react that way."

"Serves me right for taking meds not prescribed to me," I muttered, mostly to myself.

"People do it all the time," she said. "Hell, think of all the shit we did in high school."

"Yeah, but still. This was *bad*."

"Are you okay now?"

I lifted a shoulder. "Yeah. I mean, apart from wanting to die of embarrassment. But I was lucky it wasn't worse. If I worked for anyone else, I could've lost my job."

"A job you didn't even want."

"Whatever," I huffed.

"What did Wolfe do?"

I snort-laughed, remembering how wide his eyes had gotten when I'd started unbuttoning my shirt. "Threw his jacket over me as if I were on fire." He hadn't been able to cover me up fast enough.

She tilted her head to the side. "He didn't even sneak a peek at the goods?"

I shook my head, both impressed and annoyed by his response. "Perfect gentleman."

"I highly doubt that. You were probably too out of it to notice anyway. What happened after the flight? Did the rest of the evening go okay?"

"We went to dinner and then to see *Hamilton*."

"*Hamilton?*" she squeaked. "How the hell did you score tickets?"

I lifted a shoulder. I hadn't given it much thought until now; I'd just been so ecstatic about the whole thing. "I don't know. Jonathan surprised me with them."

"It wasn't a client event?"

I shook my head. "No. Just the two of us."

"Interesting." She grinned.

"What?"

"That sounds a lot like a date."

I laughed, rolling my eyes, though I wished her words were true. "I think he felt sorry for me after what happened."

"*I* think he was trying to get in your pants after watching your striptease on the plane."

"Please." I held up my hand, closing my eyes. "Don't remind me. God, it was mortifying."

"I bet he thought it was hot. Where is he now?"

"Probably in his room, as he should be." I stood, grabbing my toiletries and heading to the bathroom. "I told you—there's nothing happening between us."

"But we both know you want it to," she said. I hesitated, and that was enough to make her point at the screen. "Wait. Did something already happen?"

"No." I did my best to keep a straight face as I propped my phone against the bathroom mirror.

"Liar." Her smile widened, and she tucked her leg beneath her. "Spill."

"What are you up to?" I asked, noticing makeup set out beside her. "A new video to film?"

"It can wait." She waved a hand through the air. "So... what happened?"

"This is going to sound so cheesy," I said, covering my face with my hands. "But it felt like we had a moment."

"What kind of moment?"

"I'm sure it was all in my head. It was silly, really." I removed my contacts.

"I need details, Sumner."

"Well—" I leaned against the counter. "He sort of kissed my cheek."

"What does that mean?"

"Well, he also kissed the corner of my mouth, but it could've been an accident. I mean, you know how it is when someone kisses you on the cheek and you both move at the same time, and…" I was rambling.

"Sumner." My attention snapped to her. "Did you move?"

I thought about it a minute, but I already knew the answer. "No."

"Oh my god!" she squealed, kicking her feet. "Then what happened?" I was waiting for her to bust out a bucket of popcorn.

"Nothing. He pulled back and walked away."

"Did he say anything? Do anything else?" she asked, to which I only shook my head.

"But you wish he had. You wanted something to happen." It wasn't a question.

"It doesn't matter what I want. It will *never* happen."

"Because of your dad?"

"That's a big part of it, but Jonathan still views me as the child he watched grow up." He'd said as much—several times.

"Hm." She paced the floor of her room, then stopped and tapped a finger to her lips. I knew that expression.

"Uh oh," I said, already anticipating whatever crazy idea was bound to come out of her mouth. Preparing to shut it down.

"Now, hear me out."

"No, Piper. He's my boss, and he's letting me coach him. How would that look to future clients? How would my dad feel?"

"That's all going on the assumption that anyone would find out." She smirked. "And who's going to find out? You're in New York. You're two consenting adults. This is your opportunity to show him the sexy, confident woman you are. This is your chance to make him *see* you."

"To what end?" I hedged.

"Oh please. Don't insult both our intelligence."

I laughed. She had me there.

"What happened to seizing life by the balls? To doing what you want and not going along with what everyone else expects of you?" She let her unspoken challenge hang in the air.

"Yeah, but he's my boss. My dad's best friend…" I said, as if repeating the reasons keeping us apart would make me want him any less.

"And the only man you've been in love with since forever."

*Yeah. There's that.*

"Love?" I scoffed. "It was an infatuation, and a childish one at that."

"Mm-hmm. So, you're telling me he wouldn't still make your list of kiss, marry, fuck?"

I hesitated too long, and she said, "I knew it. He's totally on your list of dream fucks."

"Which is where he'll stay. I mean, how would you feel if you had a chance to be with…one of the Hemsworth brothers."

"Are we talking Chris or Liam?"

"Does it matter?" I asked, thinking they were both hot and this was a freaking hypothetical question.

"Yes." She stared me down. "It absolutely matters."

"Fine," I huffed. "Pick your favorite Hemsworth and imagine if you had the chance to be alone with him for an evening."

She purred, and I resisted the urge to roll my eyes. "Focus, Piper."

"I am focused. And I'm telling you to go for it."

"Go for it?" I snorted. "Be serious."

"I am serious. It's not like I'm telling you to proposition him. Just…maybe add a little oomph to the hair and makeup. Wear a sexy dress. Allow yourself to flirt with him and explore what's between you two. Because there's clearly *something* there."

"Piper." I stared at her through the screen, but she didn't back down.

"Sumner." She glared back at me, holding my gaze a moment before saying, "You want him to see you as a woman, you have to see yourself that way first."

"Oh my god." I rolled my eyes. "You sound like my mom."

"The woman knows her stuff. Have you read her latest book?"

"No." My shoulders slumped. "I haven't had time. But thanks for telling me. And, yes—in the words of my mom—I have stepped into my feminine power."

She shook her head. "Not with him, you haven't. You filter your relationship through the same lens of hero worship you always have. You need to stop thinking of him as Jonathan Wolfe," she said, deepening her voice. "And start treating him like you would any other man you were interested in."

I considered her words, but she didn't understand. Sure, she'd dated guys in the past. But it was never serious. Not like how I felt about Jonathan. And half the time, I worried it was all one-sided.

"This is it," she said, her tone more somber. "This summer. You don't act now, you never will."

I swallowed hard, knowing she was right. But still… "Maybe I shouldn't act. May—"

"I'm going to stop you right there. Sumner." Her gaze was intense, even from nearly 3,000 miles away. "Do you want him?"

I nodded. "Yes."

"Even if it's only for one night?"

I nodded again, though this time, my voice was breathless. "Yes."

"Then go for it. A few months ago, you nearly died. Do you really want to live with regrets?"

"No, but...my dad."

"Has no room to judge. He cheated on your mom."

I jerked my head back. "That's..." I swallowed. "You know it's more complicated than that."

I wasn't mad at my dad for what had happened. Maybe I had been at the time, but as I'd gotten older, I understood. I actually thought he'd made the right decision. And I loved Lea, even if their relationship had come at a cost.

"Yeah. Yeah." She waved a hand through the air. "True. But the fact remains that your dad, of all people, should know better than to judge. Besides, there's no need for him to find out, is there?"

"No, but still...it feels wrong somehow."

"Ignoring your dad and the situation for a minute, how does it feel when you're with Jonathan? Does it feel wrong?"

I shook my head. "Nothing has ever felt more right."

"Then there's your answer."

Maybe Piper was right. Maybe...maybe my dad's opinion didn't matter. It had never mattered to me with the guys in my past. But he'd never had a personal connection with them. They'd never been his friend first.

"It doesn't matter," I finally said. "Because nothing will ever happen. Even if Jonathan wanted me, he'd always stop himself before giving in."

"If he does," she said, and I opened my mouth to shut her down. But she held up her hand. "If something did happen between you two, you need to be prepared."

"I'm on the pill, and I'm sure we'd use a condom." I wasn't even sure why we were discussing this.

"Yeah. Not talking about birth control, but thanks for the update." She laughed. "Good to be safe. But I'm talking about your heart—protect it."

I had a feeling it was too late for that.

## CHAPTER TWELVE

*Jonathan*

"You really like to push yourself." Kelli raked her nails down my chest. My cock didn't even stir. "It shows."

"Thank you." I told myself to move, yet my feet remained glued to the wood floor of the empty yoga studio.

Kelli knelt to the floor, giving me the perfect view of her sculpted ass and lifted breasts. She was...exactly like the women I usually went for, I realized. Beautiful. Easy. Someone who expected no strings. Fucking her should've been a no-brainer.

But her voice wasn't the one I wanted to hear moaning my name. Her hands weren't the ones I wanted caressing my skin. And her mouth... The moment she pulled down my shorts and licked her lips, I knew I couldn't go through with it. I wanted to. I needed a release, and my workout hadn't done it. Jacking off in the shower this afternoon hadn't done it. But I had a feeling this wouldn't satisfy me either.

"Wait." I gripped her shoulders, holding her steady. Her face was perfectly positioned. If I hadn't stopped her, her lips would already be wrapped around my cock, sucking me down.

"What's wrong?"

"I, um—" I backed away, tucking myself back into my pants. "I can't do this."

"I don't see a ring." She gave my hand a pointed look.

I shook my head. "I have an early meeting, and I should get to bed."

"This will help you relax." She reached out for me, but I evaded her grasp. "Because—no offense—but you seem pretty uptight."

"No, but thanks." I turned and headed for the door, speeding away from her.

It was only when I was safely back in my room that it hit me. That woman—Kelli—had handed herself to me on a platter. And I couldn't go through with it. I groaned, pulling on the strands of my hair.

Why?

Because of Sumner?

How could an almost-kiss with Sumner, something so hilariously chaste, make me feel more than anything the yoga instructor had done?

A glance at the clock on my nightstand told me it was even later than I'd realized. With a heavy sigh, I headed for the shower. The hot water streamed over my skin, and I lathered up the soap, washing my arms and shoulders, chest and lower still until I was gripping my cock.

*Why?* Why Sumner? Why couldn't I get her out of my head?

My cock grew in my hand, and I told myself I was just going to soap up and then rinse off. *Just...* I squeezed, closing my eyes briefly as an image of Sumner flooded my mind. Her lips. That smile.

I'd resisted this for so long. Jacking off to images of my

best friend's daughter was so wrong. So *dirty*. And yet, my body craved it. Craved her.

Another stroke. *Just one more,* I told myself.

But I could feel my control slipping, need overpowering me. This summer had been torture. Watching her from afar, wanting her from afar.

*I should stop.*

I placed my palm against the cold tile, my breath coming in short pants as a war raged within me. I *should* stop. I couldn't stop. I... *Oh fuck.* I ran my hand down my chest, imagining it was Sumner's small fingers. Her hand tugging slightly on my balls. Her lips wrapped around my cock as she blinked up at me. And then, the muscles of my stomach tightened, and *oh shit,* I exploded.

I squeezed my eyes shut, the world spinning. My thoughts like a merry-go-round that someone had pushed faster and faster and faster, until I was ready to throw up. Yet beneath all that was a deep sense of release, of a need finally sated.

And fast on its heels—disgust. I shouldn't have done that. I couldn't let it happen again. I finished showering and then toweled off, unable to meet my eyes in the mirror. Fuck, this was going to be a long week.

❧

I ESCORTED SUMNER DOWN THE HALL TO HER ROOM, RUBBING my temples as if it would ease the tension building there. The tension building...everywhere. My whole body felt as if I might explode. I was a grenade, and the pin had been pulled. I was merely waiting to detonate.

I'd been short-tempered all day, despite how well our meetings had gone. We'd closed another big deal even though I'd been distracted. And Sumner had seemed different. More confident, somehow. Though I couldn't put my finger on the exact reason for it.

Or maybe I was just even more attuned to her, my guilt and self-loathing ratcheting up to an all-time high after what I'd done in the shower last night. But, damn. The dress she'd worn today, the way it clung to her curves, hinting at all that luscious skin...it was all too much.

She paused. "You okay?" Nothing ever escaped her notice, at least not when it came to me.

"Yeah." I forced a smile. "I should've had something else to drink or maybe had more water today." Between another punishing workout this morning and then consuming more coffee and alcohol than water, I knew tomorrow was going to be a bitch. "I'm going to regret it in the morning."

Occasionally, I'd go out for drinks with clients, but it was rare. That said, I found myself more inclined to do so this trip, using it as an excuse to prolong my time with Sumner. I figured if we were in a group, it was safer. I could still enjoy her company without feeling like I was doing something wrong because, technically, it was a work event.

"I have just the thing." She grinned, practically skipping down the hall ahead of me. I shook my head with a laugh, envious of her energy.

She unlocked the door to her room and pushed it open. "Give me a second to find it."

I remained at the doorway, watching her, so fucking drawn to her. The way she brushed her hair away from her face. The way she pulled her lower lip into her mouth when deep in thought. The way she moved—as if she owned the world and dared anyone to challenge her.

"Ah. Here it is!" She held up a box, victory written in her smile.

"What's this?" I couldn't take a step closer. I couldn't. Or else I'd go over the edge.

"Failproof hangover remedy," she said.

I turned the box over and glanced at the ingredients. Didn't seem too awful. But would it work?

Perhaps sensing my skepticism, she said, "You'll be thanking me in the morning." Even though her statement was intended to be innocent, it felt anything but. Or maybe that was just my thoughts—my imagination running wild with the possibilities, my brain lighting up like a slot machine.

"You sure you don't need it?"

She lifted a shoulder. "I'm buzzed, and it wasn't tequila. So, I should be fine."

I scoffed, envying her.

"What?" she asked, eyelashes fanning over her skin.

"I remember when I was in my twenties. I never got hungover. Not so much now that I'm an old man."

"You're not old," she said, swatting my chest playfully.

"I am, compared to you." She arched an eyebrow, and I wondered what she was thinking. "What?"

"I don't know." She lifted her shoulder, a coy smile gracing her lips. "I guess I never see someone's age or title—I see them. And to me, you've always just been Jonathan." She shook her head. "Does that make any sense?"

It made a lot of sense because when we were alone, away from the office, away from Ian, it was easy to forget she was his daughter. It was easy to see her as a woman I was attracted to and not my intern. She was so mature and wise; it was easy to overlook her age, especially with all the deep, soul-searching conversations we'd had this summer.

"It does." I leaned in to kiss her cheek, unable to stop myself. Alarm bells blared in my head. I needed to go before I did something stupid. Something unforgivable. "Good night, Sumner," I whispered, lingering there a moment after I'd pressed my lips to her skin.

I told myself to move, but it was as if I were tethered to her, unable to break free. The smell of her shampoo filled my lungs, clouding my vision. The heat rolling off her body made me delirious. Made me believe I could have her, even when I knew it was impossible.

I was standing on the edge, peering down into the abyss, but I wasn't sure which was scarier—stepping back or forging ahead. Stepping back was safe. Boring. But forging ahead...

"Jonathan," she whispered, moving ever so slightly so our lips were lined up, noses touching.

My blood sang from her proximity, but my mind reeled. I clenched my fists at my sides and closed my eyes, inching closer to that invisible edge. But when her lips brushed against mine, pillowy-soft and inviting, I was a goner. I fell into the abyss, not caring if or when I'd hit the ground. All I cared about was kissing her.

I groaned when her tongue flitted out to meet mine. She tasted even sweeter than I'd imagined. Kissing her was like the high I'd get after a good workout, but better. And I craved more.

I took control, gripping her hips and backing her into the room. The door closed behind us, but my focus was on Sumner. She felt so good in my arms, so right, and I couldn't stop exploring her with my hands, my tongue. I was a dying man, and she was my salvation.

My salvation and my damnation.

*Oh fuck. What am I doing?*

"Kissing me," she said, making me realize I'd spoken the words aloud. "And doing it quite spectacularly, I might add." She grinned, lips plump and red from where mine had been moments before.

"I-I—" I gripped her biceps, prying myself off her. We stared at each other, panting.

This was wrong. She was my intern. She was...fucking stunning. My thoughts were muddled from the alcohol, but mostly from this woman. She made it difficult to think clearly because all I saw—all I wanted—was her. I *needed* her, consequences be damned.

"What do you want?" A sexy smile I hadn't seen before. "All you have to do is ask."

I couldn't resist her. Not anymore. I yanked at the material of her dress, impatient, desperate. "Off. Need this off."

"Yes," she hissed, unzipping it before allowing the material to fall to the floor.

Her blush-colored bra was similar to the one she'd been wearing on the plane, the lace cups kissing the curves of her breasts. The color so close to her skin tone, I'd almost thought she was naked. I was so busy watching her that it took me a minute to realize she was sliding my jacket down my shoulders, loosening the buttons of my shirt.

Her small fingers fluttered about my chest like butterflies, her hands shaking ever so slightly. Was she nervous? *Oh shit.* My chest constricted. Was she a virgin?

I blinked a few times, clearing some of the fog of lust clouding my brain. "What are we doing?" I asked. "We need...?" She palmed me through my pants, and any attempt at coherent thought went out the door along with any remaining morals. "Fuuuuck," I said, dragging out the word. *Fuck. Fuck. Fuck. Fuck. Fuck.*

I slid my hands up her torso, teasing the bottoms of her breasts, lifting her bra ever so slightly and prompting her to gasp. I loved how responsive she was. How needy she was.

"This is a terrible idea," I murmured between kisses. Someone had to say it.

"Is it?" She giggled as I kissed my way down her neck. "Oh god, that feels so good. Don't stop, Jonathan."

The breathy way she said my name had blood rushing

south at an even faster rate. I was light-headed and happy, and making her feel good became my sole focus. If she'd asked me to define success, this would be it. Making her orgasm again and again.

"What do you like?" I sucked her nipple, noting the way she arched her back in response. I wanted to memorize every detail, every heady look and breathless sigh. Every dip of her skin, every freckle.

"You," she said.

I chuckled, loving that answer. "Yes. But what gets you off?"

"*You*," she said again, this time more forcefully.

"Me?" I asked, as if I couldn't quite believe my ears. "You're a naughty girl, aren't you? Fantasizing about your boss."

"You have no idea," she said on a whispered hush. "I've wanted you for...all summer." Her hesitation had me wondering if she'd intended to say something else.

But when she dragged the straps of her bra down her shoulders, unhooking it and releasing her breasts, all I could say was, "Unh."

They were gorgeous. *She* was gorgeous.

She laughed, and I backed her toward the bed, my hands on her hips. I stopped thinking about anything but her, me, this moment. I dipped my head to feast on her, exploring her with my fingers and my lips, teasing her with my tongue. Need for her gnawed at me, until I removed her panties, unable to resist licking her clit. She bucked her hips, and I realized I should lay her down on the bed before we fell.

"You're so fucking stunning," I growled, enjoying the way she arched her back, her body splayed out for me. "Such a pretty little WAP."

She laughed, her breasts jiggling from the motion. "Oh my god. Did you really just say that?"

"You want me to treat my nose like my platinum Amex?" I teased, nudging her folds with my nose, her laughter eclipsed by a gasp.

A gasp that turned into a moan as I brought her to the brink of pleasure, knowing I was already too far gone to stop this. We were too far gone. If I was already going to hell, I might as well enjoy this one night because it would never happen again.

"I want you," she pleaded, clawing at my belt.

"Patience," I cautioned, the sight of her lower lip jutting out testing the limits of my own. I wasn't sure I could deny her anything, especially not in this moment.

I kissed her then stood, removing the rest of my clothes, but not before grabbing a condom from my wallet. A little gasp had me chuckling. "You're not a virgin, are you?" I asked, gratified by her reaction.

She shook her head quickly, and I silently thanked the universe. "You don't have to be gentle with me."

"Good." I had a brief moment of hesitation, a realization that we were truly approaching the point of no return. "Sumner, I—"

She climbed up to her knees, crawling to meet me at the edge of the bed. "Shh." She placed her finger to my lips, the other hand wrapping around my cock, testing, teasing, gliding. "Don't ruin it."

I leaned my head back, releasing a tortured groan. "Your dad…"

"Isn't here right now." She kissed my neck, making every hair stand on end. "Doesn't need to know." An openmouthed kiss to my chest that had me ready to pounce. "We're both adults."

I nodded, wanting to believe her words. Wishing it were that simple.

"I want you. And you want me, right?" She smirked when

my body confirmed my answer, my cock twitching in her hand.

I was so entranced that I moved as if under her spell. She took the condom from me, and I watched in awe as she smoothed it down my length. I shivered at her touch, and I glanced up to find her studying us, liquid heat pooling in her eyes.

"Fuck me." Her lips were swollen from my kisses, hair perfectly mussed.

I couldn't have resisted even if I'd tried. I lifted her leg, angling us so I thrust into her with one punishing move. For a moment, I'd feared it was too much, but then she moaned.

"Oh god. Oh fuck," I cried.

And then we started moving, hard and fast, our bodies working together as if they'd been made for each other. Despite how frantic we were, our connection burned bright, bringing us both closer to each other and climax.

I'd never felt so desperate for a woman, muscles clenching as I pumped harder, faster. I held out as long as I could, kissing her, biting her neck, her nipples, whispering all the filthy things I wanted to do to her. She dragged her nails down my back, bringing me that much closer to release.

And then she came apart in my arms, unraveling, screaming my name. Her climax was a beautiful sight to behold, head thrown back, mouth open in ecstasy. But it was the way she looked at me as she came back down to earth, the way our eyes connected as we shared something unspoken. Something…intangible that struck me the hardest.

I rubbed her clit with my thumb, wanting to draw out as much pleasure from her as possible. Wanting her to feel as amazing as she made me feel, not just in bed, but every day.

When she spasmed around me, I couldn't take it anymore. With a string of curse words, I held fast to her, unloading all my pent-up desire, all my guilt, all my need, all my pain. And she took it; she took it all until we were both panting and exhausted.

When we collapsed to the bed in a heap of sweaty limbs, I knew I'd never be the same. I connected with Sumner in a way I hadn't with other women. And the sex... Fuck, the sex had been amazing.

But then reality slammed into me with the force of a sledgehammer—I'd slept with my best friend's daughter.

*What have I done?*

# CHAPTER THIRTEEN

*Sumner*

"This can't happen again." His deep voice rumbled through his chest and into my ear.

I lifted my head, my dark tresses falling over my face like the wings of a raven. "Be serious, Jonathan."

"I am serious, Sumner." He shook his head, rolling away from me and swinging his legs over the side of the bed. "This shouldn't have happened at all." He cradled his head in his hands.

"But it did." I crawled across the bed on my knees. The plush hotel room smelled of sex and desire, the rumpled sheets undeniable proof of what we'd done. "It happened, and we both know we want it to continue happening."

I trailed my fingernail along his shoulder, studying the way his muscles bunched beneath the skin. His body was incredible. And even though I'd now licked and kissed every inch of him, I wanted more. One night wasn't enough.

Hell, it had taken us months to get to this point. Months of accidental brushes in the elevator and heated gazes across the conference room. Months of pent-up tension begging to break free. But that wasn't even the worst of it, because the truth was, I'd been waiting years for this man to notice me.

*Jonathan Wolfe*, I sighed, admiring the hard planes of his back. My father's best friend—and my boss for the summer.

To everyone else, he was Wolfe. A successful business-man. A perfectionist. Demanding and shrewd. But to me, he'd always just been Jonathan. Beneath the cool façade was a man of warmth and kindness, a man who'd always been caring and insightful.

Which was why I still couldn't believe he was lying in my bed. After a night I'd fantasized about countless times. The reality had been even better than I'd imagined. His beard scratching the delicate skin of my thighs. His hands canvassing my body. His lips...

He stood, and I grabbed his hand, my lower lip jutting out. "Where are you going?"

We still had a few hours until our first meeting, and I didn't want to waste a moment. I wanted to make love and eat room service. Shower together. Just enjoy this freedom away from Los Angeles. Away from the office. Away from my father.

It was as if a switch had been flipped. Now that I'd had sex with Jonathan, I knew what I wanted, and I wasn't afraid to say it. My confidence had been building all summer thanks to his encouragement. But last night, I'd finally taken what I wanted. And it felt good to admit it.

Jonathan slid out of my grasp, evading my gaze as he grabbed his suit pants from the floor. "I'm returning to my room to get ready." He pulled them up, buttoning the top before yanking his shirt from the dresser, his movements aggressive, angry. "I suggest you do the same. I'll see you in the lobby at nine."

*He's serious.* I frowned. I was still coming down from the

euphoria of my latest orgasm, and he was ruining it. He was ruining everything.

"What about the rest of the trip?" I'd wanted this—*him*—for so long. And feeling emboldened after last night, I couldn't let the opportunity pass us by. We were going to be in New York for almost an entire week. Did he really intend to ignore this thing between us and pretend it had never happened?

"Sumner. I—" He pinched the bridge of his nose, closing his eyes briefly. "You're my best friend's daughter. My fucking intern. Not to mention, you're twenty years younger than me."

*Twenty-one years younger.* But I wasn't going to remind him of that. Besides, what difference did it really make?

I lifted a shoulder, enjoying the way his eyes flickered to my breasts. "So?"

"So you have to understand why this can't happen again."

Age didn't matter—at least not to me. I wouldn't be an intern at his company much longer. The summer was nearly over, and then I'd start grad school. As to his final objection, I couldn't change who my father was, but as Piper had reminded me, it wasn't like he needed to know.

I climbed off the bed, gratified by the way Jonathan scanned me hungrily. He might claim we were done, but his body said otherwise. I closed the distance between us, grabbing his tie from the armchair and looping it around his neck.

He clenched his jaw so hard, I thought he might crack a molar. "*Sumner.*"

"Jonathan." I arched my brow, pulling him closer. "If all we have is this week, then we should make the most of it."

He squeezed his eyes shut, inhaling a deep, shaky breath. "We—"

"*Can,*" I said, already anticipating his protest. "We can, and we should. Now—" I leaned up on my toes, pressing my lips to his jaw "—I'm going to shower." I spun and sauntered toward the bathroom, adding a little extra sway to my naked hips. It was an open invitation, and I hoped he'd take me up on it.

I started the water and wondered if I'd pushed him too far, asked for too much. We'd been buzzed when we'd fallen into bed together last night—on a high after closing another big deal, which was celebrated with drinks. Despite the alcohol coursing through our veins, we'd been sober enough to know what we were doing. But now in the harsh morning light, things were different—at least for him. And I hated the idea that he regretted it, regretted *me*.

I reached out to steady myself. I could never regret our night together, even if he currently wanted to pretend it had never happened. I dropped my head to my chest, disappointment washing over me.

But then a pair of warm arms slipped around me, his scent invading my nose. I sighed, closing my eyes as I leaned into his touch. As much as he tried to deny it, he was just as desperate for me as I was for him.

"I knew you couldn't resist me," I teased, smirking at him over my shoulder.

He growled, pulling me closer. His hard-on sought me out through his slacks, the buttons of his shirt digging into my spine. I welcomed it, welcomed the bite of pain. Because I wanted to etch this week into my memory, tattoo it on my brain the way this man was imprinted on my heart.

"Resist you? When I'm done, you'll be begging me to fuck you." He whispered the dark promise into my ear, and I shivered.

As steam billowed out of the shower, he ran his hand over my breasts, my hips, my thighs. I leaned my head back against his shoulder, my thoughts as clouded as the bathroom mirror. I wanted him. I'd wanted him for so long. But his touch was rough, as if he were angry with himself for wanting me.

"Get in," he rasped.

He released me, and I stumbled forward, into the huge walk-in shower. It was tiled in marble with multiple shower heads—decadent and opulent just like my night with this man had been. But like the shower, Jonathan could be cold, hard.

I pushed those thoughts away, stepping beneath the spray of water so it blanketed me with warmth. My body was on high alert, the droplets running down my skin nearly erotic. I watched as he stripped out of his shirt, soaking in every inch of him as if it were the last time. Because I knew it very well could be.

He was... God, he was so handsome. In my mind, he'd always been the most handsome man I knew. Whether I'd realized it or not, I compared every guy to him. How could I not? Jonathan was intelligent, confident, successful. And now, this summer, I'd gotten to know him as a man. We'd shared things with each other, things I'd never shared with anyone else.

Jonathan swept his hair away from his face, silver smattering the temples and throughout his beard. Did he even realize how crazy he made me? Did I have anywhere near the same effect on him?

I ran my hands down my chest, over my stomach, and he watched, Adam's apple bobbing. He stripped out of his button-down shirt, his blue eyes hooded with desire. They mirrored my own. His pants were next, his cock bobbing toward his stomach. My mouth watered at the sight.

No sooner had he stepped into the shower than he smashed his mouth to mine, his kiss insistent, demanding. I met him stroke for stroke, his beard scratching my skin. His body firm against mine as he crushed me to him. I couldn't breathe unless he did. Couldn't move unless he wanted me to. And I wouldn't have wanted it any other way.

He dipped his head to suck on my nipple, teasing my clit with his fingers. I reached out for him, taking him in my hand, stroking him. Water streamed down my face, and I tilted my head back and opened my mouth, letting the water fall over my lips, my skin, his skin. It made it seem as if he were everywhere, and it certainly felt that way as he pushed me higher and higher. With every nip of his teeth, every swipe of his fingers, I was that much closer to coming.

He slid one finger inside me, then another, and I grasped his shaft tighter, pumping him faster. Panting. Groaning. Punishing.

He met my eyes, his dark with lust and anger. I craved it, wanted it all. And when he gripped the back of my neck, groaning my name before slamming his mouth against mine, I came. He followed a minute later, painting my stomach with his desire.

༂

AFTER A DAY OF MEETINGS THAT SEEMED TO STRETCH ON endlessly, I climbed into the back of the town car. We'd barely pulled away from the curb, and Jonathan's attention was already glued to his phone screen as if his life depended on it. It had been like this most of the day—he did his best to stay busy, to put distance between us. I'd hoped things would be different once we were alone again, but it looked like I was wrong.

I turned toward the window, glancing at the passing scenery. Not a palm tree in sight. As far away from LA and my dad as we could get without leaving the country. And it still wasn't enough. At least, not for him. For me... Well. I pursed my lips, watching a street performer as we waited for a light to change. I hated the idea of hurting my dad. I'd never want to drive a wedge between him and Jonathan. They'd been friends since high school. Over the years, Jonathan had been an ever-present fixture in our family. But this summer had changed everything.

"Are you hungry?" he asked, startling me from my thoughts.

I lifted a shoulder. I wasn't going to push him if he was freaking out like I thought he was. Maybe some space would be good for both of us. "Not really. I might grab something near the hotel."

"Nonsense. I made reservations at La Mer."

"Are we meeting a client?"

"No."

I studied his expression to determine his intent, but it was useless. I wanted him to do something, say something, *anything* to acknowledge what had happened between us. But he was silent the rest of the ride, and so was I.

When we arrived at La Mer, Jonathan exited first, waiting for me to emerge. He placed his hand on my lower back, his touch sending sparks up my spine. Inside the restaurant, the host greeted us with a smile and then led us to a table in a secluded corner.

Jonathan held out my chair. When he rested his thigh against mine beneath the table, I wondered if it was intentional. But then I remembered how cold and aloof he'd been all day. And told myself it was likely just an accident.

"Did you enjoy yourself today?" he asked.

"I'm not sure enjoy is quite the word I'd use to describe it, though I did enjoy this morning." *So much for not pushing him.*

"Sumner..."

The waiter came by, telling us about the specials.

Jonathan ordered a bottle of wine, and I stole glances at him over the top of my menu.

"What?" He laughed after the waiter had gone.

I shook my head, returning my attention to the words printed on the page. "Nothing."

"Now you have to tell me," he said, pulling the top of my menu down so he could see my face.

"I guess I'm wondering…is this what it's going to be like between us from now on? Awkward and stiff. Our conversations limited to surface matters?"

He closed his eyes briefly, his watch glinting from the table as he gripped the stem of his wineglass. "It's not how I want it to be. Believe me."

I toyed with my napkin while I attempted to process his confession.

"Then why are you doing this to us?" When he opened his mouth, I waved a hand through the air. "I know, I know… I'm too young, I'm an intern, I'm your best friend's daughter." I rolled my eyes, not even sure why I'd asked.

He glanced around as if anxious someone would overhear then blew out a breath. "That's definitely a huge part of it, but…" He dragged a hand through his hair. "Did you know I came to the hospital after you were born? Did you realize I was there for every important milestone in your life? I watched you grow up."

"What we did isn't wrong," I said, so tempted to place my hand over his before thinking better of it. Even so, I wasn't ready to let this go. Let him go. "We're not biologically related. You're not *actually* my uncle."

"Be that as it may, you have to understand why this is a terrible idea. Your dad has always been like a brother to me. He's family, and I can't lose him. Even if you are fucking incredible."

I dipped my head. I wanted to bask in his compliment,

but my mind kept returning to his words about my father, about family. I didn't know everything about Jonathan's past, but I knew enough. He really didn't have anyone else.

Conversation returned to more "appropriate" matters— our meetings, the week ahead, registration for my fall classes, and productivity hacks. It was fine, nice even, but it wasn't what I really wanted. If anything, it only reminded me of just how good we could be together.

The ride back to the hotel was silent, and I wondered if he—like me—was thinking of last night. I couldn't stop thinking about it. Him on top of me, beneath me, inside me. His hands all over me.

We rode the elevator in silence, both of us retreating to opposite corners. By the time we reached our floor, I'd already resigned myself to the fact that I was going to bed alone and it was for the best. But that didn't make it any easier.

"You don't need to walk me to my door," I said when he didn't turn the opposite way to go to his. "I'm not a little girl." It was childish, but I was hurt and frustrated and not just a little horny. I understood his reasons, but that didn't mean I had to like them.

"No." His voice was gravelly. "You're not. But I'd like to all the same."

The hallway was empty, but it scarcely seemed big enough for the tension vibrating between us. When we reached the door to my room, I already had the keycard out and ready. I held it up to the reader and stepped inside. "Good night."

I didn't wait for him to say anything. Didn't want to have him reject me again or explain—yet again—all the reasons we couldn't be together. Instead, I closed the door and leaned my forehead against it. I breathed hard, my breath warming my skin as it bounced off the door and back into my face.

*Just this once, couldn't he...*

I shook my head with a heavy sigh, pushing off the door. Jonathan was nothing if not a man of his word. Once he set his mind to something, there was no use hoping otherwise.

I kicked off my shoes before pulling down my ponytail and shaking out my hair. I was halfway to the bathroom when there was a knock at the door. My heart stumbled over itself, my breath catching in my throat.

*Surely...*

For a minute I thought I'd imagined it, but then I heard that soft knock again. My heart started pounding, my body hyperaware. I was afraid to get my hopes up, but I couldn't help it.

I peered through the peephole, wetting my lips at the sight of him. I swung open the door. His arms braced the doorway as if he were holding himself back. His breathing was ragged, and I could feel the storm brewing within him.

He slowly lifted his head, eyes dark and tortured. "All we have is this week."

His words were an echo of mine from this morning, and I wondered what had changed his mind. Whatever it was, I wasn't going to question it.

"Then we should make the most of it."

He gripped the back of my neck, crashing his lips to mine as he backed me into the room and shut the door behind us. Our bodies collided. And I knew that no matter how hard we tried to fight this—we were inevitable.

# CHAPTER FOURTEEN

## Jonathan

"Where are you going?" Sumner groaned, reaching out from beneath the covers.

"I have to get ready."

"It's..." She pushed up on her elbows, the sheet sliding down and giving me a glimpse of her breasts. They swayed from the movement, and I licked my lips, remembering the sounds she made whenever I pulled the rosy buds of her nipples into my mouth. "Four-thirty in the morning. Our first meeting isn't until nine."

"Yes." I grabbed my pants from the floor. "But I need to work out and review some files."

"Come back to bed. I'll give you a workout." She rolled over with a yawn, but it was clear she was exhausted. Between the time difference, the long days, and the even longer nights, I knew she needed her rest.

I chuckled, bending down to kiss her forehead. "Go back to sleep. I'll see you in a few hours."

"Okay. So long as you don't go back to ignoring me." She yawned and turned the other way, but her movements, like her words, were tinged with exhaustion.

I grimaced, grateful the room was still dark enough to conceal my features. I nuzzled her forehead, so fucking tempted to undress and climb back under the covers. The only thing I wanted to ignore was work. I wanted to ignore it all and go back to focusing all my attention on Sumner. She was all I could think about anyway. Whether I was at work, working out, or lying in bed at night, she was always on my mind.

"Get some rest," I whispered, sensing that she was slipping back into sleep. "I have plans for you tonight."

"Mm," she murmured into her pillow.

I pressed my lips to her shoulder, her breathing already evening out before I left. As I walked down the hall toward my room, button-down shirt in hand, I tried to ignore the curious glance from a hotel employee. Was it that obvious? That I was a forty-four-year-old man doing the walk of shame? I could only imagine the shame and self-loathing I'd feel if Ian found out. My stomach roiled.

"Fuck," I hissed, dragging a hand through my hair. *What the fuck are you doing?*

It was as if I could forget about reality when I was with her. But the moment I was alone, the truth of what I'd done came crashing back down. My carefully constructed lies and excuses collapsed under the weight of it all.

I stared at my door a moment before remembering to pull the keycard from my wallet. I held the key up to the card reader and then slipped inside. My room looked just like Sumner's, apart from the rumpled sheets and the fact that the bed was vacant. But I felt the same emptiness, the same longing as I had the night before at the prospect of returning to my room, alone.

I'd never felt this *need* to spend every spare moment with a woman. It was both strange and nice. And a terrible idea. What I'd done was unforgivable, yet I couldn't seem to stop myself. She was... God, she was impossible to resist. Everything about her called to me, captivated me.

*Just this week,* I reminded myself as I changed and headed for the hotel gym. She was mine for the week. And then we'd go back to LA, and everything would return to normal. We'd pretend as if this week had never happened. Even if I knew it was one I'd never forget.

I was relieved that Kelli was nowhere in sight, and I cranked up the treadmill, putting myself through a punishing run and lifting heavier weights to make up for my missed workout. At least, that's what I told myself it was for, but I knew the truth. It was penance.

I showered and ate in my room, heading down to the lobby at a few minutes to eight. I leaned against one of the pillars, responding to an email from Alexis when I heard the ding of the elevator. I glanced up as the doors slid open to reveal Sumner.

*Holy...*

I scanned up her legs, her ankles studded with spikes. Her black dress stopped just above her knee, and despite the conservative cut, the dress was fucking sexy. Or maybe it was the woman wearing it. The material clung to her curves, a black leather belt emphasizing her waist. Her cleavage peeked out from the notched neckline, making my mouth water. But it was her smile that had me faltering as I stalked toward her. That knowing grin that was both demure yet naughty.

"Good morning." Her voice was breathy, and I scanned her lust-darkened eyes. There was no way I was going to make it through the workday without touching her.

*Right. The workday.* We were here to work. She might be mine at night, but during the day, it was business as usual. Something I had to keep reminding myself.

"Morning." I slid my phone into my pocket. "You ready?"

She nodded, but she slipped on the tile, nearly toppling in the process. I grabbed her elbow, steadying her even as my heart tumbled and fell to the floor. What was it about her? Why could she so easily disarm me?

"You okay?" I asked, reluctantly removing my hands when I felt she was stable once more.

"Yep," she chirped. "Let's go."

As we walked to the car, my hand on her lower back, I said, "You ready for another fun day?"

"Of course."

I watched as she slid into the back seat of the hired car. I climbed in beside her, smoothing down my tie. If I'd found it difficult to keep my hands off her in the lobby, it was damn near impossible in the back seat of the car. Her scent was everywhere, enveloping me in memories of the last two nights.

"So, we're meeting with Bass this morning, right?"

"Yes." I cleared my throat, impressed with how easily she seemed to have switched to work mode. Despite the fact that we were alone, despite the fact that my thigh was pressed to hers, our arms aligned, and tension clouded the air, she was focused, professional.

"Yeah," I said, mentally chastising myself to get it together. "They're looking at some properties in downtown LA."

"Is this typical?" she asked. "Traveling to the client, even when they're looking at properties in California?"

I lifted a shoulder. "No, but he's an old friend. So, I made an exception."

"An old friend," she mused, and I wondered what she wasn't saying. I didn't have to wait long because she asked, "Does he know my dad?"

"No." I shook my head, swallowing hard at the mention of Ian. The very man I was trying to avoid thinking about. "But we should be careful. You're still my employee." Even if sleeping with her wasn't strictly forbidden, it would definitely raise some eyebrows.

"Careful…" Our eyes met, breaths syncing, as she uttered the word, "Right."

I wasn't sure anything I did was careful when it came to Sumner. The more time I spent with her, the more I let her in, the more reckless it seemed.

"And then lunch with Anderson at the Ritz," she said, interrupting my thoughts.

I nodded, trying to ground myself in the plans for the day instead of reminiscing about last night or looking forward to later. "Followed by drinks with Sheffield."

"Right." She sucked her lower lip into her mouth, and I wanted to pull it between my teeth. *Just kill me.* "Did you have a chance to look at the former Masonic lodge?"

"Briefly. It could work. Securing his business would be huge for the Wolfe Group."

"Why don't you sound excited?" she asked, and I didn't know why I was surprised that she'd picked up on my tone. She always seemed to sense my moods, even if she didn't know or understand the reason for them.

*Maybe because I'd rather spend the day exploring the city with you.*

I sighed. "It just seems like more of the same."

She nodded, her expression contemplative. "Have you thought any more about your vision of success? I know we got distracted with the trip and everything, but it's important."

"It feels wrong—the things that I want." Both in business and in life.

"Why?" Her tone wasn't judgmental, merely curious.

"Because I've worked so hard for so long to accomplish all that I have." I blew out a breath. That was only part of it.

"What do you want?" she asked. "And it's okay if you don't

138

know. Sometimes it's easier to know what we don't want instead of what we do."

"I—" I hesitated. "I honestly haven't given it much thought." I hadn't allowed myself to go there. To allow myself to envision a life without the Wolfe Group, without the things and the people that currently defined it. Just as I hadn't allowed myself to imagine her as part of my future.

She nodded then glanced out the window, the smell of her shampoo infiltrating my lungs and penetrating my heart. I needed to get these thoughts and feelings under control. This was a fling—ill-advised, short-lived, no strings. We both knew where we stood.

*Get your head back in the game.*

"Was I dreaming, or did you mention something about tonight?" she asked, throwing me off once more.

I nodded, glancing out at the skyscrapers, a city full of potential. The complete opposite of our relationship, if you could even call it that. If our relationship had been a building, I'd say it was one that was shiny and looked good from the outside, but the foundation had been poured incorrectly, and the floor plan didn't make any sense.

"Another business dinner?" she asked.

I shook my head, the curl of my lip visible in the window. I was happy. For the first time in months, maybe years, I was happy. Light. At least when I ignored the reality of our situation. "We're going out. Just the two of us."

"Where?"

"You'll see."

"That's it? That's all I'm getting? A one-word answer?" she teased, feigning outrage.

"Excuse me," I chided. "That was two words."

She arched an eyebrow, her green eyes glittering with an unspoken challenge. "I have a feeling I'll be able to persuade you to tell me."

I gripped my thigh to keep myself from touching her, my cock stirring. "You can try."

"Mm." She leaned back against her seat. "Maybe."

After that, our conversation turned to business matters. Somehow, I made it through our morning meeting and lunch without touching her. Well, nothing beyond what could be considered professional—a hand on her back, brushing against her in the elevator when no one was watching. It was the most exquisite form of torture, and the closer we got to the end of the day, the more anxious I was for us to be alone. I wanted her all to myself. I wanted her thoughts, her words, her kisses, her smiles for my own.

"You okay?" Sumner asked from next to me in the booth. She laid her hand over mine, and I relaxed momentarily before sliding my hand out from under hers under the pretense of checking my phone.

"Yeah. Fine." We were waiting for Tom Sheffield, and I was impatient to get this meeting over with.

I spotted him in the doorway and waved him over. He smiled at me as he approached, but then he turned his attention to Sumner and his lips spread into a predatory grin. My hackles immediately rose, but I reminded myself how important the meeting was. How important his business could be for the firm.

After I made the introductions, I waited for Sumner to slide back into the booth and then joined them. Tom boasted about his latest acquisition and the private schools his kids attended. I glanced at my watch, wondering how much longer I'd have to put up with this pompous ass. Wondering if I ever sounded like him—bragging about all the "things" in my life. What was the point? He already had everything he could ever need and then some. What would he even do with more money?

"Seeing anyone?" he asked after Sumner had excused

herself to the restroom. Hell, I was half tempted to join her. So far, the meeting was going well, though it had mostly been small talk. I wanted to dig into the meat of the matter. I wanted to wrap this up so I could be alone with her.

I shook my head, surveying the crowded restaurant. "You know how it is. Busy with work."

"What about your intern?" Tom nudged me, and I tugged at my collar, wondering if he suspected there was something between Sumner and me or was merely suggesting it. Or— worse, still—was feeling me out to see if I'd cockblock him if he pursued her. I got the feeling he was attracted to her, but who wouldn't be? She was confident, beautiful, and she had a presence that drew everyone in.

"What about her?" I asked, attempting to sidestep his question.

"Is she seeing anyone?"

"None of your business," I all but growled.

"Ooh." He winced, sucking air through his teeth. "Someone's touchy. That's why you let her tag along to New York, isn't it?"

I jerked my head back. "No. I invited her to join because apart from Eric, she knows this portfolio better than anyone else."

He leaned back in the booth, completely at ease. "Relax, Wolfe. I'm just messing with you. But I wouldn't blame you if you mixed a little business with pleasure." His attention was focused on something across the restaurant, and when I turned to follow his gaze, I saw Sumner.

She was a knockout, her black dress clinging to her hips like my hands had been mere hours ago. The neckline dipping low enough to hint at her gorgeous tits. Her lips curling in a smile when our eyes met.

"Ah." Tom stood when Sumner approached. "Here she is now." He placed his hand on Sumner's shoulder—ratcheting up my tension another notch. "I don't know how you work for this guy," he said to her. "He's always so uptight. Always so focused on work."

She smiled at him, but I saw through the saccharine façade. "That's what I love about Wolfe. He's relentless when he's passionate about something." Was it just my imagination, or had her voice sounded huskier?

"Hm," Tom mused, studying Sumner a moment longer before releasing his hold on her. "Someone's clearly drinking the Kool-Aid."

"Try the vodka punch," Sumner corrected, taking a seat and downing the rest of her cocktail.

Tom stared at her a moment then threw his head back with a hearty laugh. "Don't let this one go."

Too bad our internship, our relationship, everything with Sumner had an expiration date.

After that, Tom behaved himself—mostly. And Sumner certainly proved herself more than capable of holding her own. She answered his questions with ease, deflecting any inappropriate comments and shutting him down without being rude or off-putting. It was impressive, and the longer we stayed, the harder it was going to be to conceal my desire for her.

"What do you think, Wolfe?" Tom turned to me.

I sipped my Rusty Nail, realizing I'd been so absorbed with Sumner that I'd completely zoned out. "What do I think about what?"

"Sumner's proposal for me to lease the old Masonic lodge."

Sumner appeared to be holding her breath, practically vibrating in her seat. I'd spent some time this morning looking over the specs, and she was right. It could be a great fit—both the size and location. Though it would need some work.

"It's a great option," I said. "What do you think, Tom?"

Tom stood and offered me his outstretched hand. "Consider it a done deal. Send the papers over, and we'll make it happen."

I nodded woodenly, my head spinning as I glanced to Sumner. Holy shit. Had she just closed one of the biggest deals of the year?

"And thank you, Sumner." Tom shook her hand after we'd both stood. "If you ever get tired of this schmuck—" he hooked his thumb toward me "—I'd be thrilled to have you."

I nearly growled at the suggestion in his tone. Instead, I placed my hand on her lower back, possessiveness surging through me. And yet...all we had was this week, and it was slipping away.

"Thank you," Sumner said, turning to me. "But I'm very happy with Wolfe."

I smirked to myself, enjoying the way she'd put him in his place and so very clearly established she was with me. She was young, but she was a skilled negotiator. She was classy and professional, and I was falling for her.

*Fuck.*

CHAPTER FIFTEEN

*Sumner*

"You're awfully quiet," Jonathan said as we stopped at another red light.

I'd been quiet during most of the ride, absorbed in my thoughts. I should've been exultant, celebrating the huge deal we'd just secured, thanks to my research. But the mood was decidedly less joyful. It was our last night in New York, our last night *together*. And I wasn't ready for it to end. Did he feel the same way?

"Just thinking." I brushed a strand of hair away from my face.

"About what?"

"Dinner. Business," I said, though I had a lot more on my mind than that. The past. The future. Men and my questionable decisions when it came to them.

"You were amazing tonight. Tom was an ass, but you handled him with grace and poise," he said.

I barked out a laugh, thinking of how much Tom had reminded me of Nico. "Boys will be boys, right?"

"Bullshit." A muscle twitched in his jaw. "Are you telling me something like this has happened to you before?"

I lifted a shoulder, turning my attention toward the window and the city beyond. I loved the lights, the movement, the noise. Everybody had a story to tell. Everyone had a dream. I had a dream, and I'd let one man try to talk me out of it. And another had encouraged me to pursue it.

"Sumner," he growled.

"I..." I swallowed. "I haven't always made the best decisions when it comes to men. And my last relationship—if you could even call it that—well, I wish I'd done things differently."

His voice was gentle when he spoke. "Different how?"

"I wish I'd stood my ground more often. Wish I hadn't allowed him to make me doubt myself." I turned my attention to the skyline once more. "Why are we even talking about this? It's our last night in the city, and I can think of literally a million things I'd rather be doing."

"You don't seem to have any problems standing your ground with me." I could hear the smile in his voice, the pride.

I considered it a moment. "I do, but it's not as much of a struggle as it used to be."

"I've noticed that too, especially this summer. Why do you think that is?"

I twisted my hands in my lap. "Because I promised myself that I'd start using my voice and trusting my gut."

"I'm glad you did," he said, placing his hand over mine, stilling my movements.

I turned to look at him, and he held my gaze a moment, something unspoken passing between us. "But also, I think a lot of it is thanks to your encouragement."

He tilted his head to the side. "Mine?"

"Yeah. Having your support, especially for my coaching business, has really given me a lot of confidence."

"I'm glad, though you were always talented and smart.

You just had to see it for yourself." His expression softened and he leaned in, his lips brushing the shell of my ear. "Did I tell you how unbelievably sexy you were—putting Sheffield in his place?"

I laughed, though it turned breathy as he slid a hand up my thigh. The calluses on his skin left goose bumps along the smooth flesh of my leg, anticipation thrumming through my core.

"You seemed annoyed with him. What did he say while I was gone?" I asked, remembering Jonathan's thunderous expression.

He stilled, my blood whooshing through my ears. "He asked if you were seeing anyone."

"And that bothered you?" I asked, gasping when he placed openmouthed kisses down my neck.

"More than it should." Despite his rough tone, his touch was tender. "Thank you for being honest with me. I hope you never feel like I've pressured you into anything," he said, returning to our earlier conversation.

"Pressured?" I laughed, turning to meet his eyes in the darkened car, having wondered the same. "You always make me feel so safe. I've wanted this. I've wanted *you* for…so long."

"Really?"

Did he really not know? Our first night together, I'd told him I'd fantasized about him, but I hadn't let on the full extent of it.

"Oh my god, yes. This is embarrassing to admit, but I had the biggest crush on you growing up."

He smirked, clearly bemused by this revelation. "Oh, did you now?"

I nodded, my breath hitching when he ran his nose along my neck. "I used to fantasize about what it would be like to taste your lips. To have you slide your hands over my breasts, tease my nipples. The pressure of your hand as you slipped it beneath my shorts."

He groaned. "Oh god. Don't tell me that." But the way he pressed his hand against his crotch told me he wanted me to continue. And I felt emboldened to do so.

I expected him to tell me to stop. But then he rasped, "What else?"

I closed my eyes briefly as the memories overtook me. The past and the present melding together, making my world spin.

"I'd imagine you teaching me what you wanted. Showing me how to please a man. How to please *you*." I stroked him through his pants, loving the feel of his teeth on my neck, his control close to snapping. "I'd lie in bed after you'd gone home, touching myself as I imagined you there with me."

"Fuck." He hissed. "You make me so fucking crazy. You make me question everything." He cupped my breast, sliding his hand inside my dress to pinch my nipple.

I gasped, both from his words and his touch. "You make it sound like that's a bad thing," I panted, equally affected.

Unable to hold back any longer, I unbuckled his belt, the hiss of his zipper filling the car with promise. His eyes were intent on my lips as I freed him, my thoughts focused on making him lose his mind. I slid to the floor and bent over, licking him from root to tip before peering up at him.

"Tell me what you like. Tell me how to please you." I stroked his length, a dot of precome beading on the tip.

"I like your mouth." He traced my bottom lip with his thumb. "These lips. These past few weeks, I've imagined fucking them countless times."

I took him in my mouth, watching him the entire time. Suppressing the urge to gag as I swallowed him down.

"Yes," he hissed. "Just like that. Keep looking at me."

He threaded his fingers through my hair, tightening his grip when I grazed his length with my teeth. All the while, he maintained eye contact. He traced my lips with his thumb and told me how beautiful I looked, how incredible it was.

I'd never felt more powerful or aroused, rubbing my thighs together as if that would help. I needed him between my legs. I needed to feel him inside me.

I massaged his balls, feeling them tighten in my hand. And I knew he was close. I could tell from the way his hips jerked, his breath coming in short bursts. It was clear from the way he groaned when I hummed around him.

"Sumner." It was a warning, a courtesy, and one I ignored.

A moment later, he came, and I took it all. I swallowed it down until he finally loosened his grip on my hair, his body relaxing on a powerful exhale.

"Wow." He blinked a few times. "That was…"

I laughed, patting him on the chest before leaning back against the seat. "Good."

He chuckled and leaned over to kiss me, the taste of him still on my tongue. "You're incredible." He gave me another peck. "You know that? Don't let anyone ever convince you otherwise."

My chest filled with warmth. How did he always know exactly what I needed to hear?

He tucked himself back into his pants then leaned over to kiss me as the car pulled to a stop. I hadn't even paid attention to where we were headed, but we were parked next to a large apartment building.

"Where are we?" I asked, glancing around. And then I saw it—the giant red gondolas high above, "Roosevelt Island" emblazoned on the side in white paint. I turned to him, my lips spreading into a smile. "Seriously?"

He nodded. "I've never been, and it seemed like something you would enjoy. Want to play tourist with me?"

"I—yes." I wrapped my arms around his neck. "Thank you."

I adjusted my dress and then followed him out of the car. It was a balmy evening, and we climbed the stairs to the boarding platform, horns honking as they paused on the street below. The station was relatively empty, and I hoped we'd have a car to ourselves. This was our last night together, and I didn't want to share him with anyone else—even strangers.

"Do we have time for this?" I asked as we waited for the next gondola to arrive.

He cupped my cheeks, threading his fingers through my hair. "Yes. Thanks to you."

I tilted me head to the side. "What did I do?"

"You helped me see what was really important." He pressed his lips to mine, shocking me with the public display. But I was even more stunned by his words because it felt as if he was saying that I was important.

We boarded the tram, and it felt as if we were in a bubble gliding over the city, past bridges and cars. I moved from window to window, enthralled by the view. Jonathan chuckled.

I tilted my head to the side, unable to decipher his expression. "What?"

"You're cute." I scrunched up my nose, and he added, "It was a compliment."

He came to stand behind me, bracketing my body with his arms. I turned to face him, and he slid his hand between us, inching it up my thigh. My body quivered with anticipation, desire pooling in my core.

"Would you be happier if I told you you're the sexiest woman I've ever seen?"

"Maybe." I melted into his touch, his lips grazing my neck.

He slid his fingers beneath my panties, wasting no time. I shivered from the contact and the idea that anyone could be watching.

"Did you ever imagine me doing this?" He teased my clit, the bundle of nerves thrumming with need.

I shook my head, biting my lip as I held back a moan. My imagination had been limited by my inexperience. But now...*ohmygod.* "Jonathan," I begged.

"What do you want, baby?" he rasped in my ear.

I closed my eyes, swallowing down the emotion that one word brought with it. *Baby.* Not Sumner or Sum, but baby.

*I don't want this to end.* The words were on the tip of my tongue, but I knew better than to say them. I'd told myself that I would accept this for what it was. I would ask for nothing more.

Even so, with my hands clutching his jacket, I was completely at his mercy in every sense of the word—my body and heart on display for him. Available to him to do his bidding.

"You." I swallowed. I felt even more frantic than usual, the knowledge that our time was running out in the forefront of my mind.

He shook his head, a smile teasing his lips. "Later. Back at the hotel."

I pouted, but then he thrust a finger inside me, and I gasped. "Oh..."

"We're almost there," he said, pumping harder, faster, and I wondered whether he meant my orgasm or Roosevelt Island. "Give it to me, baby. Give me everything."

Goose bumps erupted over my skin from his words. And when he nipped at the skin of my neck, I was lost. My desire almost overpowered me as he thrust his fingers in and out of me. In and out, making my legs shake. Blinding white light followed by one of the most intense releases of my life.

My knees nearly buckled, but he held me, pulling me close to his chest. He rubbed circles on my back, giving me a moment to catch my breath as the tram came to a stop. Passengers waited on the platform, and my body flooded with warmth at the idea of what we'd just done.

The doors opened, and Jonathan turned, tucking me into his side before guiding me out of the tram.

"That was close," I breathed.

"That was hot."

I glanced down to his pants where his bulge was definitely more prominent.

"You hungry?" he asked.

"Are you asking if I want to eat your sausage again?"

He started laughing, the sound bellowing from deep within. "And you teased me for referencing 'WAP' in bed. But no, that's not what I meant. Not everything is about sex."

We continued along the street, taking some stairs down to a boardwalk lining the water. A breeze blew off it, the lights of the city blinking from across the river.

"Isn't it? That's what this week is, right?"

We stood there a moment, before I couldn't take it anymore. I realized I didn't want to hear his answer, and when my eyes caught on an ice cream stand, I rushed ahead. "I'm starving."

When I glanced back, he was staring after me, and I couldn't read his expression. Finally, he shook his head. "For ice cream?" He frowned. "We haven't even had dinner."

"So?" I challenged, knowing all about his strict rules on dessert. And wanting to see if I could push them. I tugged on his hand. "Come on. Live a little."

"I'm not sure my heart can handle much more 'living,'" he teased.

I rolled my eyes. "It's one meal. And you know you want it."

"You're a bad influence."

"Oh. So, this is all my fault?" I teased, to which he nodded. "Next thing I know, you'll be blaming this week on me. Saying I seduced you."

He lifted a shoulder, giving me an expression that said, "If the shoe fits."

My jaw dropped, and I waited for him to retract his implied statement. "What?"

"*What,* what?" His nonchalance was unnerving. Was he serious? "You did kiss me first."

"Um." I shook my head, closing my eyes briefly. "That's not how I remember it."

He stalked toward me, wrapping his arms around my waist. His scent was all around me, his lips inches from mine, and I softened. "Okay, then. How do you remember it?"

"Come closer," I whispered, our eyes locked. His darkened, swirling with desire.

"Yes?" he whispered, noses nearly touching.

It was our last night together, and I could feel time slipping away. "Thank you for this week." I kissed the corner of his mouth, lingering there a moment. "For letting me come with you."

"I'll let you *come* with me as many times as you want."

I rolled my eyes, pushing against his chest. The moment was gone. I walked farther down the path.

"Sumner," he called.

I wasn't upset, not really. At least, not with him. I knew this was the end, but I didn't want it to be.

"Sumner." He caught up to me, pulling me aside so I was trapped against the metal railing. He tucked a strand of hair behind my ear. "Talk to me."

I didn't want to talk, so I gripped the lapels of his jacket as if I could hold on to him. Keep him. He tangled his fingers in my hair, angling my head, and I could barely stand or remember my name. He kissed me until I'd forgotten that we were temporary. Until I'd forgotten about anything but him.

## CHAPTER SIXTEEN

*Jonathan*

"If we keep this up, we're going to miss our flight," I said, though the words lacked any heat.

I was more focused on the feel of Sumner's naked body wrapped around mine. Her hair brushing against my skin. The fact that I didn't want this to end.

Sumner's green eyes peered into mine. "Would that really be such a terrible thing?"

*No.* "Yes. I have meetings, and…" I lost all train of thought when she rocked her hips against me. My heart was racing, and I was still trying to catch my breath from our latest round.

She laughed, and I breathed her in, closing my eyes as I tried to memorize everything about her. All the while, knowing this was the last time. The last time I'd hold her in my arms or kiss her. The last time she'd be mine.

I was tempted to stall. To miss our flight back. To do anything for more time with her, but I knew that was foolish. It would only be delaying the inevitable.

"Come on." I slapped her butt before rolling us so that I was on top. "Let's shower."

I climbed out of bed and paused, pressing my lips to her bare shoulder. She was beautiful in the early morning light, the sun warming her skin through the slit in the curtains. The sheet draped her body, revealing her curves and making me want to sink my teeth into her skin.

She glanced at the clock on the nightstand and hurried out of bed. "Crap. It's even later than I realized." She shoved my clothes at me, scrambling to pick up her own. "I'll meet you in the lobby in thirty."

I was so tempted to follow her to the bathroom, to join her in the shower like I had our first morning together. But when my phone buzzed with a text from the car service, I knew she was right. It was time.

It was also time to clarify where things stood between us.

I was buttoning my shirt when she returned to the room, riffling through her suitcase.

"No one can ever know about this. You understand, right?" She nodded, her movements rushed like my thoughts. "We go back to how we were. As if this week never happened. Because if anyone…" I scrubbed a hand over my face considering all the ways this could go sideways. "This has to be our little secret because the optics would—"

Her sharp intake of breath gave me pause.

"Optics, right," she repeated, though I didn't understand the edge in her tone. "Of course. I understand."

I hesitated a moment, then asked, "Are we good?"

"Yep. Fine." She disappeared into the bathroom.

I took a step forward, tempted to follow her. To press her. But another glance at the clock had me thinking better of it.

"Okay. See you downstairs," I called out before the door shut behind me.

When my phone buzzed with a new email, I frowned and hurried down the hall, my mind already back on work. Back on the things that needed to get done, many of which I'd put off this week to be with Sumner. One of the permits had been rejected on an office building, and the client was freaking out. In the past, I would've spent most of the ride to the airport responding to emails on my phone. But I now had more confidence in my team thanks to Sumner, and I was pleased by how they handled the situation.

When I glanced over at Sumner, her shoulders were tight, lips drawn. I assumed it was because of the impending flight and her nerves.

"You okay?"

"Mm-hmm. Yep." She continued typing on her phone as she had been before. "Just catching up on work."

"Same," I said, feeling as if both of us were using it as an excuse. It made me question whether we were even capable of going back to how things were after everything that had transpired this past week. The idea of returning to how things had been made my gut clench with dread.

When the driver pulled up to the airport, Sumner shot out of the car before he could open the door. He unloaded the bags, and she grabbed hers before I could. She struggled with her tote and her bag, the tote continually falling off the side.

"Here," I said, holding out my hand.

"I'm fine." She smiled brightly, repeating that damn phrase again. I was beginning to hate the word "fine." Then she was off, and I wondered how she could walk so quickly in those heels.

I shook my head, ignoring the way my cock stirred at the sight of her ass in that skirt. Her hips swaying as she marched through the airport. I glanced down, adjusting myself discreetly. *This is all your fault.*

I finally caught up to her, but between the chaos of checking in and then security, we didn't speak again until we were waiting to board. "Did you send Eric the updates from our meetings?" I asked, scrolling through a chain of emails.

"Yes."

"Alexis tells me there's a water leak at the house," I said after we were seated, mostly in an attempt to distract her.

"Mm." She stared at her phone, practically ignoring me.

I could see her anxiety building as the crew prepared for takeoff. I hated it. Hated feeling so helpless. She was afraid of flying. I was afraid of falling.

So, I took her hand in mine, holding on tight even when she tried to take it back. "It's going to be okay. *We're* going to be okay." I wasn't sure whether I said it more to comfort her or me.

She whipped her head to look at me, her tone even and calm when she said, "There is no 'we,' remember?"

She removed her hand from mine and returned her attention to her phone, gripping it tightly as the plane took off down the runway. With every second that passed, Sumner's tension seemed to ratchet up a notch. Or maybe that was just my own anxiety over the situation.

Suddenly, I felt desperate to make her smile or laugh. To have her acknowledge me. I wanted to blame this on the flight, but I got the feeling this widening gulf between us wouldn't just disappear when we landed in LA. I was beginning to think I'd been foolish to assume we could go back to the way we'd been. But what choice did we have?

I thought back to the flight out to New York and her erratic behavior. "You didn't take anything, right?"

We'd finally leveled out, the roar of the engines fading to a dull hum.

She rolled her eyes, those green orbs flicking to the "Fasten Seat Belt" sign that had just been turned off. "I think I learned my lesson last time."

"Yes, but—"

"Excuse me." She stood and headed for the bathroom without a backward glance.

I stared at her retreating figure, anger and desire swirling in my blood. Before I realized what was happening, I was following her, my steps pounding the aisle. I pushed open the door before she had a chance to close it.

She glanced up quickly, her eyes turning from shock to anger. "Get out."

As angry as she was, I knew Sumner well enough to sense that her emotions weren't solely related to what had happened between us. Yes, she was upset, but I had a feeling it was heightened by her fear of flying. My nerves certainly felt exposed—my need to protect her, to help her, driving my actions.

I ignored her and closed the door behind me, locking it. "I'm done with this passive-aggressive bullshit. If this isn't about the flight, then it's about me. *Us*."

*Us?* There was no "us," and there never would be. But I couldn't seem to get it through my head. I wasn't ready to give her up yet, even though I'd been the one to insist this had to end.

"You're right. Passive-aggressive isn't me. I just say yes, and I give and I give and I give. But you know what? I told myself I wouldn't do that anymore. I wouldn't please others at the expense of myself. So yeah, I am upset. Are you happy now?"

"No."

She scoffed, turning away to the mirror, not that she could go far. She inspected her makeup, and I watched her. I was pretty sure she muttered something about "I don't know what you want from me."

*You. I want you.*

If only she'd look at me, surely she'd see…

But instead, I forced myself to say, "I want...I *need* for us to be friends."

She scoffed, turning to face me and crossing her arms over her chest. "Jonathan, I know what you taste like. I know the sounds you make when you come." She let out a jagged breath. "So, excuse me if I need a minute to try to erase this week from my brain."

*Fuck.* I gritted my teeth, clenching my fists so as not to touch her. Her words were so filthy coming from such pure lips. Lips I'd tasted. Lips I'd fucked.

I'd never seen her so upset, so passionate. And while part of me wanted to applaud her for speaking up, the other part hated myself for putting her in this position in the first place.

"You think I like this?" I asked, crowding her in the already tight space. "You think I *want* to stay away from you?"

She turned her head to the side so that my breath grazed her cheek. I leaned in, knowing I'd regret this later, but at the moment, I didn't give a damn.

"I want you so fucking bad, I can barely breathe," I panted. I pulled her into me, letting her feel just how much I craved her.

"Jonathan. Please." She placed her hand on my wrist as if to stop me or to urge me on, which, I wasn't sure. From her tone, it sounded more like she was begging me to continue, even as her eyes glittered with anger.

I leaned in, kissing my way down her neck. Savoring every inch of her.

"Aren't we supposed to be *friends*? Colleagues?" Despite her protest, she panted, pressing her hips to mine.

"We are. But right now..." I nipped at her collarbone, and she gasped when I slid my hand into her skirt, sliding through her slick, wet heat. "High above the world... You're mine."

She gripped the edge of the sink, pressing herself into my hand. "I thought this ended in New York."

"It does. *Did*," I said, dipping my tongue into her mouth for a kiss. "We're still on New York time. This doesn't count."

She panted as I teased her clit. I swallowed her moans with kisses, wondering if the other passengers could hear us.

"Tell me to stop," I whispered. "If you tell me…"

She gripped my forearm, holding me in place. "Don't you dare stop."

I drove her to the breaking point, my movements frenzied, my thoughts disordered. "This is the way it *has* to be. You understand, right?"

"*Right.* Because I'm bad for your image." She pushed me away, jerking out of my hold, but not before I'd seen the flash of pain in her eyes.

"No." I crouched down so I was at her eye level. "Is that what this is about?"

"Yes. No. Ugh." She clenched her fists, her skin still flushed with desire. "The last guy I dated wouldn't introduce me to his friends, wouldn't meet my family, wouldn't…" She sagged. "Well, let's just say that *I* wasn't good for 'optics.'"

"Sumner. That's…shitty. I'm sorry. I wasn't trying to make you feel like—"

"The dirty little secret I am?" She straightened her clothes, and I could see her rebuilding her armor.

I dragged a hand through my hair. *God, I am such a hypocrite.*

"That's not—" I let out a deep sigh. "More than anything, I worry about how this would affect your relationship with Ian."

"And yours."

"That too," I admitted.

"I know. You're right. Just…" She sighed. "Give me a minute. I'm amped up from the flight and everything. I promise that by the time we land in LA, I'll have my head screwed on straight."

I wasn't sure I'd ever have my head screwed on straight when it came to this woman. My feelings were so conflicted, want and need overriding my better sense. Making me betray my best friend in a way that would've seemed unthinkable. And yet…I couldn't seem to stop myself when it came to his daughter. I was going to end up hurting them both. I was going to end up hurting us all.

᭝

"How was New York?" Cody asked, standing from his desk as I stalked toward my office. After the flight, I'd come straight to the office, but it still felt as if my head were in the clouds.

"Fine." God, there was that fucking word again, though this time, the memory of it brought a smile to my face, fleeting as it was.

I smoothed a hand over my hair as if to soothe my guilt. All the while, I wondered how the hell I was going to make it through the rest of the summer. I'd have to see Sumner every day, all while knowing what she tasted like, felt like. Those sexy moans she made when I touched her in all the right places. It was going to be torture.

"Just fine?" He followed me into my office.

"Yes," I ground out. I barely glanced up at him, busying myself with plugging in my laptop and turning it on.

"How'd it go with Sumner?"

I stilled but then realized he meant business-wise. "Fine."

"Interesting." I didn't like the smug little note to his tone.

"Cody," I snapped. "Do you need something?"

I had countless emails to go through for the Wolfe Group, let alone the stuff on my latest project with Alexis. A workout. A podcast interview to prepare for. All things I'd been putting off in New York. Putting off to be with Sumner.

But the truth was, none of it mattered. These past few weeks, I'd come to realize that my team was more than capable of running the Wolfe Group. It was why I'd hired them after all. And I was using work as an excuse to avoid my feelings about Sumner.

"Sheffield returned the contract. I'm surprised you were able to sell him on the former Masonic lodge."

I lifted a shoulder. "That was all Sumner."

"Impressive."

I nodded. It was an impressive feat, especially considering how shy she'd been as a child. But she was nothing like that child now. She was assertive and confident, negotiating with ease and closing deals.

"Anything else?" I asked.

He shook his head, excusing himself from my office. I immersed myself in work and lost track of time, catching up on everything that had happened while I was gone. When there was a knock at the door a while later, I glanced up and my heart stalled.

"Ian?"

"You don't seem happy to see me," he teased, walking into my office and sitting across from me.

"No. What?" I shook my head. "Of course I am. It's just—"

"Now's not the best time," he finished for me with a wry grin.

I furrowed my brow. "Um. Yeah. Work is crazy. You know what it's like when you're gone for a day, let alone a week," I said, hoping he'd empathize and let me off the hook.

"You work too much." He stood. "Come on. Cody told me you haven't had lunch yet, and I want to hear about New York."

"New York?" My voice came out squeaky.

"Yeah. I texted Sumner a few times, but it sounded like you guys were pretty busy."

I tried to swallow, but it felt impossible, my throat was so tight. A boa constrictor was wrapped around my windpipe, squeezing. "We... Uh, yeah."

"What's up with you? You're acting weird."

"Am I?" Another squeeze. I was struggling to string two words together. My heart pounded, and I was convinced he'd known what I'd done just from the sound of my voice. I couldn't avoid him the rest of my life, but I hadn't expected to have to contend with him so soon after returning from New York.

"Come on," he said, and I knew there was no getting out of it.

I stood and followed him to the door. Maybe we could get a quick bite at one of the food trucks down the street. Perfect. No sitting meant less time to talk.

"Should we swing by Sumner's desk on the way and invite her?" he asked as we headed toward the elevators.

"No," I blurted, then quickly backpedaled. "I mean, I think she had lunch plans already with one of the associates."

I had no idea what her plans were, but I knew that Sumner, Ian, and me alone together was a terrible idea.

"That's good." He smiled. "I'm glad she's making friends. She seems a lot happier lately."

"Yeah?"

"Yeah." He nodded, his expression contemplative. "Thank you again for bringing her on this summer. I hope it hasn't been too much of a burden."

I wanted to laugh, but I was too busy trying not to throw up. "Not at all."

God, I was a terrible friend—the absolute worst. I'd slept with his daughter, and now I was lying to his face. This was exactly why I had to stay away from her.

163

## CHAPTER SEVENTEEN

*Sumner*

"How was New York?" Lea asked, while Dad plated the salad.

"It was…yeah. It was good," I answered, not entirely sure what to say. Jonathan and I had returned from New York earlier in the day, and everything had gone back to normal. Well, as normal as things could be after you'd slept with your boss.

Lea poured three glasses of wine. "Did you learn a lot?"

"Yeah. I mean, I loved being in the city. I got to meet some clients." But it was the things Jonathan showed me in the bedroom that had my toes curling. Him pressing me against the shower, finger-fucking me in the back of the town car.

"And Jonathan?" Dad asked, carrying two plates over to the table and setting them down. Lea brought over the third and took a seat.

"What about him?" I asked quickly, a little too quickly. I sipped the wine, my cheeks heating as I quashed those memories.

"How did he seem?"

"Good." I swallowed the truth as I continued spilling lies.

I'd told myself that my dad wasn't part of the equation, but that was easier to believe when he wasn't sitting in front of me, asking about his best friend.

Sure, I'd kept things from my dad in the past, but I couldn't imagine he'd be thrilled if he knew I'd slept with Jonathan. Not that it mattered. We were back to being professional and acting like it had never happened. After we'd returned to the office, he'd spent the rest of the day catching up, and I had done my best to keep my head down and get my job done.

"Did he..." Dad cleared his throat. "You know, say anything? Confide anything to you?"

"Like what?" I asked, though sweat dripped down my back. Did he suspect something?

"I don't know." He lifted a shoulder but continued to cut his chicken. "You guys spent a whole week together. I just figured..."

"Dad, it was a business trip."

"Yeah. I know." He recoiled, and I immediately regretted the way I'd snapped. "But after work, surely you guys talked."

I shook my head. "Not really. The hours were pretty crazy, and any talk was focused on the clients and what was coming up next. Besides—" I sipped my wine and set the glass back down "—he's my boss. He's not going to spill all his secrets to me, even if you two are besties."

"Oh." His expression fell, and I felt even worse for my lie. "Right. Of course."

"Honey, is something wrong?" Lea asked Dad.

"He was acting really odd today."

I nearly choked on my chicken, coughing a few times before gulping down some wine. "Sorry." Another cough. "You saw him today?"

"We had lunch. I would've invited you, but he said he thought you had plans."

"I...yeah." I tried to school my expression even as my mind churned with questions. They had lunch? *Did Jonathan say anything?* "I did."

"Odd, how?" Lea asked Dad, and I wished they'd just drop it.

"Just really evasive or something. I got the impression he wasn't particularly happy to see me." Dad stared into the distance, brows furrowed. Lea placed her hand atop his.

"I'm sure it's nothing." Lea forced a bright smile. "You said he seemed good in New York, right, Sumner?"

"Yes." I forced out the word. "Really good."

Dad shook his head, his earlier expression clearing as he smiled. "You're right. I'm probably overanalyzing."

I nodded and kept my attention focused on my meal. The rest of dinner was uneventful, and I spent most of it pushing the food around my plate. When they'd finished, I volunteered to do the dishes, grateful for an escape.

I thought I was in the clear until Lea sat across from me on one of the barstools. "Sumner, is everything okay?"

"Yeah," I chirped. "Yeah. I'm just tired. It's been a long day."

She nodded slowly, though she continued to appraise me. She glanced around, and I realized Dad was nowhere in sight. Even so, she lowered her voice. "Did something happen in New York?"

"No." I jerked my head back, heart racing. "Why would you think that?"

"I don't know." Her lips turned down, and I wondered if she could hear my heart trying to beat out of my chest. "I guess I thought you'd be more excited after the trip. And when your dad mentioned Jonathan—"

I tried to maintain a neutral expression, even though I feared she could see right through me. "It's nothing, promise. I'm just tired," I said, settling on a version of the truth.

She placed the back of her hand to my forehead. "You sure you're not coming down with something?"

I nodded. "I'm good. Really."

"Good, because I'd hate to cancel our spa day this weekend."

I cringed. I'd totally forgotten about it, but there was no way I could spend an entire day alone with Lea and maintain this charade. "I, um, I actually have to work," I lied, desperate for an escape.

"On the weekend?" she asked, and I nodded, wishing I'd thought it through. "Surely you deserve a day off, especially after stepping up and helping with the New York trip."

"I wish." I wiped down the counters before folding the dish towel.

She nodded, crossing her arms over her chest. "For an intern, you sure are working long hours."

I took my time draping the towel over the oven handle. "Not really. It's no different from anywhere else. Anyway—" I yawned, though my weariness was genuine and bone-deep. "I'm exhausted. I'm going to shower and head to bed."

Before she could press me further, I darted upstairs and into my room, shutting and locking the door behind me. I showered, wishing my lies would wash down the drain along with the dirt from my skin. I hated lying to my dad. I hated lying to Lea.

Did I regret sleeping with Jonathan?

I didn't know that I could ever say I regretted it, but my current predicament was less than ideal. And I couldn't see how I was going to make it until the end of the summer, the end of my internship.

I tossed and turned, my mind even more restless than my body. And when my alarm went off, my eyes were dry and scratchy, my body felt like it was weighted down with stones. I dressed before dragging myself down to the kitchen to make some coffee. It was early, and I was hoping to escape the house before my dad or Lea got up. I'd struggled through the conversation at dinner last night, and I didn't know how I could keep up this act.

But I soon realized that being at the office was no better. I wasn't sure whether I wanted to see Jonathan or avoid him. Both prospects seemed equally daunting, though I knew I'd have to face him eventually.

I headed toward the conference room, when my phone vibrated with an incoming email. I glanced down at the screen, startled to find a new message from Nico. I was about to hit delete, but curiosity had me skimming the contents.

SUMNER,

I'll be in LA next week for a conference, and I'd love to see you. I've missed you.

Best,

Nico

I HADN'T HEARD FROM HIM IN MONTHS. OR AT LEAST, NOT since I'd blocked his number. And I was so shocked to hear from him now that I barely noticed where I was going until someone cleared their throat.

I glanced up to find Jonathan staring at me from down the hall.

"Hey," I said, hitting the Power button on my phone so the screen went black.

Jonathan shoved his hands in his pockets and shifted on his feet. "Hey."

We both moved to the right, blocking each other's path.

"Oh, um," I moved left, and so did he, continuing our awkward dance. "Sorry."

I was so caught off guard—by Nico's email, by this man—that I couldn't think straight. I moved right, and then finally, he brushed past me, careful not to so much as glance my direction.

"Excuse me." Jonathan's tone was brusque.

Was it really just a few days ago that he'd been eating me out, fucking me on every surface in the hotel room? And now he couldn't seem to bear the sight of me. I understood his reasons, but that didn't mean I liked them. Didn't erase the hurt. I missed our conversations. I missed his laughter. I missed *him*.

When I reached the conference room, I sank into an empty chair, busying myself with work. At least Nico was a good distraction for the moment. What the hell did he want anyway? And why did I even care?

Thinking about Nico only reminded me how naïve I'd been, how naïve I still was, when it came to men. Why did I keep falling for the same kind of guy—older, accomplished, emotionally unavailable? I mean, didn't it say something that I kept picking men I could only ever have a secret relationship with?

I'd dated Nico in secret for a little over a year, but I was finding it more difficult to hide my feelings around Jonathan. I'd done my best to remain professional and polite, to act as if nothing had happened. But it was exhausting, and I didn't know how I could maintain this act for the rest of the summer.

The seats around me filled in, and I deleted Nico's email just as Jack kicked off the meeting. I tried to focus on the presentation, but my mind was elsewhere. And when Jonathan opened the door, slipping into an empty chair near the front, I swallowed hard then quickly glanced away.

My phone vibrated with an incoming text. I snuck a

glance at the screen, careful to keep it concealed beneath the table.

**Piper: Party tonight. Klaus's yacht.**

My gut reaction was to tell her I was busy, but part of me wanted to go out. Wanted to let loose and have fun. To forget about Jonathan and flirt with guys my own age. Guys who would be proud to date me, not try to pretend I didn't exist. Maybe a party on Klaus's yacht was just the thing I needed.

Wasn't that what twenty-three-year-olds did on a Friday night?

Even if he didn't admit it, I knew part of the reason Jonathan didn't want to be with me because I was too young, too...*whatever*. I glanced over at him, taking the opportunity to watch him while his focus was on the speaker. His profile was as painfully gorgeous as I remembered—kissable lips, scruff that tickled in all the right places, and those eyes. Blue eyes as endless as the ocean, and just as deep and mysterious.

He didn't look at me, didn't even acknowledge my presence. This was how it had been since we'd returned. He avoided me, wouldn't meet my eyes, was cordial and cold. It was even worse now that I knew how it could be. How affectionate and warm he could be, but also how rough and demanding. And I wanted it all. I wanted the Jonathan I'd seen in New York. The man who took what he wanted. The man who *lived*. Not this shell of a man who seemed burdened by guilt and regrets.

I closed my eyes briefly and took a deep breath. This was so fucked up.

I let my breath out slowly, returning my attention to my phone. Maybe it really was time to let go. I'd fulfilled my fantasy. And it could never be anything more.

**Me: Count me in.**

**Piper: Awesome. I'll send you the deets.**

I returned my attention to Jack, grateful that he seemed

to be wrapping up. When the meeting was adjourned, I pushed out my seat, gathering my things. Out of the corner of my eye, I saw Jack approach.

"Hey, Sumner." He leaned against the conference table.

"Hey." I kept my attention on my bag, eager to leave.

"A group of us are going out for drinks after work. Want to join?"

"Thanks, but I can't." I held up my phone and grinned, wondering if it looked more like a grimace. "I have plans."

Even without looking, I could feel Jonathan's glare searing me from across the room. I had the fleeting thought that maybe he was jealous, and then it was gone. Of course he wasn't jealous. And even if he was, he had no right to be.

"Maybe next time, then." Jack's expression was hopeful, and I tried to imagine myself saying yes. Tried to imagine what it would be like to go out with him, but I couldn't. I couldn't picture myself with anyone but Jonathan.

By the time I met Piper at the dock, the party was already in full swing. Music streamed through the boat's speakers, guests dotting the decks on both levels.

"I'm so glad you could finally make time for me in your busy schedule," Piper teased, air-kissing my cheek. She linked her arm through mine, and we proceeded toward the yacht, where a security guard checked our IDs, marking us off on a list.

"How sick is this?" she asked, staring up at the vessel. It was pretty nuts. I smiled, excitement replacing some of my earlier dread.

We boarded the yacht, and Piper gripped my arm tighter. "Oh. My. God," she hissed. "Is that Stellan Mclane?"

"Who?" I frowned.

"He's only, like, the hottest singer this summer. How have you not heard his song—'Buy Me'?"

"I've been a little busy."

"What's up with you tonight?" she asked, guiding me over to the bar where we ordered drinks. "You seem tense."

Instead of answering, I surveyed the crowd. I recognized a few celebrities. Piper had told me about these types of parties before, but it was different experiencing it firsthand rather than through her Instagram posts.

When the bartender returned with my drink, I thanked him and took a few sips. The flavor of the cocktail reminded me of one I'd had in New York, and I stared into the glass as if it held the answers. Between pretending everything was fine at work and keeping the secret from my dad and Lea when I couldn't avoid them, I was exhausted. The only reason I hadn't told Piper yet was because I wasn't ready to dissect what had happened. But I couldn't hold it in anymore. If I didn't talk about this with someone, I was going to explode.

"I did something stupid."

"Are we talking kissing-Carson-with-braces stupid or…"

My thoughts immediately went to Jonathan caging me in in the airplane bathroom. His breath hot on my neck, my muffled pants. I swallowed back those thoughts, heat flooding my cheeks.

"I slept with my boss."

"Oh shit." Her eyes went wide. Then she settled back into her seat, seeming to realize I was serious. "Well, was your dream man everything you hoped he'd be?"

I took a deep breath and let it out slowly. "And more."

She squealed, drawing the attention of some men nearby. "Yas, girl. Get it." She took a sip of her drink. "Wait. Why do you seem so upset, then?"

I hung my head. "Because it's over. Well, it never really started, to be honest. And now everything is such a mess."

"Aw, Sumner." She wrapped her arm around my shoulder and pulled me into her side. "I'm sorry. I know you've always had a thing for him." She pulled back to look at me. "He wasn't an asshole about it, was he?"

I shook my head, my eyes stinging. Even though I was mad at him—at the situation—I couldn't honestly say he'd been an asshole. "No. Not really. He was never anything but honest."

She nodded, then seemed to consider something. "Hey, do you want to get out of here?"

I did, but I also knew how excited she'd been about the party. "Already? We just got here."

"So?" She lifted a shoulder. "There will be other parties. I only have one best friend."

And then I really did almost cry. "Aw, Piper." I tugged at the corners of my eyes. "You're going to ruin my makeup."

"Come on," she said, escorting me toward the deck. "Let's blow this joint." Her heels clicked against the deck. "Wait—" She turned to me. "Maybe that's what we should do."

"What's that?" I asked.

"Smoke."

I shook my head with a laugh, though the idea was tempting. How nice would it be not to care about anything for a while?

"At least now you've gotten him out of your system. You've checked off that fantasy, and you can finally move on."

The problem was, I didn't know if I could.

## CHAPTER EIGHTEEN

*Jonathan*

"**W**olfe?"

"Isla." I glanced up when I heard a knock at the door. "What can I do for you?"

She stepped inside, taking a seat across from me. "I just wanted to stop by and say thank you for the coaching lessons. Sumner's been wonderful."

I nodded, thinking that I couldn't agree more. Sumner was wonderful. "Good. I'm glad."

"And...well, I hate to do this, but I'm going to have to tender my resignation."

I leaned forward, resting my hands on the desk. "Did something happen? Have you accepted a job elsewhere?"

"No. I mean, sort of. I've always enjoyed working with the Wolfe Group, but Sumner made me see where my true passion lies. And she helped me figure out a way to level up my business. With a few life changes, I can make my passion project my full-time job."

"Wow. That's..." I swallowed, overcome with pride for Sumner and what she'd accomplished. This was bigger than any deal; she'd changed someone's life. "That's great, Isla."

"And it'll give me more time with my new grandbaby."

I nodded, knowing how close she was to her children. I almost envied her—having such a strong sense of purpose, especially when it came to her family. "I'm happy for you."

"I don't mean to overstep," she said. "But have you considered hiring Sumner as a coach yourself?"

I nodded, thinking about how much I'd missed working with Sumner lately. The past few weeks—at least until New York—I'd been happier, lighter. And that was due to her suggestions. I wanted our friendship back. Our long conversations about productivity and time audits and anything and everything else.

I still didn't trust myself to be alone with her, so I'd avoided her since returning from New York last week. That didn't mean I wasn't thinking about her.

*Fuck...* I slid my hands down my thighs, wishing they were on her body instead. It felt as if I could think of nothing but her. If she'd asked me to do a time audit of my thoughts, there'd only be one entry for every single block: Sumner.

Sleeping with her had been a mistake for obvious reasons —I was her boss, her dad's best friend, the list went on and on. But the true reason was something I could never tell her. Now that I'd had her, I couldn't get her out of my head. I thought maybe I'd scratch the itch and be done, but it was like a rash. The more you scratched, the worse the itch, until it was all you could think about.

"Anyway..." Isla smiled, standing. "Thank you, Wolfe."

"Thank you, Isla." I stood, shaking her hand.

After she left, I glanced at my calendar. I could skip several of the afternoon meetings, which meant...

"Cody," I called.

He came to stand in the doorway. "What's up?"

"What's Sumner working on?"

"Medical facilities with Jack."

"Can you ask her to come to my office?"

"Sure," he said. "If she asks, what should I tell her it's about?"

"Just ask her to come, please."

He nodded, then disappeared. I responded to a few emails and was closing my laptop when Sumner appeared in my doorway. I froze, my blood roaring to life for the first time in a week. This was torture. Being so close to her but feeling so far away. Everything stilled as our eyes locked, and I scanned her, searching for any changes, any clues that she missed me as much as I missed her. That she was as miserable as I was.

But all I saw was a confident, professional young woman who looked more beautiful than ever. Why did she have to be so tempting? So off-limits?

"Hey," she said, hanging back at the doorway. "You wanted to see me."

"Isla's resigning."

"What? That's great!" She smiled but quickly hid it. "I mean, well, sorry for you." She cringed. "I guess that plan backfired."

I stood, keeping the desk between us as if it were a shield. "Honestly, when she told me, all I could think was how jealous I was."

She furrowed her brow. "Jealous?"

"Yeah." I rounded the desk and sat on the edge. "She was so fired up, so passionate about what she was doing. I want that."

"Okay…" She stepped farther into the office, and I took it as a sign to continue.

"I want you to help me find that. I want to work with you again—like we did before…"

I faltered at the reminder of our time together. It had been amazing, but it couldn't happen again. It shouldn't have happened in the first place. And if Ian ever found out…

"*Before.*" She nodded slowly, and I knew she understood everything I wasn't saying. "You mean before you started avoiding me?"

My eyes darted to the open door, where I imagined Cody was sitting just outside. I walked over quickly and closed it.

"Don't act like you weren't avoiding me too."

I knew it was immature, and she wisely ignored the jab. Instead, she crossed her arms over her chest. "Have you defined success on your own terms yet?"

I frowned, meeting her eyes once more. "No, but—"

She turned and walked to the door, hand poised on the knob. "Come see me when you have. Then, maybe we can talk." And then she walked out.

*Damn.* Why was she so adamant about this? I *was* successful; did I really need to define it? Apparently so, at least if I wanted her to coach me.

So, I sat down behind my desk with a pad of paper and a pen. I opened her email with the prompts and proceeded to stare at it. My ideal day. *My ideal day.* A vision of Sumner in bed flashed before me. A memory? A fantasy? I wasn't sure whether it was something that had happened or something I wanted to. Maybe both.

Sumner's words from all those weeks ago floated back to me. "Have you ever felt torn between what you think you should want and your true desires?" All. The. Time.

She'd told me to decide if I could live without what I wanted. And if I couldn't, to find a way. To do whatever it took. I wanted her.

I shook my head. *Be realistic.*

I reread her prompt, wrote a few things. Struck through them. Crumpled up the paper and tossed it in the trash. Tried again. And again. Until finally, with a huff, I stood from my desk and grabbed my suit jacket.

I wasn't getting anything done. I was wasting my time in

every sense of the word. I needed to clear my mind. I needed to do something with my hands. So, I headed over to the latest house I was working on with Alexis.

On the drive over, my phone rang through my car speakers, and I pressed the button to connect the call. "Wolfe."

"Jonathan?" Ian asked. "Have you seen Sumner?"

"No." I frowned, tightening my grip on the steering wheel. "Why?"

"I just thought she'd be home by now. We were supposed to have dinner. Oh—" He paused, and I could hear a door open and shut in the background. "Here she is now. Never mind. Hey, kiddo," he called.

"Ian…"

"She's been so secretive lately," he whispered with a laugh. "I think maybe she's seeing someone."

I clenched my jaw so hard I was surprised I didn't crack a tooth. "Seeing someone?"

Was that why she'd brushed me off for coaching?

"Anyway, sorry to worry you." He chuckled. "I guess it doesn't matter how old she is, she'll always be my baby."

I cringed, chest tightening as if there were a band around it. *Fuck.*

She was his baby, and I'd wanted to call her "baby." God, I was a shitty friend.

The following afternoon, I called Sumner into my office again. My visit to the jobsite yesterday had given me an idea. I'd realized that perhaps part of the reason I couldn't envision my future was because I was stuck in the past.

"Are you busy?" I asked her.

"Jack is expecting—"

"Right now? Do you have any meetings this afternoon?" I asked, unable to hide the impatience from my tone.

"No, but—"

"Good." I grabbed my keys from the desk. "Come on."

"Where are we going?" she asked, her eyes wary.

"Out. Bye, Cody."

"See you later, Wolfe. Bye, Sumner." He smiled brightly at her, and my attention whipped between them. Was she sneaking off to date Cody? I shook my head as if to clear it. What the fuck was wrong with me?

"Are you seeing someone?" I blurted as soon as the elevator doors closed.

"So what if I am?" she asked, hands on hips.

"Is that why you won't coach me?"

"What?" She jerked her head back. "No." She laughed, and I watched her face transform from spectacular to exquisite. "There's no point in coaching you if you won't put in the work."

Wasn't it enough that I was trying?

The doors slid open to the parking garage, and I marched toward my truck, her heels clicking on the pavement behind me. I opened the passenger door for her and watched her legs as she climbed in. Watched the way she moved.

I rounded the hood, hopping in the driver's seat and starting the truck before throwing it in reverse.

"Where are you taking me?"

"I need to show you something," I said, knowing it would be more impactful if she saw it with her own eyes. Maybe then, she'd understand.

During the drive, I asked her about what she was reading, the projects she was working on at the office. Despite the awkward, terse silence of the past week, I was relieved that we seemed to lapse so easily back into our friendship. More than anything, I was grateful that Sumner had been mature and professional despite what had transpired between us.

"Another fixer-upper?" she asked as I slowed, pulling up to a curb next to an abandoned house. Boards covered the windows, and the grass was littered with trash, an old toilet sitting prominently among the weeds.

I shook my head. "This is where I grew up."

Sumner lifted her hand to her mouth but kept her eyes focused on the house a moment more before returning them to mine.

"And, no, it didn't look much better back then, though my mom did everything she could to make it beautiful."

"What happened to them?" she asked, her voice as gentle as the hand she'd placed on my forearm.

"Car accident," I said. "We only had one car. My mom dropped me off at school and then went to pick up my dad from the graveyard shift…" I shook my head, squeezing my eyes shut as if I could push away the sadness, the regret as well. I never talked about my parents. "They never made it home.

"Anyway," I continued. "This is why I'm having a difficult time with your assignment. Because, to my parents—to the version of myself growing up. Struggling. Scraping to get by. The life I'm living is… Well, it would be beyond their wildest dreams."

She nodded. "And wanting something else for yourself feels somehow…selfish."

"Not only that," I said, relieved that she understood. "But ungrateful."

"Don't you think your parents would want you to be happy? However that looks for you?"

I glanced back outside, back at the crumbling house and the memories it contained. Memories of sacrifice and hardship, sure. But also, happy times. Days filled with love and laughter.

I nodded, unable to even choke out a simple "Yes."

"And don't you think that they, of all people, would realize that money doesn't always equate to happiness?"

"I—" I shook my head, captivated by the intensity of her green eyes. The wisdom housed there. "You are a wise woman, Sumner Gray. Has anyone ever told you that?"

She laughed, and I could feel my muscles relax after they often did following a deep tissue massage. "It's okay to want something else. To want something different. That doesn't diminish your hard work nor make you seem ungrateful. If anything, it shows that you have a growth mind-set."

"I want to," I said. "I don't think I realized it, but I'm tired of feeling chained to the past."

"Wanting to move on and making different choices is different from actually doing it."

"And how's that going for you—making different choices?"

"Honestly?" she asked. "Not so well. I thought I was making progress, but then I kind of had a setback." I wondered if she was referring to me, but I was too afraid to ask.

"Thank you for showing me this," she said as I put the truck in drive and pulled away from the curb, leaving the past behind.

"Why do you want to go to business school?" I turned on my signal, checking my blind spot before changing lanes as we headed back toward the office. "You have clients. You don't *need* an MBA to do what you want to do."

I knew how hard Ian had pushed for her to go to Stanford. And I knew what it was like to make choices based on your parents' expectations. How easy it was to go down a path without realizing the full implications of your decisions.

"True, but I think it would be beneficial. Especially if I'm counseling small business owners. And as a younger coach, I think it could lend me some credibility."

"I can see that," I said. "But that shouldn't be your only— or even your main—reason for going."

"It's not," she bit out.

I glanced over at her before returning my attention to the road. Her shoulders were tight, eyes straight ahead. "Have you told Ian about your coaching business?"

"No," she said, confirming my suspicions.

"Why not?"

"Because—" She blew out a breath. "I'm afraid he'll try to talk me out of it."

I nodded, though I wasn't sure I agreed. And even if he did try to convince her it was a bad idea, I wanted her to have faith in herself and her ideas. Or at least have the confidence to try something, even if it resulted in failure. Sometimes that was the best way to learn. "You're young. You should create the life of your choosing. Not the one everyone else expects for you."

"I wish you could follow your own advice when it comes to us." The words were said so softly, I'd almost missed them.

Out of the corner of my eye, I saw her shake her head. "Sorry. I shouldn't have said that. I knew what I was agreeing to. And I know you're right."

"What am I right about?" I asked, pulling into the parking garage for the Wolfe Group and putting my truck in park. This time of night, the garage was mostly empty.

"You, me, my dad. All of it. It may not seem like it, but I'd never want to come between the two of you. And…" She let out a breath. "I've done a lot of thinking since we returned from New York, and I'm sorry if I pushed you into something you didn't want."

I chuckled. "Something I didn't want?" I placed my hand beneath her chin, guiding her gaze to mine. She was so goddamn beautiful, it stole my breath. Black hair that hung in waves, those jade eyes that captivated me. "First of all, I wanted you." *Want you.*

I released her chin, placing my hands on the console.

"Don't ever think I didn't. And push me into something?" I chuckled again. "Sumner, no one pushes *me* into anything."

"I know and thank you. That means…a lot." She placed her hand on mine, and I didn't know how it was possible to feel both tenser and more relaxed at the same time. Perhaps because my body and head were at war. If it were up to my body, we'd already be undressed in the back seat.

"Fuck, you're gorgeous," I blurted, feeling closer to her than ever.

She sucked in a jagged breath and removed her hand. "You're not making this easy, and I-I'm really trying to respect your wishes here."

I was trying to remember what those were. Because at the moment, all I wished for, all I *wanted*, was her in my arms.

She leaned across the console to place the softest of kisses on my cheek. "Good night, Jonathan."

I gripped her shoulders, holding her in place. I was tired of living for my parents. I was tired of being bound by my past. By my guilt over the situation with Ian. For once, I knew what I wanted, and what I wanted was Sumner.

"I want you," I rasped.

Her eyes searched mine, and I nodded. She pressed a hesitant kiss to my cheekbone. Another to my temple. With each kiss, she gained more confidence, and I'd never felt so worshiped or adored.

"Sumner," I groaned when she kissed my forehead, giving me a straight shot down her blouse. "We should—"

"Shh." She pressed her finger to my lips, her own pouty and begging for my kiss. "Don't ruin it."

I swallowed, the cab filling with tension ready to explode. She reached down and palmed me through my slacks, and I squeezed my eyes shut. *Fuck. Yes. More.*

I glanced around, but we were alone. My belt was released, my zipper drawn, and my cock freed. God, it felt amazing to have her hands on me again. The past week had been torture, plain and simple.

"Sumner—" I reached out with every intention of stopping her. Of telling her we should go back to my place, a hotel, anywhere but the office parking garage. *Christ.* But my willpower crumbled the moment she wrapped her lips around my cock, swallowing me down.

Her head bobbed in my lap as she worked me into a frenzy. "Fuck, baby. Fuck," I hissed, gripping the door with one hand for support while I threaded the other through her hair. The curtain of black silk fell over my fingers, and I knew I was done for.

I pushed my feet against the floorboard, muscles tensing. Her mouth was warm and wet...and then she hummed, and I couldn't take it anymore. I needed to be inside her.

"Back seat. Now," I growled.

I proceeded to take her in the back of my truck like a horny teenager unable to control himself. And despite my age and supposed wisdom, I knew it wouldn't be the last time I took her that way. She made me feel young, powerful, wanted in a way no other woman in the past had. It was why I couldn't stay away. Hard as I'd tried, I couldn't fight this anymore.

*Just for the summer,* I told myself.

# CHAPTER NINETEEN

*Sumner*

"Come home with me," Jonathan whispered in my ear, kissing just below it.

I shivered from his touch, the aftershocks of my orgasm making me delirious. Had he really just asked me to come home with him? God, how I'd longed to hear those words. It might not seem like a big deal, but it was to me. He was inviting me in, asking me to stay.

But was he? A little voice in the back of my head asked.

Nothing had changed. We were still sneaking around.

A light flickered in the distance, and I was grateful for the dark tint on the windows of his truck. Despite the harsh fluorescents illuminating the parking garage, we were hidden. Well, as hidden as we could be, considering what we'd just done. Talk about bad for optics.

God, I hated that word and all it implied.

"Are you sure that's a good idea?" I searched for my panties in the back of his truck while he disposed of the condom.

"You mean because of Ian?" His lips were flat, his posture rigid.

I'd realized that Jonathan didn't like talking about my dad, at least not with me. And definitely not when I called him "Dad." He seemed to do better when I referred to my dad as Ian. And I'd found it best to simply avoid the topic altogether.

"Yeah."

He pulled me to him, my back to his front. He inhaled deeply as he gave me a soft squeeze. "God, I missed you. Missed this."

I closed my eyes, a sense of calm washing over me just from his words and his proximity. I'd missed him too, and not just the sex. I'd missed our friendship and easy banter. We'd only recently started talking again, which was part of my hesitation for diving back into bed with him. Despite what we'd just done.

"What?" he asked.

"This past week has been a roller coaster. And now that we're in a good place again, I don't want to jeopardize that."

"Neither do I." He brushed my hair aside, adorning my neck with kisses.

"Besides, I'm not sure I should be sleeping with my client," I teased, needing to make light of the moment.

"And I'm not sure I should be sleeping with my intern. You might sue me for sexual harassment."

We both had a lot to lose. Not to mention, the biggest risk of all—my heart.

"Except it would have to be unwanted. And it's not."

"But you're still not sure this is a good idea." He wrapped a strand of my hair around his finger.

I thought back on how difficult life had been since returning from New York. At the office, at home, I'd felt trapped—like a fly caught in a spider's elaborate silken web. "This past week—lying to Lea and my dad—it's been harder than I expected."

The prospect of choosing between my dad and Jonathan, between smothering my desires or lying and embracing what I wanted, was giving me heartburn.

"Fuck, you're right." He leaned back, his deep exhale filling the cab with everything unspoken. "I'm constantly dodging his questions or avoiding him altogether."

"Same." I let out a deep sigh. "I feel like the world's worst daughter."

Silence filled the cab, but the desire was still there. The need too.

I thought back on how he'd opened up to me tonight. The way we'd connected so seamlessly, and I twisted around to face him, so I was straddling his lap. "How can this feel so right but be so wrong?"

"I don't know, baby." He gripped my hips. "I don't. I keep telling myself to stay away, but—"

"It's impossible," I finished for him, and he nodded.

He rested his forehead against mine. "I've tried."

How could I possibly say no? Even if I knew I was setting myself up for heartbreak, I would never turn down an opportunity to be with this man. But I'd also promised myself to speak up, to use my voice. And so even though it was hard, I forced myself to tell him what I wanted. What I needed.

"If we do this, I have a few conditions. While we're together, we won't see anyone else." I didn't want anyone else, and I hated the idea of him with another woman.

"Agreed," he answered readily, putting my mind at ease. "And obviously, discretion is key."

"Obviously," I said. "And you have to promise not to be a dick."

His jaw hardened, and I wasn't sure whether he was pissed off or turned on. At least until his cock nudged my center. "When did I act like a dick?"

"Um—" I glared at him. "Most of last week."

He bent forward, peeling my neckline aside so he could kiss the area he'd revealed. I sighed, goose bumps breaking out along my skin.

"Did you say you want my dick?" he asked, continuing to drive me wild even as I laughed.

"Jonathan," I chided.

"Yes." It was said with such conviction, but his eyes were focused on my cleavage. He slid his hands up my rib cage, teasing the bottoms of my breasts, testing their weight.

"Jonathan," I said in a more stern tone.

He snapped his head up to meet my gaze. "Yes?"

"I'm serious."

"So am I." He cupped my breasts, pinching my nipples and making me lose my train of thought. "And, yes. I promise not to be a dick. But just to be clear, this is only for the summer. So, if you can't handle that—"

"I can handle it." I would handle it. "Can you?"

"Yes." He nodded, his expression solemn. I wanted to know what he was thinking. Was he dreading the end of the summer as much as I was?

I maneuvered off his lap. "I need to grab a few things at home, and then I'll meet you at your place." I finally found my underwear and held them up victoriously.

Jonathan snatched them out of my hand and fingered the delicate lace material. "Mine." His eyes darkened and stayed locked on mine as he slid my underwear in his suit pocket.

I shook my head with a laugh as we both finished making ourselves presentable. "You're crazy."

"And it's all your fault." He leaned in for a quick kiss, and he seemed so much more relaxed now. Was it just the sex, or had he made peace with our relationship? If you could even call it that.

"Just come straight over. You don't need any clothes. Not

for what I have planned." His wicked grin made my body hum with promise.

"Maybe not, but I do need my birth control pills."

"Then you may as well grab some clothes for Monday while you're there," he said as I opened the door and descended from the cab.

I furrowed my brow. "Monday?"

He grinned. "So you won't have to go home before work."

Was he really—

He chuckled. "Yes, Sumner. I want you to stay for the weekend."

Wow. Okay. I hadn't been expecting that. Though, in all honesty, I hadn't expected anything that had happened in the past thirty minutes. Not the sex in the back seat. Not him asking me to come home with him. Not...anything.

"That is, if you want to." He glanced through the windshield, dragging a hand through his hair.

"Yes." I laughed at his sudden bashfulness. "Of course I do. I'll be there soon."

I climbed out of the truck, and he rolled down the driver's window. I was tempted to lean up on my toes and kiss him, but we were in the parking lot, in view of security cameras and anyone who happened to walk by. Somehow kissing under the bright lights seemed like a bigger risk than what we'd done in the back of his truck. It made no sense, and it made complete sense. But that was how it was with Jonathan —everything was a risk.

I smiled and turned for my car, eager to get home, get packed, and get back to his place before he could change his mind. I shouldn't have worried. The moment I climbed in the driver's seat, there was a text message waiting for me.

*Jonathan: I'll be sure to have our song playing when you arrive.*

If we were going to sneak around for the rest of the

summer, I needed to change his contact in my phone, make it something less obvious than "Jonathan" or even "Wolfe." Something where no one would guess his true identity if they saw the name flash across my screen. After racking my brain for a minute, I finally settled on using Jack's name. He was a coworker, and it wouldn't be suspicious if I were working late with him or even dating him.

**Me: We have a song?**

**Jack: I'm insulted.**

I opened the link in his next message, and "WAP" by Cardi B started playing.

I laughed to myself as I pulled out of the garage and headed for my dad's house. All the while, hoping no one was home. My phone rang on the way there, Piper's name appearing on my dashboard.

"Hey, Piper," I said, answering the call through Bluetooth.

"Hey. Where are you?"

"Driving home from work. Why? What's up?"

"This late? Geez. You need a life."

"I have a life!" I protested.

"A life outside of work. Which is why you're coming out tonight. There's this guy I want you to meet, and—"

"Piper, I appreciate the invitation, but I already have plans."

"What plans? I'm your only friend in LA."

"Hey! That's not true."

"Fine. The only friend you actually hang out with. So, what are your plans? More spreadsheets? Movie night in with your dad and Lea?"

I was both bursting and afraid to tell her. "Jonathan wants me to stay with him for the weekend."

"What?" she shrieked, and I winced, wishing I could've turned down the speaker volume faster. "Jonathan, as in

Jonathan Wolfe? The man who dropped you faster than a hot potato?"

I tightened my grip on the wheel as I tried to ignore the sting that accompanied her words. That wasn't quite the reaction I'd been anticipating.

"He didn't drop me. We agreed to end things when we left New York."

"So, what...he's flying you to New York for the weekend?"

"No." I laughed, mostly to cover my annoyance with her tone. "He invited me over to his house."

"Mm-hmm. So he can get what he wants and then go back to ignoring you and acting like a dick."

My hackles rose. "You're the one who encouraged me to sleep with him in the first place. No regrets, Sumner," I said, attempting to mimic her voice.

"Yeah. But then I saw how upset you were after you came back from New York. I mean, have you forgotten about the night on Klaus's yacht? It wasn't that long ago."

"No." I hated how meek my voice sounded. "But...but—"

"Sumner, listen to yourself. You said you wanted to use your voice, and you're letting him walk all over you. You're making excuses for a man who will never choose you."

"Jonathan and I have an agreement. And anyway, we both know I'm leaving at the end of the summer."

I was lying to both of us, but at least part of it was true. I *was* leaving at the end of the summer.

"Just..." She sighed, and I could feel her disapproval through the phone. "I think this is a bad idea for so many reasons."

I gnashed my teeth, ignoring the kernel of truth her words contained. "Bad idea or not, it's my choice."

"I'm not trying to piss you off. I just don't want you to get hurt. And you're *going* to get hurt because I don't think you're capable of separating your feelings from sex when it comes to Wolfe."

I pulled into the driveway and shut off the car, yanking my tote out of the passenger seat and nearly dumping the contents on my lap. I didn't want to talk about this. I'd made my decision; I wanted to be with him. "I have to go."

"Sumner," she pleaded. "Don't be like that."

"It's fine," I said. "I get that you're annoyed because you're not used to me saying no."

"That's not—"

"Gotta go." I disconnected the call before she could press me further.

I hated arguing with Piper. And I hated that a small part of me wondered if she was right. Wondered if this was a mistake.

I shook away the thought. I'd learned my lesson with Nico, and I knew what I was getting into with Jonathan.

I took a deep breath, checking my makeup in the mirror. My hair was a little messy, so I smoothed my hands over it then stepped out of the car. Dad's car was parked in the garage, but Lea's wasn't. I wasn't sure whether that was a good thing or not. I gave my clothes a once-over, smoothing down my skirt before heading inside.

"Sumner?" Dad called out as soon as I opened the back door. I squeezed my eyes shut briefly, a silent curse on my tongue. So much for sneaking in. "Is that you?"

"Yep." My voice sounded bright to my ears, and I knew I needed to get it together or he'd see right through me.

"How was work?" He set his glasses on the kitchen counter, rubbing at his temples.

"Good," I said. "Busy day. I'm working on some residential properties."

"Oh boy." Dad chuckled. "Jonathan and his little side project." He shook his head.

"You don't approve?" I asked, trying to keep the edge from my voice.

He rounded the counter to give me a hug. "I think it's just another way for him to bury himself in work, but I'm not sure why."

"Maybe because he loves what he does?" I offered, unwilling to share Jonathan's reasoning with my dad.

"Maybe," he said. "But there's more to life than work. Spending time with the people you love is more important than money. You can always make more money. Time is limited."

"I know."

"Are you sure?" He gripped my shoulders. "Because it seems like all you've done this summer is work."

"That's not true." My shoulders tightened, and I wondered if he could feel the tension I held there. "I went out with Piper, and..."

"And you bailed on Lea for your spa day last weekend." He peered down his nose at me, and I felt like a child being scolded. "She was really disappointed. And honestly, I think it hurt her feelings that you didn't make it a priority."

"I know," I sighed, deflating. "I'm sorry, Dad. I hate feeling like I let either of you down."

"Did something happen between you two?"

I jerked my head back. "Between Lea and me?" When he nodded, I said, "No. I love Lea."

"Maybe you should show her that by spending time with her."

I nodded. "Okay. Yeah. Of course."

"How about this weekend? We were thinking about going to the Huntington Gardens, maybe taking a picnic."

I cringed. "I, um, I'm going to be gone all weekend." I didn't know which was worse—the fact that I'd hurt Lea's feelings or that I was lying to my dad, *again*. Guilt twisted in my gut, and it made me question what Jonathan and I were doing. We shouldn't be lying. We shouldn't feel the need to lie.

"All weekend?"

"Yeah, um, Piper invited me to go with her to Palm Springs," I said, totally pulling it out of my ass. I felt awful, so I rushed to add, "I haven't gotten to spend much time with her since I went away to college," which only made me feel worse.

"Of course. I know you have a life of your own. I guess, sometimes, I forget. I still see you as my little girl."

"Dad." I laughed, needing some levity. "I haven't been little for years."

"I know." He frowned. "But maybe I want to spend some time with you before you leave again. It wasn't easy—you living across the country. I missed you."

Oh my god, I was going to cry. He was the sweetest, most loving dad. And how was I repaying him? By lying and sneaking around so I could sleep with his best friend.

"I missed you too, Dad." I sniffled, hoping he wouldn't notice as he pulled me into a hug. "And we'll spend time together."

"Soon," he said, releasing me but not before kissing the top of my head.

"Definitely." I nodded. "There's actually something I've been wanting to talk to you about."

Concern etched into his features. "What's that?"

I decided to do it. I'd just rip of the Band-Aid and tell him about my business plan. "I want to start a coaching business."

He chuckled, ruffling my hair like you would a cute puppy. "*You* want to tell other people what to do?"

I straightened. "Not tell them what to do. Help them navigate business and life. I have a business plan, and—"

"That's great, sweetie," he said, but it felt like a brush-off.

"I'm sure business school will help you hone those ideas and decide if it's a viable plan."

I opened my mouth as if to say something but realized there was no use. He'd already made up his mind on the matter.

"Shouldn't you get packing?"

I nodded and turned to head upstairs but then paused. *No.* I was not going to let this go so easily. If this was my dream—and it was—I needed to own it. "I already have a few clients, including Jonathan."

"Mm-hmm," he said, but his attention was focused on the TV.

I huffed and headed up the stairs. As soon as I got to my bedroom, I texted Piper, knowing I needed to cover all my bases.

**Me: *If my dad asks, I'm with you in Palm Springs.***

Three dots danced on the screen then disappeared. Reappeared once more. Then a message came through.

**Piper: *This is a bad idea.***

I gripped the phone, my fingers flying across the keys as I typed out my reply.

**Me: *If you don't want to cover for me, it's fine. I'll come up with a different story.***

**Piper: *You know I've always got your back.***

I scoffed and tossed my phone down on the bed. It sure didn't feel like it. Her lecture made it seem as if she most certainly did not have my back. But there was nothing more to say. So, I riffled through my drawers, intent on carrying out my plan. I was already in too deep to stop. What was one more lie at this point?

# CHAPTER TWENTY

## Jonathan

I paced the living room, wondering where Sumner was. I would've thought she'd be here by now. And I was beginning to worry she was having second thoughts.

I wouldn't have blamed her. The past week or so since returning from New York hadn't been exactly smooth sailing, though my plan had seemed simple enough—avoid her. Forget about New York. But I'd quickly realized it was easier said than done.

I'd tried to stay away. When I couldn't avoid her, I'd been an asshole. And then, talk about the ultimate backfire—I'd had sex with her—*in the parking lot.* I scrubbed a hand over my face. What was I thinking?

That she was amazing.

That I wanted her.

That we'd already slept together, so what was one more time?

All that and more. Besides, hadn't she proved that she could be mature about the situation—discreet and level-headed? She'd called me out for being a dick, but I couldn't say it was undeserved. At least now, we both knew where things stood.

I glanced at my phone again. No new messages or calls. *Huh.*

I padded over to the kitchen and pulled out a bottle of whiskey before remembering it was one Ian had given me for my birthday. It felt wrong—drinking the whiskey he'd given me while waiting for his daughter to sneak over so I could spend the weekend with her.

I shook my head and pushed it to the back of the cabinet along with my guilt before grabbing another bottle. It wasn't as decadent, but it would do. I had a feeling it would go down smoother than the one from Ian.

I poured myself a glass and stared at the amber liquid before taking a sip. It tasted of vanilla and caramel, but it wasn't the flavor I wanted on my tongue.

I glanced toward the door, peering through a window to the street. *Where is she?*

My phone dinged with a new email, and I skimmed the contents. *Meh.* I moved on to the next and the next, feeling as if I were reading the same thing over and over. None of it excited me anymore.

I finished my glass and rinsed it before putting it in the dishwasher. I returned to the counter and stared at my phone screen, thinking back on everything Sumner and I had discussed about success. Was this what success looked like? Was this what I wanted the rest of my life to be like? Alone. Living in a big house I didn't even like with things I didn't care about.

Finally, mercifully, the doorbell rang, and I jogged over to answer. *God, I'm pathetic.*

"Hey," I said, opening the door for Sumner. "Everything okay?"

"Yep!" Blink. Blink. Blink. *Lie.*

"Mm-hmm. Why don't you come in, and we'll have a drink?"

She kicked off her shoes and followed me into the kitchen before dropping her bag on the counter. I reached into the fridge and pulled out a bottle of white wine before grabbing two glasses.

"What? No whiskey?" she teased, settling onto one of the barstools.

"I have whiskey if you'd prefer," I said, corkscrew poised above the bottle. "Though I didn't get the impression it was your favorite."

"But it's yours. Well, Blanton's, more specifically. You think Pendleton tastes too much of juniper."

"I—" I tilted my head to the side. "Yes."

She'd noticed all that? Remembered those details about me?

"I want you to show me what you like," she said, and I had a flashback to New York. To her mouth wrapped around me in the back of the town car. It was a scene I'd played over in my head again and again. Her eyes peering up at me. Her lips and tongue.

I had a feeling neither of us was thinking of whiskey, but I also got the impression she was deflecting.

"Whiskey, right," I said, hoping it would loosen her tongue.

I went over to the cabinet where I stored the liquor and pulled out several bottles before lining them up on the counter. "Okay. So, I have a few for you to try." I turned the bottles so they were facing her. "Maker's Mark."

She stuck out her tongue. I laughed, but I couldn't help sharing how whiskey was made, the differences between them, and more.

"Blanton's." I slid the next bottle over. "And Knappogue Castle."

"Are you sure that's how it's pronounced?" she teased.

"Ninety-percent sure." I laughed, as did she.

I grabbed some glasses, one for each whiskey plus another for water. As well as some tortilla chips and a cup I'd filled with ice.

"This is... Wow. Okay. You're even more passionate about whiskey than I realized."

I thought of all the whiskey tastings I'd dragged Ian to. All the memories we'd shared. The Kentucky Bourbon Trail came to mind as a highlight.

"Jonathan?"

"Yeah." I picked up one of the bottles and started to open it before setting it back down. "I did promise you a proper tasting, but are you sure you're up for this?" I asked, though I wasn't sure whether I was referring to the whiskey or us. "You seemed upset when you got here."

"I..." She blew out a breath, shoulders deflating like a balloon. "Yeah."

Suddenly, she seemed too far away. The counter separating us too wide, and my need to touch her too great. I rounded the counter as she turned to face me. I stepped between her legs, relaxing when she wrapped her arms around my neck. The entire movement was fluid, as natural as breathing.

I smoothed my hands up and down her arms. "You can talk to me, baby. What's wrong?"

"I had a fight with Piper. Then I had to lie to my—Ian, because he's disappointed in me. And Lea..." With a deep breath, she pushed her hair away from her face and smiled. "Anyway. I'm sure you didn't invite me here to talk about my drama."

All along, I'd worried about my relationship with Ian if the truth came out, but I was beginning to see just how shortsighted I'd been. Ian's relationship with his daughter was being strained. Sumner's relationships with nearly everyone else in her life were suffering because she was with me.

I rubbed a hand up and down her back. "I asked you to stay because I wanted to spend time with you."

"Yeah—but, like, in the bedroom."

"Sumner." I dipped down to meet her eyes. "I wouldn't have invited you over for the whole weekend if I didn't enjoy your company. I don't—" I pinched the bridge of my nose. "I've never done this."

"Done…*what* exactly?"

"Spent time with a woman other than for short periods."

"You mean for sex," she said, to which I merely shrugged. "But Rachel—"

"We were always going out on the weekends, hanging out with friends, or I was working. We were rarely alone. I think we both knew that if we actually stopped and spent time together, we'd have to admit how wrong we were for each other."

She nodded but said nothing, and I wondered if I'd said too much.

"Did I just freak you out or break some rule about bringing up the past?"

She laughed. "No. I was surprised, that's all. Do you ever talk to her?"

"What would be the point?"

"I don't know. I just… You guys were together for a long time. You were *engaged*."

"Yes, but she wasn't the one."

"Interesting." She cocked her head to the side. "You believe there's one person for each of us? A soul mate?"

"Let's just say, I'm open to the possibility."

"Aw. Maybe you are a romantic after all. Well, a cautious

one anyway." Her mouth tilted up tantalizingly, and I wanted to kiss the smirk from her lips.

"I don't know that I'd go that far," I teased. "But I do know that I like spending time with you."

"I like spending time with you too," she said, smiling briefly before her expression fell. "I just wish we didn't have to lie and sneak around to do it."

"I know. And I hate putting you in this position—where you feel like you're disappointing the people you care about."

"I'm just as guilty for putting myself in this position." She sighed, perhaps realizing I wasn't going anywhere or expecting anything. "I have a difficult time saying no to people. It's something I've been working on—boundaries. But it's more difficult with the people I'm closest to."

I nodded, encouraging her to continue. She'd always been a people pleaser. Even as a young child, she'd sought the approval of her parents and authority figures.

"I told my dad about my coaching business."

I leaned back so I could get a better look at her. "You did?"

"He brushed me off."

I gnashed my teeth. "I'm proud of you for telling him. Hopefully, he'll see how brilliant it is, but even if he doesn't, you shouldn't let that deter you."

"Thanks. I can't tell you how much your encouragement means to me." She swallowed. "For so many years, I felt caught between my parents. And knowing that our family could break apart made me want to keep the peace even more. I think that's a big part of the reason why I hesitate to say what I think, especially with my parents."

"I'm sure that wasn't easy." Maybe I'd always underestimated just how difficult it had been.

"It wasn't." She peered up at me, toying with the hair at

the back of my neck. "It wasn't, but you always made every-thing better."

I grinned, loving the fact that she was here. In my home. In my arms. I kissed her. "I realized something recently…" I hesitated, wondering if I was admitting too much. But then I decided to just go for it. "All my happiest memories involve you."

She smiled, her eyes full of adoration. "Mine too."

"So…"

"So?"

"Do you want to watch a movie? Do something else?" I asked.

"Don't laugh, but now I kind of want to try some whiskey."

"Really?" I grinned, backing away.

"Yeah." She hopped down from the stool. "You were all fired up, and it was sexy."

"You're sexy." I gave her a quick tap on the ass. She glanced at me over her shoulder and smiled. My heart seized in my chest, and then it pounded so fast I was light-headed.

Was it possible to pinpoint a moment you fell in love, or did it happen slowly? With Sumner, it had happened slowly, but in that moment, in that one look, I knew. I loved her.

But love wasn't part of the deal, so I focused on the whiskey. "Okay. Where should we start?"

"This one." She pointed to the bottle of Knappogue Castle. "The one with the funny name."

"Did you pick it based on the label?" I teased, popping off the top and pouring some into a glass.

"I tend to find that if the label is appealing, the taste will be too. Don't you agree?"

"Sometimes. Let's see if it holds true for this whiskey." I sniffed the contents before sliding the glass over to her. "This is a twelve-year-old single malt, and it was designed to capture the flavor of Irish whiskey."

I watched as she swirled the glass then took a sip. She cringed. "It's...yeah. Burns."

I chuckled. "Yes, but try to concentrate on the flavors, the individual notes." When she continued to stare at me, I added, "Sometimes it helps to close your eyes. Then your remaining senses really have to focus."

She lifted the glass to her lips and closed her eyes, and I watched her, completely enraptured. The column of her neck, the way she swallowed. Her tongue flitting out to lick her lips. "It's a little...spicy. And maybe something citrusy?"

"Let me see." I pressed my mouth to hers, exploring with my tongue, the taste of malted barley mixing with Sumner's. It was better than any whiskey I'd ever tasted. "Mm. Yes. Spicy."

I could feel her smile against my lips, which prompted my own. Finally, I pulled back and offered her a chip. "To cleanse the palate," I said, taking one myself.

"Oh. So distinguished." She lifted it to her mouth, her pinkie finger elevated.

"Up next, we have Maker's Mark." I uncapped the bottle and poured some in a fresh glass and slid it over to her.

"Did you know on the plane, when you sipped my whiskey, I thought you were going to kiss me."

"I was tempted to."

She grinned down at the glass, her expression so fucking coy. "Was that the first time you were tempted to kiss me?"

"Honestly?" I shook my head. "No. I was tempted to kiss you the moment you walked through the door of my office."

"You..." She stared at me, slack-jawed. "Seriously?"

I took her hand in mine, kissing her palm, the inside of her wrist. "Yes. And nearly every day since."

"You can't say things like that." Her voice shook, and

when I glanced at her eyes, they were as warm as the whiskey had been going down my throat.

"Why not?" I rasped, dipping a cube of ice into the whiskey before trailing it down her neck.

She shuddered, her chest rising and falling in quick succession as a drop of water trickled its way down her skin. I licked it off, the vanilla and caramel of the whiskey mixing with the taste of her. Forget Blanton's; I had a new favorite.

I dipped the ice back in the whiskey, this time getting a little more of the alcohol on my fingers before painting her skin. From now on, I would forever associate the taste of whiskey with Sumner. My two favorite things—linked together.

"Because— Ahh…" She moaned when I dipped the ice cube lower, chasing the flavor with my tongue between her breasts. "You'll… Oh god." She tugged on my hair. "Make me forget about anything else."

*That's what I'm hoping.*

# CHAPTER TWENTY-ONE

# Sumner

"Good morning." I jumped at the sound of Lea's voice, and she emerged from the pantry a moment later.

I knew I shouldn't have let Jonathan talk me into staying over again last night. But how could I say no? Ever since "whiskey weekend," as I'd taken to referring to it, I'd been staying over more and more. He'd take me out to see a site, and then we'd end up having sex on his kitchen counter. He'd ask me to come to his office to look at something, and next thing I knew, I'd be pressed against the wall. It was as if we both thought if we kept busy enough, fucked enough, we'd forget about all the lies between us.

"You're up early." I yawned, placing my travel mug beneath the coffee machine.

"A spot opened up in a yoga class I've been dying to try." She tucked her yoga mat beneath her arm, her hair tied back low on her neck.

"Oh." I pushed the button on the machine, attempting to blink away the sleep from my eyes. I'd snuck in only an hour ago to get ready. "That's exciting." I yawned.

"Someone was out late. I didn't hear you come in until... well, not that long ago."

"I, um—" I shifted from one foot to the other, feeling like a teen who'd been busted sneaking in after curfew.

"Wait," she whispered, stepping closer. "Are you seeing someone? Is that why you're sneaking around all the time?"

"I—uh—" I felt like a deer caught in the headlights but decided maybe I could work with this. "Yeah. Yes."

"Oh, this is so exciting!" Her ponytail bounced with the movement. "What's his name? Where'd you meet?"

"I'll—" I glanced at the time on my phone. "I can't be late to work, but I promise to tell you all about him later."

She grinned then opened her mouth as if to say something, but I grabbed my mug and rushed for the door, calling, "Have a good day!"

I couldn't get out of there fast enough.

Work was busy. I checked in with Jack and Eric on a few assignments. Eric was still recovering at home, but he was doing better. The day passed quickly enough, and I smiled to myself when Jonathan called me into his office just after lunch.

"Hey." I paused at the door, enjoying the way his eyes raked over my figure. "Are you going to reprimand me for being late this morning?"

"Were you?" His raised brow conveyed amusement. He shut the door behind me, quickly placing his hands on my hips.

"Lea cornered me on the way out and asked if I was sneaking around because I was seeing someone."

His fingers dug into my skin, and I wondered if they'd leave a mark. "What did you tell her?"

"That I'd tell her all about him later. Jack," I added. "I'm going to tell her I'm dating Jack."

"What?" He jerked his head back. "Why Jack?"

"I could go for a blond with a Captain America vibe," I teased, sensing the tension coursing through him.

"Sumner," he growled.

"I needed a story that would be realistic and somewhat close to the truth."

"Still... *Jack?*"

"Is there someone else you'd prefer for my fictional boyfriend?" I smoothed my hands over his chest. "Maybe Chris Hem—"

He captured my mouth with his, cutting off my words. With every swipe of his tongue, I knew that he was claiming me, marking me as his own. I was desperate for him, need making me forget where we were. Making me forget anything but him.

His movements were frantic, our kisses messy and rough. His touch hurried, our clothes an annoyance as we clawed at each other.

"Wolfe," Cody's voice called through the intercom. We ignored him. "Wolfe," he said again, the insistence of his tone breaking through the haze. "Ian's here."

We broke apart, lips swollen, clothes askew. "Ian?" I panted, frantically tucking my shirt back into my skirt. "As in my dad?"

"Fuck," he hissed, and I wasn't sure I'd ever seen him so flustered. "Fuck. I forgot we're supposed to have lunch."

He straightened his shirt and went over to the intercom. "Just a minute." He turned to me, smoothing down some of my hair before cupping my cheeks, his expression full of tenderness. "You good?"

I nodded. "This was too close."

"Stay here." He marched over to the door and swung it open, allowing me to stay hidden.

My heart was pounding, and I remained in the shadows, debating whether to show my face or not.

"Wow, you're actually ready for lunch?" I heard my dad ask.

"Starving," Jonathan said.

"You've been playing hard to get lately," Dad teased, but my stomach soured.

I hated that I'd put them in this position. Jonathan was jeopardizing his relationship with my dad for me. And every time Jonathan lied to be with me, or avoided my dad because of his guilt, it was chipping away at their friendship.

Their voices faded, and I didn't hear anything more after that beyond the rush of blood in my ears, the distant ring of a phone. I sagged against the wall.

Cody walked through the door, a piece of paper in hand. He didn't see me, not at first. But when he did, we both startled.

"What are you still doing in here? Wait—" He glanced toward the open door and the hallway beyond. "Were you... hiding from your dad?"

"What?" My voice came out as more of a shriek. "No." I laughed. "Of course not." I glanced around, searching for an excuse as if one would materialize. "Yes. Okay. I have a lot to get done, and you know those two with their bromance. I didn't want to get dragged into lunch."

He laughed. "Actually, I've been meaning to talk to you about my sister's bakery. Well, it's more of a food truck at the moment."

I sighed with relief, grateful for the change of topic. I followed him out of Jonathan's office and over to his desk, where he procured a business card.

"This is it—Cutie Pies." He handed it to me.

I grinned down at the business card where images of small, hand-sized pies were displayed. "Cute."

"And delicious. But she's going through some growing pains and could really use some advice."

"I'd be happy to talk to her." I smiled. "Gotta go." I jetted down the hall.

It felt like that was all I did this summer—avoid people.

❧

"WELL, THIS IS NICE," LEA SAID AS WE SMOOTHED OUT THE picnic blanket. "Though I wish Jack could've made it. I was really looking forward to meeting him."

"Me too," I said, moving my bag so it would hold down the quilt.

"I still don't understand why you felt the need to hide that you were dating someone." She flipped the corner back so it laid flat on the grass.

"I don't know," I sighed, thinking the longer the summer dragged on, the more lies I told.

Lie. Avoid. Deflect. Those had become my default. It felt a lot like dating Nico, except Jonathan was nothing like Nico.

And Lea was thirsty for information. She'd been peppering me with questions the past few weeks. Where was Jack from? When did we first start seeing each other? Was it serious?

My dad stood nearby, crunching a chip between his teeth. "Yeah. I was prepared to grill him."

"Dad." I rolled my eyes.

"Hey." Lea swatted at him when he popped another chip in his mouth. "No eating yet."

He pulled her in, giving her a quick peck on the lips. I wondered what that would be like—to be with someone who openly showed affection. Someone you didn't have to hide your feelings for. Though that hadn't always been the case for my dad and Lea, it certainly was now. But it had come at a price, and I knew their happiness had been hard-won.

And their love story—unconventional as it was—gave me

hope. Hope that maybe there could be a future for Jonathan and me. A future where I didn't have to lie and sneak around. A future where we could be together. Because every time I thought about the end of the summer or leaving for Palo Alto, I felt sick to my stomach.

"You have to wait for Jonathan," Lea said, and I froze, wondering if I'd spoken my thoughts aloud. I was paralyzed with fear, but then I followed her gaze and saw the very man I'd been thinking about.

"Jonathan?" My voice was hoarse, eyes practically bugging out of their sockets. *Thank god for sunglasses.*

"Yeah. I thought I told you I'd invited him," Lea said.

I shook my head. She definitely had *not* mentioned it. But it was too late now.

"Hey, Lea." He grinned, giving her a side hug. She seemed so tiny in comparison to him. He and my dad shook hands before my dad pulled him into a hug, patting him on the back a few times.

*What the heck is he doing here?*

And then it was my turn. I just stood there, mouth agape, staring at his stupidly handsome face. "Hey."

"Hey, Sumner." He gave me a side hug just like the one he'd given Lea. "Good to see you."

We settled onto the blanket, and I busied myself with the food while everyone else talked. How could he seem so at ease? I thought I might burst out of my skin. This was too much—too risky. We were playing with fire.

A family walked by in the distance, the children skipping along as they sang a song. I picked at my salad and tried to avoid looking at Jonathan. I was afraid if I did, my attraction to him—or worse still, what we'd done—would be completely obvious. My guilt painted across my features for all the world to see.

I was so lost in my thoughts, I didn't hear much of the

conversation. Eventually, Dad left with the trash, depositing it in the bin before heading off in the direction of the restrooms.

"While Ian's gone, I wanted to talk to you guys." Lea leaned in, lowering her voice.

"What's going on?" I asked, suddenly alarmed.

"Well, your dad's forty-fifth birthday is coming up, and I'm planning a big weekend for him."

I laughed, feeling more at ease. "Of course you are. Just tell me what you need from me."

"I just need you to show up—both of you. And maybe give a short speech about Ian." She glanced at Jonathan. "I've hired one of the best event planners in LA—Juliana Wright." She said the name like it would mean something to us.

"Alexis's friend?" Jonathan asked, surprising me.

"That's the one." Lea smiled. "Anyway, it's going to be epic! But please keep it a secret."

"Of course," we both said in unison.

"So, Jonathan—" she leaned in, placing her hand on his forearm "—what can you tell me about this Jack guy Sumner's been spending so much time with lately?"

Jonathan looked at me, head tilted. "Jack?"

"Yeah. You know—" I widened my eyes, silently imploring him to play along "—Jack. Tall. Good-looking." I wanted to laugh when a muscle in his forehead twitched. "Looks like he could be a professional surfer."

"Oh dear," Lea said, placing a hand to her chest, her features filled with concern as she glanced between the two of us. "Was it a secret that they were dating? Sumner assured us they weren't violating any rules, so I just assumed it was common knowledge."

"I typically try to steer clear of gossip," Jonathan said, sidestepping the issue. "But good for you, Sumner."

"So, what can you tell me about him?" Lea prodded. "She's been very secretive."

Jonathan chuckled, leaning back on his hands as if he didn't have a care in the world. "Jack. Jack. Jack." Lea bent forward, hanging on his every word. I thought I was going to be sick.

"Jack is..." he said, then turned to me. "Well, Sum, how would you describe him? What do you like about him?"

I glared at him, though it was unlikely he could see my eyes from behind my sunglasses. So, I forced a smile. "Oh no, I'd much rather hear what you have to say about him."

"What'd I miss?" Dad asked, taking a seat on the ground next to Lea.

"Jonathan was just telling us about Jack."

Dad furrowed his brow then nodded. "Oh, Jack. Right."

"You have no idea who Jack is," Jonathan ribbed him.

"I—" He held up his pointer finger. "Yes. Jack is the guy Sumner's dating. I just didn't think it was very serious."

"Not very serious?" Lea laughed. "She's spent almost every night with him the past few weeks."

Dad lifted his shoulder, clearly not wanting to be drawn into the conversation. I could only imagine how he'd feel if he knew that Jack was actually Jonathan. I doubted he'd be so blasé about it. But Lea was right—we weren't serious. I was leaving soon, but that hadn't stopped me from developing some serious feelings for Jonathan.

"Ah, well. An office romance is fun as a summer fling." She turned to my dad, placing her hand over his heart. "The best love stories always have a touch of the forbidden. Don't they, dear?"

"Huh?" He glanced away from Jonathan and shook his head as if to clear it. "Oh yeah." He grinned, pulling her into his side.

"And what about you, Jonathan?" Lea asked, turning her attention on him.

"What about me?" He sipped his water, the sun glinting off his sunglasses.

"Are you seeing anyone?"

"If I say no, you're not going to try to fix me up with another one of your friends, are you?"

I swallowed hard, blinking a few times as I tried to dislodge the cracker from my throat. *Fix him up? With her friends?* And worst of all, it didn't sound like this would be the first time.

"Need some water, kiddo?" Dad asked, handing me a bottle.

I accepted, gulping it down. Some dribbled out of my mouth, sliding down my chin before dropping between my breasts. I could feel Jonathan's eyes on me, watching that droplet as if he were a man crawling through the desert desperate for water. I wondered if he, like me, was thinking back to the night of the whiskey tasting. He'd spent more time sampling my body than the alcohol, dripping the liquor onto some of my most sensitive parts before lapping it off. I'd done the same until we were drunk off each other.

"The offer's always there." She grinned.

"Thanks, but I'm good."

"So...does that mean you're seeing someone?" she asked.

"Lea," Dad chided. "Leave the poor man alone."

"Okay." She shrugged. "All right. I'll leave him be. Though you do seem happier lately."

I couldn't help stealing a glance at Jonathan, pride filling my chest as he smiled. "I am happy. It's been nice reconnecting with Sumner this summer."

Dad smiled. "I'm glad it worked out so well."

I swallowed back my guilt. My poor dad had no idea.

# CHAPTER TWENTY-TWO

## Jonathan

"Well, this is unusual," Ian joked as I joined him at the table. "You inviting me to lunch."

I took a seat and began perusing the menu, though my mind was elsewhere. This was Sumner's last week at the Wolfe Group. A week after that, she'd be moving to Palo Alto.

"I actually wanted to talk to you about Sumner," I said, sweat prickling at my forehead.

"Hm." Ian glanced up from his menu, completely oblivious. "Is this about the coaching business? She told me you'd let her take you on as a client. That was generous of you."

I frowned, not sure I understood his tone. "It wasn't *generous* of me. If anything, she's being generous with her time. And she's good at it."

"She's always had a big heart. Always wanted to help people," he said with an offhand tone.

"This is about more than helping people," I said. "It's her passion. And I think she could make a good living doing something she loves."

"I can appreciate that, but she's always talked about

getting her MBA. I don't want her to give up on that dream now. Not when she's so close."

"What if her dreams changed?" I asked, thinking of myself. Thinking about all the conversations Sumner and I had had. Maybe I was overstepping, but I was the one she'd confided in. And every time she'd tried to talk to Ian about it, he'd been dismissive of her ideas. Which was why I'd felt the need to bring it up with Ian myself, not that she wasn't fully capable of handling herself. But I knew Ian better than anyone. I wanted to believe I knew Sumner better than anyone.

He shook his head, taking a sip of water before setting the glass back down. "She's young. She's still learning about the world."

I gnashed my teeth. "She's smart, confident. Hell, she's completely made me reevaluate my life."

"That's great," he sighed. "And I know you care about her and have her best interests at heart."

I nodded, though I wasn't sure we had the same definition of what was best for Sumner.

"Which is why I'm asking you *not* to encourage her coaching business any more than you already have." His words landed with a thud, and I didn't hear a word he said after that, my ears ringing, blood pulsing. I... *He* was asking me *not* to encourage her? Surely he didn't understand the magnitude of his request.

"After she gets her MBA, *then* she can decide what kind of business to start, if any."

"What do you mean—if any?"

"I just—" He sighed, rubbing the back of his neck. "I think she'd be better off working for someone else. In a more stable job. It's part of the reason I asked you to take this on in the first place."

"I'm not sure I agree," I said. "And anyway, isn't that

Sumner's decision to make?"

"I don't know that she's in the right frame of mind to consider her future logically. I'm afraid she's getting too attached to this Jack. It feels like that fiasco with the douchebag all over again."

I frowned. "What douchebag?"

"I never told you." He leaned in, lowering his voice. "But she was dating a professor."

Dread curled in my gut. It felt wrong—obtaining information about her this way. But it wasn't like I'd asked Ian about Sumner's dating history. Ian was the last person I expected to be talking about this with.

"Well, he was her professor before they started dating. And he was wrong for her on so many levels." Was this the ex she'd been referring to on the flight back from New York?

I could see the similarities in our relationship. Older. Professional. Secret. I didn't want to know, but I had to ask, "Because of the age difference or their roles?"

He sighed, scrubbing a hand over his face. "Both." He shook his head. "She always goes after these guys who seem to have it all together, but who are a mess. They have the emotional maturity of a goldfish. Yet she bends over backward to be with them."

I gripped my thigh beneath the table, hating the idea of Sumner with another man. Hating the thought that I might fall into the category of men Ian described. I didn't want to admit it, but I wondered if I was hampering her ability to take care of herself. To be happy.

"Anyway, I'm concerned this Jack guy is clouding her vision when it comes to grad school. It just feels like the situation with the professor all over again. I mean, he won't even make the time to meet Lea and me."

"Maybe he's not ready to take that next step," I offered, wishing I could tell him the real reason "Jack" wouldn't meet him and Lea. The more Ian spoke, the more I realized how impossible that idea truly was.

"It's dinner. Not a marriage proposal." He shook his head. "I expect more for my daughter. She deserves better."

"I agree," I said. She did deserve better than me.

"But she won't listen to me." He sighed, leaning back so the waiter could place our meals before us.

My heartbeat slowed, and it felt as if I were underwater. It was difficult to breathe, to think. I had a feeling I already knew where this was headed, but I wanted to hear him say it.

Ian cut into his lunch. "I know the two of you have grown close this summer, and I wondered if maybe you could try talking some sense into her." When he peered up at me, his eyes questioning, three thoughts flitted through my mind in quick succession.

*Does he know?*

*Don't look away.*

*Don't flinch.*

"She respects you. Admires you. And I think receiving career advice from her mentor would carry more weight than from dear old dad."

I laughed, tugging at my collar. "I'm not so sure about that." Whether Ian realized it or not, his approval mattered to Sumner.

"She's been skipping things with Lea, ignoring Piper. All for...some guy."

I tightened my grip on my fork and knife, the need to justify myself and my relationship with Sumner rising with every passing second.

"Maybe they're happy together. Maybe they love each other." We'd never said the words, but I loved her. I was pretty sure she felt the same way.

"It's been—what? A few weeks?" He shook his head, skepticism marring his features. "No." He scoffed. "It's not love. It's lust. Why are you defending him?"

"I just... Maybe he has good intentions, even if it doesn't seem like it."

He said nothing, though his expression conveyed everything—doubt, disgust, concern. I had a feeling it didn't matter what I said, Ian wouldn't be swayed.

We fell silent for a moment, the noises of the restaurant filling the gap as he ate and I picked at my food. What I felt for Sumner went well beyond infatuation. She was so embedded in me that I didn't know how to separate where I ended from where she began.

"How has she been at the office?" he asked. "I mean, you've seen them together, right?"

"Fine," I answered quickly, perhaps a little too quickly. My chest squeezed, and I tugged at my collar again. *Is it hot in here?* "What I mean is—they're nothing but professional at work. I don't think I ever thanked you for suggesting I bring her on. I'm really glad you did. She's done an amazing job— both with projects for the Wolfe Group and coaching. Everyone loves her."

*I love her.* And I didn't want to lose her.

Could I fill her position at the Wolfe Group? Sure.

But no one could fill the hole in my heart created by her absence.

I didn't want to let her go. But what about Sumner? I knew what she wanted—at least what I thought she wanted. But maybe I'd been the one pushing her to pursue her coaching business when she wasn't ready. When she wanted more education. She'd admitted she had trouble saying no, that she hated disappointing people. Was I doing more harm than good?

His features softened, a proud smile crossing his lips. "I'm glad. She is pretty remarkable."

"That she is," I said, unable to hide the wistful note in my voice.

We spent the rest of lunch discussing other matters, though my mind was on Sumner, as it often was. I'd seen her growth this summer. She was confident. She wasn't afraid to speak her mind. She didn't hesitate to put me—or any other man—in their place. Just thinking about our meeting with Tom Sheffield had a smile forming on my face. She'd handled him with grace and ease, and she'd closed the deal.

"She's tougher than you think," I said as the waiter returned with my credit card. I signed the check, and Ian thanked me before we headed for the valet stand.

"Perhaps. I can be a bit blind when it comes to Sumner." Apparently I wasn't the only one. "But I know that she also has a blind spot when it comes to men. And she doesn't make the best decisions where they're concerned. Anyway—" Ian clapped a hand on my shoulder, but it felt as if he'd wrapped it around my throat and squeezed. "Think about what I said."

☙

"You wanted to see me?" Sumner grinned from the doorway to my office, probably because the last time I'd called her in, I'd ended up eating her out on my desk.

"Yes." I stood, smoothing down my tie, knowing this would be nothing like the last time. "Come in. And close the door, please."

Her smile widened, and I hated myself for what I was about to do. It had to be done. And though I didn't like the idea of breaking up with her at the office, it was the only way. If we were at home, she'd find a way to persuade me otherwise. She'd already been hinting that we could keep this going beyond the summer. Much as I wanted to, I knew we couldn't continue long term.

Ian's comments at lunch the other day had made that abundantly clear. I wasn't sure why I'd ever thought he might find a way to approve of our relationship, but that conversation had brought me back to reality. Had made me realize I had to let her go.

"Sumner," I said, debating my words, even though I'd rehearsed this conversation a million times in my head. "This summer has been amazing."

"I know, and I've been doing some thinking." She threaded her fingers through mine, peering up at me with the most brilliant smile. She pecked me on the lips, and I tried to savor the taste of her, memorize it.

"Today's your last day—"

"Yes," she cut me off. "But maybe it doesn't have to be."

Hope rose in my chest and then plummeted, sinking in my gut. *Stay?* There was no way I could let her stay. Even though I'd tried to ready myself for this, I was woefully unprepared.

"You once said if I weren't going to grad school, you'd offer me a full-time job. And I want to take you up on it. I love the work I'm doing here, and I've loved working with you as your coach."

Her eyes shone with hope. But I needed to quash any chance of us being together, once and for all. We needed a clean break. It was for her own good.

"I don't think that's a good idea."

She'd already paid the deposits and rented an apartment, registered for classes—not to mention, Ian would kill me.

"I don't understand." She smoothed her hands over my lapels. "Last weekend...at the Huntington Gardens, you said—"

I shook my head, denying her pleas even though I knew exactly what she was referring to. The moment I'd told her I didn't know if I could let her go, even if I had been speaking in vague terms.

"What about your dreams of having a coaching business?"

"I can do both. I was going to take classes full time. I can work full time instead."

"But you've been looking forward to grad school. And I know it's important to you to have that education."

"I can always go back later, if I want," she said.

I shook my head. This was going to be even more difficult than I'd anticipated. "It's not that simple, and you know it." I inhaled deeply, my head and heart fucking aching as if someone had taken an anvil to them. "We agreed that our arrangement terminates along with your employment."

*Smash.* I'd just smashed it all to pieces.

"Arrangement?" She jerked her head back. "'Terminates along with your employment,'" she said, attempting to mimic my distant tone. "Wow, Jonathan." She took a few steps back. "You're kidding, right?"

I shook my head.

"Just say it, then. Say the words. You're breaking up with me."

I had to stand firm. I couldn't let this continue. So, I closed myself off to her, adopting the mask I often assumed in business—cold, demanding, shrewd. It was for her own good, even if I knew she'd hate me for it. "How can we break up when we were never together?"

She looked at me as if I'd physically slapped her. It certainly felt as if I had. Fuck, this was painful. It was so much worse than I'd expected, and I was almost tempted to tell her it was a mistake. To beg her to stay and promise to tell Ian about us. *Almost.* But I reminded myself that I was doing this for her own good. She couldn't give up grad school—her future—for me.

"Never together?"

I studied her expression, watching as she crumpled but then quickly recovered. She concealed her pain with anger, and I hated myself for it. Hated myself for ever making her think she meant nothing to me. That our time together hadn't been the best ten weeks of my life.

"How can you say that?" She pressed her hands to my chest. "You don't mean that."

I had to make her believe we were over. Unless I made it absolutely clear we were done, she would never move on. And she would move on. She'd find someone else, someone more appropriate. My heart squeezed at the image of her with another man, but I quickly pushed it away. This was the only way. Because the truth would devastate Ian, ruining our friendship and ripping apart their family.

"Thank you for all your hard work and dedication this summer," I said, adopting a formal tone. "You did a great job, and I've written you a glowing recommendation."

She shook her head and scoffed, her eyes glittering with unshed tears. "You promised."

"I promised nothing."

"No," she ground out. "You promised not to be a dick." She shook her head. "I thought you were different. I thought I meant something to you. I guess I was wrong."

She swiped at her tears, squaring her shoulders before turning for the door. I wanted to grab her wrist and beg her to stay. I wanted to apologize. I wanted to… There were so many things I wanted to do. But instead, I pushed my wants aside and focused on Sumner. It was time to let her go.

And then she walked out of my office like the goddamn queen she was. She certainly ruled my heart, even if I wouldn't admit it. What would be the point? We could never be together, and I'd already let things go on long enough.

# CHAPTER TWENTY-THREE

Summer

"Um. What are you doing?" Piper asked from the doorway to my room.

"Organizing." I held up two pairs of sandals from high school. "I figured a big purge was probably long overdue. And I watched some documentaries on Netflix on minimalism, and I've been listening to a few new podcasts. So inspiring."

"How much coffee have you had?"

"I don't know." I sped around the room, folding, stacking, organizing. "Three cups? Four? I've been up all night working on this."

"That's great, but shouldn't you be packing? Classes start next week."

I ignored her question. "God, do you remember these? I wore them every day one summer? Aw. And look at this." I handed her a picture of the two of us in a "Seniors" frame.

"This trip down memory lane is fun and all..." She held it closer. "Oh my god. My makeup is awful. I'm going to have to post this on my Instagram."

"Nice."

"Okay." She plopped down on my bed. "Now quit distracting me and tell me what's really going on."

"Nothing," I chirped, folding a shirt and setting it in the donate pile.

She placed her hand over mine, stilling my movements. "No. What's going on with Jonathan?"

"The summer's over, and our fling is done."

"Just like that?" Her tone betrayed her skepticism.

"Yep!"

"Sumner, I know I wasn't the most supportive when you told me you guys were getting back together or whatever. But it's only because I care about you. If something happened or you're upset, I want to be here for you."

After four days of being holed up in my room, I couldn't take it anymore. I cracked. I kept replaying that day in his office in my head, as well as the ones leading up to it. And I couldn't make sense of it.

"He acted like we were nothing, Piper. *Nothing*," I could barely think the word, let alone speak it. "And I know this is going to sound so clichéd. But along the way, something changed. *We* changed."

"Are you sure you weren't reading more into it?" She placed her hand on my upper back, rubbing circles. "Sometimes when we want something so badly, we can make ourselves believe it's true." Her tone was gentle, but her words cut through me like glass.

I jolted upright. "No! I *know* it was more for him. I *know* he loves me."

Her expression was one of pity, and my stomach churned, dreading the words she'd say next. "Did he ever tell you he loved you? Did he ever say the words?"

"He didn't have to!" I practically shouted.

"Sumner, listen to yourself."

I turned away from her, annoyed with my friend, with the

conversation. I knew he loved me. I knew it deep in my gut. Yet he'd pulled back. Why?

"I've tried giving you space. I've tried being nice," she continued. "But I think it's time for some tough love." She crossed her legs, her appearance so at odds with the disaster that was my room. "You need to face the truth. And the truth is—Wolfe was just the latest iteration of Professor Dick. Another asshole. It's time to move on."

I shook my head, not wanting to believe it. Maybe to some, he was an asshole. I could see how others might misinterpret his silence for condescension. But that wasn't the man he truly was—the man he was with me. Or at least, the man I wanted to believe he was.

"He's not," I spluttered, a storm of emotions rolling through me. For days, I'd been numb, but now, I felt everything. It was too much. "He's—"

"Why are you defending him?" She stood, her gaze fiery.

"He's…different. That may be the man he shows in public, but it's not the true Jonathan."

"Mm-hmm." She crossed her arms over her chest, and I bristled at the skepticism in her tone. "And the man you know is?"

I couldn't say more, not without betraying Jonathan's confidence. But she didn't understand; she didn't know his tortured soul like I did.

"I don't need this." I brushed past her, intent on the bathroom.

But she wasn't deterred; she followed behind me. "You haven't showered in days. You've been 'organizing,' avoiding me. What are you going to do when your dad and Lea come back from Miami in a few days?"

"I don't know." I huffed.

"And what about grad school? Don't classes start soon?"

I gripped the edge of the counter and let out a few deep

breaths. I didn't lift my head, not wanting to glance at my reflection. I couldn't face myself, let alone the truth.

"Yes," I ground out in answer to her last question. I should already be in Palo Alto, buying my books, settling in to my apartment.

"Well—" She wasn't tapping her foot, but it felt as if she may as well be.

"Well, what?" I glanced at her, anger and defiance in my eyes.

"You're going, right?"

I dropped my head, shoulders sagging. "I don't know." I didn't know anything anymore. Was Jonathan the man I thought he was, or had I been played a fool again? Was he, as Piper said, Professor Dick Version 2.0?

She gripped my arms and shook me gently. "I *do*. And you are. Hop in the shower, and then we'll pack."

"Why?" I croaked.

"Because, my friend, the world needs you. *I* need you. And it's time for you to dust yourself off and step into your power."

That did it. I burst into tears, and she pulled me into a hug. "I know you might not believe this, but you're going to be okay. Now, will you please shower?" She stepped back, pinching her nose. "Because you smell."

I rolled my eyes, but I knew she was right. A shower would do me good.

☙

THE FOLLOWING AFTERNOON, I STOOD IN THE DRIVEWAY, Piper's arms wrapped around me. "You call me if you need anything, right?"

I nodded, stepping out of her embrace.

"I mean it, Sumner. Any time. 'kay?"

"Okay. Same for you."

"Thanks. Okay…well, have a safe drive. And try to make some friends. Maybe date some guys your own age for a change."

"Thanks, Mom," I teased, sticking my tongue out at her.

We both knew I wasn't going to be doing any dating anytime soon. I'd barely managed to make it through the past twenty-four hours, and that was only because Piper had been there every step of the way, holding my hand. Now, I was going to be alone. Alone with my thoughts. With the memories of Jonathan. I still couldn't understand. I'd thought…

*Never mind.*

With a deep sigh, I hopped in the car and wound through the streets of the neighborhood. I accelerated onto the freeway, a weird sort of giddy anxiety bubbling up through my throat when I realized where I was headed. Without thinking, without intending to, I'd taken Jonathan's exit. I hadn't seen him since my last day of work, but I'd thought about him. I couldn't stop thinking about him.

Even though I knew it was a terrible idea, I pulled onto his street, slowing as I neared his house. I hadn't done something like this since high school, when Piper was obsessed with Steven Kingsley. I parked, and before I realized what I was doing, I was knocking on Jonathan's front door.

I hadn't expected him to be home, so when he answered, we both stared, a little surprised. His T-shirt clung to his chest, athletic shorts hanging low on his waist. Damn, he looked good.

"What are you—"

I marched past him, not even waiting for an invitation. He closed the door and stared at me.

"Sumner." His tone was a warning. "I said everything I have to say. I really don't think you should be here."

He'd always encouraged me to speak up, to speak my

mind. So I ignored him and continued on. "Do you know why you're so unhappy?" I asked. "Because you won't admit what you really want—not even to yourself."

He crossed his arms over his chest. "You're not my coach anymore. I didn't ask for your advice."

"I know you want me. You know you want me. So, why won't you just say it?" I was panting, like a bull ready to charge. I wasn't quite sure what had gotten into me, but I kind of liked it. "Say it."

He grasped my shoulders, walking me backward until my back hit the wall. The cold surface was a jolt to my system. "Fine. I. Want. You," he ground out. "But I can't have you."

*I knew it.* "You *can* have me, but you won't take me. There's a difference."

He shook his head, tightening his grip on my shoulders. I welcomed the bite of pain, silently begging him to stop fighting this, fighting us. And to start fighting *for* us. In business, he took what he wanted without regard for the consequences. Why couldn't he do that with me?

"What happened to being daring and bold?" I turned his words back on him, thinking of all the lessons he'd tried to teach me in the boardroom. "Or does that only apply to business?"

"Fuck." He pounded his fist against the wall beside my head. "I—" His body vibrated with tension, and it felt as if he might explode at any moment. The fuse was lit, and I was waiting for him to detonate.

"Fuck." His voice was softer this time, almost pained. He rested his forehead against mine, loosening his grip, though the intensity remained.

I closed my eyes and let out a shuddering breath. He trailed a finger along my jaw, and I broke. A tear slipped out, gliding down my cheek. This was a mistake. This wasn't closure; it was torture.

I opened my eyes, blinking up at him. "I can't keep serving myself up to you on a platter. I just—" My chest ached, and I needed space. "I can't." I shook my head and ducked beneath his arm.

My legs were shaky, but I was determined to put some distance between us. If only he could let go of the fact that I was twenty years younger and his best friend's daughter, we could be amazing. He knew it just as well as I did, but instead, he continued to fight it.

I made it to the door before he wrapped his arms around me, holding me to his chest. I both loved and hated his attention. I craved it like a drug, but I didn't want to crave it. Didn't want to crave him.

"Don't cry, Sumner. *Please*." He brushed my hair over my shoulder, pressing kisses to my collarbone.

My body quivered from his touch, and my heart...my heart was weak. If I was going to survive, it was up to my head. Because my body and my heart would give in to this man every time.

"This is breaking me." My voice cracked. I heaved a breath, forcing out the words. Admitting it aloud was akin to ripping my heart out.

He spun me to face him, caging me against the door. His hips pressed against mine. "Believe it or not, it's breaking me too. But I can't throw away a thirty-year friendship. Your dad—"

I pressed my hands to the door, anger coursing through my veins. "Should have no say in this."

His nostrils flared. "You're his daughter, his only child. I'm his best friend. If he had any idea..."

"Give him time," I said. "Eventually, he'll accept the fact that we're together."

I knew it wouldn't be easy, but I had faith that it would work out. If only Jonathan could too.

He shook his head, resignation marring his features. "Even if I were willing to sacrifice my relationship with him, I'm not willing to sacrifice yours."

"He's my father. He loves me unconditionally. He…" I swallowed down a lump. "You're the man I love. Surely he'll understand that."

He clenched his jaw but didn't otherwise respond to my declaration. He had to have known. How could he not know that I loved him? Desperately so. The past week apart had only crystallized my feelings—I loved him.

When I realized he wasn't going to budge, I sniffed and lifted my chin. I was done. I'd laid all my cards on the table, and it was time to admit defeat.

I yanked the door open, the blue sky and cheerful sun mocking me. My chest felt tight, as if my ribs might crack open and let my heart bleed out. At least, if there was anything still left in my chest. But it was too late.

I barely made it to the car before I dissolved into sobs, my entire body aching with yearning. I screamed, pouring every ounce of anger, of hurt, of longing into the discordant sound. I'd never experienced pain like this. Never felt so helpless, not even when I'd thought the plane was going to crash.

But with the death of the scream came a release, a wave of calm—or maybe just exhaustion—washing over me. And with that, some much-needed clarity. I couldn't keep doing this to myself. It was time to move on. So, with a heavy sigh, I restarted the car and drove away, leaving Jonathan in my rearview mirror.

ॐ

WEEKS PASSED, AND I HEARD NOTHING FROM JONATHAN. NOT that I'd expected to. Still, a small—foolish—part of me held out hope.

I was headed back from campus when my phone rang, my dad's name flashing across the screen. I clenched my jaw, anger coursing through my veins. This was all his fault.

I knew I was being irrational, but it was easier to blame my dad than Jonathan. He was the one who'd made it impossible for us to be together, even if I knew that wasn't entirely true. Still, I'd been ignoring his calls, only responding to texts and pretending to be too busy to talk.

According to Piper, I was moving through the stages of grief. Apparently, I'd gone from the denial phase to anger. *Whatever.*

"Hey, Dad," I answered, knowing I couldn't avoid him forever.

"Hey, kiddo. I'm glad you answered. I thought I was going to have to send out the National Guard."

"Ha-ha." I laughed. "Very funny."

"You okay? You sound…off."

"I'm just tired," I said, glancing both ways before crossing the street.

It was the truth. Since the move and starting grad school, I'd barely slept. When I wasn't studying, I toiled away on my business plan. I'd also continued my journey of minimalism, and some of it became a game of sorts. My latest exercise— seeing how little stuff I could live with. It was a good distraction, even if it felt hollow.

"Yeah. Seems like you've been really busy lately. I hope you're not upset that Lea and I weren't there to see you off."

I wanted to laugh. That was the last thing I was upset about, but for some reason, I couldn't tell him how I really felt.

"Dad, it's fine. You didn't know I was going to be staying for the summer when you and Lea booked your vacation."

"Still…you just kind of disappeared. I thought you were going to wait until after we got home to leave."

I lifted a shoulder, fighting back tears as I unlocked the door to my apartment. "You know how much I hate goodbyes."

"I know. But you know I'm always here for you, right?"

"Thanks, Dad. I do."

"So, how are your classes going? How do you like your new apartment?"

"It's, um, fine," I said, glancing around the space.

Every day was the same. I woke up, went to class, studied, worked on my coaching business and some course offerings I was hoping to start providing for clients. I did everything I could not to think about Jonathan, but then I'd find one of his shirts in my stuff. I'd see someone who looked like him across the street, and I'd long for what we had. But then I'd see reason. I'd remember how he'd cast me aside so carelessly.

And then I'd repeat my new mantra: *I deserve more.*

# CHAPTER TWENTY-FOUR

## Jonathan

If I'd thought life before Sumner was tedious, it was absolute hell after. At my house, at the office, I couldn't escape the memories of her. And it wasn't just the sex—it was the conversation, the laughter, and the life she infused into everything. And now, it seemed as if all I did was go to work and work out. Over the past two months, my life had become monotonous and tiresome.

Someone knocked on the door to my office, and I glanced up to find Ian standing there, basketball tucked under his arm. He'd been trying to get me to meet up with him, and I kept putting it off. I was being a chickenshit, but I couldn't face him. Not without thinking about her.

"Long time, no see," he said. "If I didn't know better, I'd think you were avoiding me."

I laughed, standing to greet him. "I've been—"

"Yeah. Yeah." He waved away my words with a grin. "Busy, right? Then it's a good thing I made an appointment. See you on the roof in twenty."

I glanced at my computer, at the emails waiting for me. I'd avoided him as long as I could. "Sure."

I finished up some emails and then met him at the executive gym on the roof. We played for a while, and I tried to ignore the pain in my chest. It came and went, my heartbeat fluctuating rapidly. I didn't know whether it was due to the exercise or the company, but I was more than happy to let him lead the conversation. He talked about everything except the one thing I really wanted to know—how Sumner was.

I couldn't get her out of my head. But it wasn't the quiet moments we'd shared or the feel of her writhing beneath me; it was the haunted look in her eyes when I'd finally ended it. It was the resignation and hatred shining back at me when she realized I was serious this time.

"What's up with you lately?" Ian dribbled, and I stole the ball.

I made my way across the court, bouncing the ball, feeling the way it pounded against my skin. "A buyer approached me about selling the Wolfe Group, I took on another property with Alexis—"

"*Another* project? I barely see you as it is."

"What are you, my wife?" I teased, though when I shot the ball, I missed. *Fucking again?*

I'd needed to fill my days so I'd be exhausted at night. *Too* exhausted to think about Sumner or wish she were in my bed. Too busy to consider all the ways I'd fucked up. Fucked her over, was more like it.

God, I wanted to ask about her. I wondered if she was as miserable as I was. Though that idea only made me feel worse.

"Wait. Rewind a sec," he said. "Someone approached you about selling? Are you considering it?"

I lifted a shoulder, watching as he retrieved the ball from my latest shot. "Maybe."

He stopped dribbling, tucking the ball against his side.

"You're serious?" He shook his head. "You? The man who's married to your job."

"Maybe I don't want to be anymore."

He shot the ball and sank it in the net. "If you're burned out, step back. Don't step down."

"It's more than burnout," I said, jogging across the court to collect the ball.

"You built that company from the ground up. You're one of the most demanding sons of bitches in the field, but also the most successful. And now... What? You're just going to let it all go?"

I blew out a breath. "That's just it. I *have* been successful. It's not just about wanting a change. I need a new challenge." Flipping houses with Alexis had helped, but after Sumner, nothing seemed to hold my interest.

*Probably because you still haven't admitted what success means to you.*

"I thought that was the point of your little side project." He carried the ball over to the bench and set it down before grabbing some water. "You're not—" He tilted his head to the side. "You're not dying, are you?"

"What?" I jerked my head back.

He grabbed a towel from his bag and wiped the back of his neck. "I don't know. People usually want to make huge changes like this when they've had a near-death experience or..."

"What? Are diagnosed with cancer?"

"Yeah."

I blew out a breath. "No. I'm not dying." Though it felt like it most days, felt as if I were watching life pass me by. And if I wasn't careful, I was going to bury myself in work as Ian often liked to joke.

"Okay." He scrubbed a hand over his head. "I may tease

you about having a midlife crisis, but you know if you ever need to talk, I'm here for you."

I nodded, swallowing past the lump in my throat. "I know."

But there was no way I could talk to him about this—*ever*. He could never know I'd slept with Sumner. And the fact that he was being so supportive only made me feel worse.

"Maybe I should sell and move," I said.

"Move where?"

*Far away from Sumner.* But I knew it didn't matter. She was in my blood, stamped in my soul. Even from her first day in the office, I'd known—known she was a part of me.

"You know…" Ian rubbed a hand over his chin. "I haven't seen you this out of sorts since—"

I held up my hand. "Don't say it." *Don't.*

"You and Rachel broke up. Have you been seeing someone?" When I didn't say anything, he said, "You have, haven't you, you sly old dog?" He pointed at my face with a smug grin that made me want to punch him.

Even so, my heart rate skyrocketed, my pulse racing faster than it had the entire time we'd been running around the court.

Ian leaned in, butting his shoulder to mine, a knowing grin on his face. "*So*, who is she?"

I shook my head, sweat dripping down my back.

"Maybe I'll have to ask Sumner if she has any ideas. Hell." He laughed. "She saw more of you this summer than I did."

I choked on my water, setting it aside before wiping my chin with my shirt. "Leave it, Ian."

"Ooh. Somebody's touchy." He held up his hands in mock surrender.

I rolled my eyes and lowered my voice, knowing he wouldn't stop badgering me unless I gave him something. "No one can know, okay? We work together," I said, scrambling for a plausible reason to get him to drop it before I blurted the truth. "And she's younger."

"I didn't realize either of those was a problem. At least, you didn't seem to mind that Sumner was dating Jack."

*I am Jack!*

"She's not the CEO."

"True. Gotta love a taste of the forbidden fruit," he mused, and I wondered if he was thinking of Lea. They'd both been married when they met.

"Well, it's over now. So, will you please just drop it?"

"Fine," he sighed. "But I hope you guys will find a way to make it work. Anytime we talked this summer, you seemed so happy."

I had a feeling if he knew the woman in question was his daughter, he wouldn't be so supportive.

❧

"Um. Can we get Sumner back?" Cody asked the following morning. "Or is it just a coincidence that you're even more of a bear now that she's gone?"

"Cody," I growled, doing nothing to disprove his accusations.

"What?" He set several contracts on the desk. "She was good at her job. And I liked her. You seemed to like having her around too."

"Yes, it was nice. But she had to start grad school," I said, executing the documents with an angry flourish. "Where's the Greene portfolio?"

"Here." He indicated a file on the desk. "How's that going, by the way?"

"What?"

"Sumner? Grad school?"

"How the hell should I know?" I snapped when something fell off the desk. "Harrington?"

"I thought you guys were close. Here," he said, retrieving the item from the floor and placing it and the file before me. The invitation to Ian's surprise birthday weekend. "You still haven't RSVP'd for the party, at least not officially. Do you want me to handle it?"

I didn't respond, attempting to ignore the invitation and my problems. I needed to keep my attention focused on work. Sumner was gone, likely moved on. I was avoiding Ian. And I had no one else. Work really was all I had.

But even work wasn't much of a distraction. Thanks to Sumner's coaching, I'd effectively deleted or delegated many of my former tasks. At this point, I was beginning to think the company could run without me.

"I'll take care of it. Alito?"

"Here. And," he continued when I opened my mouth, "before you can ask—your dry cleaning has been delivered. And your flight is reporting a slight delay, but hopefully that will change."

"Thank you." I'd always appreciated how efficient Cody was, even if he could be a bit mouthy at times.

I stared at my computer screen, a jumble of letters and numbers. And I realized I didn't care. I didn't care about any of it—not the prestige, the clients, the money. I had it all, and yet I had nothing. For what was it worth without Sumner?

"Wolfe?" Cody asked.

"Yes?" I jerked my attention to him.

"I asked if you needed anything else."

"No." I forced myself to focus on the screen, but that only made me want to smash it. I was fried. Burned out beyond belief, and nothing seemed to help.

I was underwater, drowning. And with every item Cody listed, it was as if another stone were being piled on top of me. Maybe Ian was right. Maybe I needed a break. Nothing had ever sounded so tempting.

Cody turned and headed for the door, and I knew I couldn't keep living like this. I couldn't... My chest tightened, spots dancing before my eyes.

"Cancel everything." The moment I said the words, I could feel a shift, a weight lifted. And I knew in my bones that it was the right decision as I floated back to the surface.

He stared at me a moment, mouth agape. "I must have misheard you."

"Cancel everything," I said again, this time with a smile. "The flight, the meetings, all of it."

"Wolfe." He closed the door and then approached the desk. "What's going on?"

*I need a break,* I thought, knowing I was on the verge of breaking down.

"I'll be out of the office for the next week. I will not be answering phone calls or responding to emails. I will not have internet access." I stood, grabbing my suit jacket.

"What?" he gasped. "Where are you going?"

"Away," I said, not entirely sure myself. I grabbed my phone but left everything else behind, bypassing Cody as I headed for the door.

"But wh-what am I going to tell people?"

"Whatever you want," I said, not giving a shit.

I practically skipped out of the office. At least until my phone buzzed with an incoming text, totally ruining the illusion of freedom.

**Cody: What about Alexis? Want me to cancel?**
**Me: No.**

I'd always felt invigorated by my projects with Alexis. If anything, that was the one thing I didn't want to lose.

**Cody: Maybe you could just take the weekend and then go from there?**

***Me: No.***

I needed my phone for directions, of course. But as soon as that was accomplished, it was going into airplane mode.

When I reached my truck, I removed my tie, tossing it and my suit jacket in the back seat. I sped across town to meet Alexis, figuring maybe I'd use this newfound time to work on a new project. But the moment I pulled up, I realized that wasn't the case. I wanted to be free of obligations. Free of schedules. Free of…expectations.

"Hey, Alexis," I said, ascending the steps to the front door.

"Hey, Wolfe."

I had a flashback to the last house Alexis had showed me, Sumner at my side. I was trying to forget her, but she seemed to pop up at every turn. Clients and employees referencing her ideas, then there were Cody's questions, and now this. But even without those reminders, it would've been impossible to forget her. She was everywhere. I woke up thinking about her. I went about my day, remembering the way she'd smiled at me from across the conference room. Or I'd see her name on some report.

At home, it was no different. I couldn't eat dinner without thinking of the taste of whiskey on her skin. I couldn't lie in bed without wishing she were there. From the time I woke up to the time I fell asleep, she was with me, haunting me.

I followed Alexis through the house, nodding occasionally, but not really paying attention. By the time we finished the tour, I knew I couldn't be involved. I was a fucking mess.

"Thanks for showing me the house," I said. "I think it's a good investment, and I'm happy to help with capital, but I'm not going to be able to do the work myself." Not that the house wasn't awesome. I just…couldn't find it in me to care.

"Of course. I know how busy you are."

I kicked at the floor, wondering why I'd even come.

"Jonathan, are you okay?"

"Yeah." I shook my head as if to clear it. "Yeah. Why?"

"You seem really down lately. And as your friend, I'm worried about you."

I glanced toward the ceiling, rubbing the back of my neck. I had no one to talk to. Sumner had been my confidante, but we were over. I couldn't exactly talk to Ian about my feelings for his daughter. I had no other friends.

Alexis was throwing me a life raft. I could take the easy way out—gloss over everything and pretend it was fine, but I got the feeling she actually cared. That she wanted the truth and not just the "it's all good."

"I was seeing someone, and we broke up."

"What happened?"

I sank down onto a nearby crate. "I was an ass to her. I pushed her away because I was scared."

"Of what?" she asked.

I tugged on my hair. How did I explain this without going into all the details? "Hurting someone."

"Hurting her? Or getting hurt yourself?"

*Both.*

"A friend," I said, resting my arms on my thighs. "It's complicated."

"I feel you. Preston and I were complicated. Or at least, I thought we were."

"What do you mean?"

"He's younger than me. He was my daughter's nanny."

"Really?" I chuckled, somewhat surprised that straitlaced Alexis had such an unconventional love story.

"Oh yeah. You can ask Preston. I made all kinds of excuses for why we couldn't be together. My daughter. Other parents. My friends. The age difference. You name it. But in the end, none of it mattered. And once I finally realized I was the only person who cared, I knew there was no one else I wanted to be with."

I nodded, understanding completely. "Yeah. I've put up a lot of roadblocks. But there's one I'm not sure we can get past."

I didn't want Sumner to give up grad school or her dreams. But I was convinced there had to be another way. Which left only Ian standing in our path.

"The friend?" she asked, to which I nodded. "If they're truly your friend, they'll want you to be happy."

"I wish I could believe that, but it's not quite so simple."

"Have you tried talking to him? *Her?*"

"Him." I shook my head. "And I…can't."

"Because you're scared he'll disapprove?"

"That's pretty much guaranteed. But, no, it's more than that." I sighed. "Imagine it was Lauren we were talking about. Would you risk your friendship with her to be with Preston?"

She screwed up her face. "She hasn't always approved of the men I've dated, but I can't imagine her cutting me out of her life because of it. If that's what you're afraid of, maybe he's not the friend you deserve."

"I slept with his daughter," I blurted.

I'd been carrying around this huge secret for months, and I felt lighter the moment the words were released. It was so nice to finally unload this burden on someone else, even if Alexis's immediate reaction had been to cringe.

"She's legal, right?" she asked, quickly recovering herself.

"Yes. Of course she's legal. God, Alexis." I shook my head.

"Okay." She held up her hands. "Okay. Sorry."

"I mean, yes, she's young. But I often think she's more mature than I am."

"Oh, I get that." She laughed. "Preston was definitely more emotionally mature when it came to our relationship." We were both quiet for a minute until she said, "Do you love her?"

"Yes." My answer was freely given, and it was one of the few things I knew with certainty at the moment. I might not know what I wanted out of life, but I knew that I loved Sumner and wanted her to be part of it.

She nodded. "I wish I had the answers. Really, I do."

"You and me both," I muttered.

"I'm always happy to listen. But if you ever need to talk to a professional, try giving Preston a call." She handed me his business card.

"I thought he counseled pediatric cancer patients." I frowned, turning it over in my hand.

"He does, but he's trained to work with adults as well. And if you don't feel comfortable talking to him, he can always refer you to someone else."

I pocketed the card. "Thanks, Alexis. For...everything."

"Absolutely." She gave me a hug. "And, Wolfe?"

"Yeah?"

"Don't let anyone stand in the way of your happiness, least of all yourself."

It sounded a lot like the advice I'd given Sumner. And I could imagine her throwing it back in my face, telling me to stop being a hypocrite. She'd be right. I'd been an ass.

I needed a plan. It was time to overhaul my life. I was going to win Sumner back. I only hoped it wouldn't be too late.

I took a deep breath and met Alexis's eyes. "I think I'm going to need your help."

# CHAPTER TWENTY-FIVE

## Summer

I made some friends. Immersed myself in classes. I set up my website, sought out clients for my coaching business, and even started working with a few small business owners. It was invigorating, and it helped me forget about my own troubles. About everything and everyone back home.

At least until the invitation for my dad's surprise forty-fifth birthday celebration arrived. It sat on the counter for a few days before I finally opened it. And even then, I didn't immediately RSVP. I left it to collect dust, not wanting to return home. Not wanting to see Jonathan when I was finally in a better place.

Then the emails had started arriving. Lea and the party planner, Juliana, sent out the details for the weekend, assuming I'd be there. Because, why wouldn't I be?

I continued to ignore them, along with the rising feeling of dread that accompanied each new missive. Itineraries, hotel room assignment, dress code suggestions. It almost felt more like a wedding than a birthday celebration.

After a few days of ignoring Lea's calls and voice mails, I knew I couldn't put it off anymore.

"Hey, Lea," I said, answering on the second ring.

"Hey. I wanted to check in about your dad's birthday celebration. When are you coming home?"

This was exactly why I'd avoided her and this conversation. Because I couldn't say no. Despite all my talk of boundaries, I knew it was important to her, and she'd always been there for me. Plus, my dad would be devastated if I didn't show.

"Friday afternoon, though it depends on traffic."

"Great. I set aside a room for you as part of the block for the guests."

"I saw," I said.

"And...don't kill me, but..." I held my breath, bracing myself for what she was going to say next. "I set you up with a date."

"Thanks, Lea. But I'm really not interested."

"Psh. Sumner, you've been wallowing long enough about this whole Jack thing. It's time to get back out there."

"I don't know," I hedged, wishing there were some way to get out of this—both the weekend and the date.

"Damien is super cute and a musician. I think you'll hit it off."

I rolled my eyes with a smile. She said that to almost everybody she set up on a date. And then it struck me—I'd smiled. And I'd been happy, genuinely so. I'd noticed it happening more and more lately, but it still felt foreign. As if my body didn't know how to be happy without...*him*.

"Jonathan will be there," she said, and there was a tiny prick in my heart. A bursting of that fragile bubble of happiness. I wasn't sure I'd ever be able to hear his name or think of him without a tinge of sadness, but I was trying.

"That's nice," I said, all but forcing out the words.

"I'm sure he'll be happy to catch up and hear how grad school is going."

Suddenly, a date sounded a lot more appealing.

૪

I SMILED AND NODDED POLITELY AT WHATEVER MY DATE, Damien, had said. But I wasn't listening. All I could think about was the fact that I'd be seeing Jonathan again, and I'd have to pretend as if nothing had happened. As if he hadn't ripped my heart out and stomped all over it. I placed my hand to my stomach, trying to quell the nerves there.

I gulped down some more champagne while we waited with the other guests for my dad and Lea to arrive. It was going to be a long weekend, and this was just the beginning. Tonight was the surprise party with 100 guests. Tomorrow morning, I was supposed to meet up with the two of them for breakfast.

I hadn't seen Jonathan yet, and I braced myself for it. Steeled myself for the idea that he—like me—might be here with a date.

Damien excused himself to the restroom, and my phone buzzed in my clutch. I pulled it out, smiling when I saw a text from Piper.

*Piper: How's it going?*

*Me: Fine. I think you'd like my date.*

*Piper: You don't?*

*Me: He's nice, just...not my type.*

*Piper: Too young?*

I laughed, watching as the ellipsis danced on the screen just before another message came through.

*Piper: Any wolf sightings yet?*

I typed a quick reply as my aunt sidled up to me, asking about grad school and life in Palo Alto. I didn't seek out conversation but was drawn into it anyway. Some of my dad's friends, my grandmother. Everyone seemed to want to talk, and I played the part, even if my heart wasn't in it. I kept glancing from face to face, wondering what they'd think if they knew about Jonathan and me. Not that we were together. But if we were, would my family and friends ever be able to accept our relationship? More importantly, why did I care? He'd made it abundantly clear that whatever had been between us was over.

"Quiet, please," a tall blonde said from the front of the room. "Lea just texted that they're pulling up to the hotel."

She dimmed the lights to the ballroom, and everyone quieted down. I glanced around for Damien, knowing Lea would expect me to at least be a good host, even if I wasn't a very good date.

When the doors to the ballroom swung open, light from the hallway filtered in. My dad's and Lea's silhouettes blended together, and I could hear my dad say, "Ooh, Lea. You know I love it when you get frisky."

While others in the crowd laughed, I cringed. And then the lights came on, and everyone shouted, "Happy birthday!"

My dad paused, slowly removing his lips from his wife's and turning toward the room. He grinned when he spotted everyone and straightened. Lea's cheeks were dark pink, and she smoothed a hand down her dress. I laughed despite myself.

Damien appeared at my side and continued to charm everyone throughout dinner, including my grandmother. After we ate, the party moved to the hotel lawn. I still hadn't seen Jonathan, and I was beginning to think he wasn't coming. So, I focused on my date, resolving to put the summer behind me. To move on once and for all.

Damien seemed nice, and he was "appropriate." And I tried—honestly. But he wasn't Jonathan.

"Whoa," Damien said. "Your dad looks pissed. Did I do something?"

I followed his gaze and discovered it wasn't my dad but Jonathan who was glaring at us from across the hotel lawn. The sight of him nearly stole the breath from my lungs, but I was determined not to show him how affected I was. So, I played the part—waving with a smile before turning away.

"That's not my dad. It's his best friend." *And my former boss. Former...everything.*

"Oh." Damien furrowed his brow. "Okay. Is he like really protective or something?"

"Something like that," I said, more to myself. "Come on." I linked my arm through his and flashed him a smile. "Let's grab a drink."

We made the rounds, his hand on my lower back the entire time. He was nice, a talented musician, and I was... bored. God, I was *so* bored. And when I couldn't handle the tedious conversation anymore, couldn't force one more smile, I excused myself to the restroom.

My dress swished about my legs, my strides hurried as I rushed to escape. Finally, mercifully alone, I let my shoulders sag. I pressed my palms to the sink and took a deep breath, relief coursing through me that it was a single restroom and I wouldn't get dragged into another conversation with one of the women in my family.

A few breaths later, I lifted my head to evaluate my appearance in the mirror. The material of my dress hugged my curves, emphasizing my generous breasts before flaring over my hips. I knew I couldn't stay in here all night, but I wasn't ready to leave yet. So, I dug in my purse for my lip gloss.

The door to the restroom opened, and I called out, "Just a minute."

But they didn't hear or didn't listen.

A moment later, Jonathan stepped inside the bathroom, closing the door and locking it behind him. His suit fit him to a T, and it reminded me of our time in New York. Of the flight back and everything since. Which only made me angry.

Why had he tempted me with the promise of what could be when he knew we'd inevitably break up? And worse still, why had I agreed?

I used to think we were inevitable—fated for each other. Now I realized I'd been wrong. The only thing certain about Jonathan and me was that we were destined to hurt each other.

"Um, excuse me." I glared at him, lip gloss poised midair. "What are you doing?"

He leaned against the door, crossing his legs at the ankle. Crossing his arms. I shrugged and returned my attention to the mirror, needing to avoid his powerful gaze. I took my time, leaning forward slightly and pressing my lips together. I could feel his eyes on me, scanning my legs. *Good*—I hoped he was thinking about the fact that they could be wrapped around his head, his waist. I hoped he was regretting his decision.

"What are *you* doing?" he asked in a tone that conveyed boredom. Or was that distaste? Either way, his placid demeanor was a façade. He was annoyed with me, and I knew him well enough to know that he was fighting for control. And losing.

"Applying my lip gloss," I said, intentionally misinterpreting his question.

He let out a deep sigh, pushing off the door and stepping closer. I could see him in the reflection, feel his presence. "Sumner," he chided. "I thought you were better than these immature games."

"I'm not playing." My blood boiled. He'd accused me of playing games, but he was the one yanking me around. He was the one who ran hot then cold. He was the one who lured me in with compliments and encouragement only to push me away. To act like we were was a mistake. Like it couldn't happen again.

"Did you bring him to make me jealous?" His voice was low, the words said with an edge of malice.

I pressed my lips together, making sure the color was applied evenly. "Not everything's about you, Jonathan."

I'd agreed to come with Damien as a favor to Lea, but Jonathan didn't need to know that. But also, a small part of me wanted to see what it would feel like to give another man a chance.

"Ask him to leave. Tell him you're not interested." Though the words were said quietly, the force behind them ricocheted them around the bathroom, bouncing off the tile walls and reverberating into me.

I scoffed. "You'd like that, wouldn't you? If you can't have me, no one else can?" I glared at him, challenging. I leaned forward so I was in his face. The air sparked with anger and passion, desire and duty—a storm brewing between us. "Well, you can't have it both ways." I dug my finger into his hard chest, wondering if there was actually a heart in there or not. "I'm done. Let me go."

He stepped closer so our bodies were pressed together, my breasts crushed to his hard chest. Our pelvises kissing. His gaze was so intense I nearly looked away.

My heart danced within my chest, hope and fear and desire and every other emotion warring within me. *Just do it. Just kiss me. Claim me*, I screamed in my head.

I didn't know what he was waiting for, but I was holding my breath. I'd been holding my breath until he finally pressed his lips to mine, giving me the oxygen I so desperately needed. The breath, the life, only he could give. It was as if I'd been drowning, and he'd saved me.

I gasped when he released my lips to kiss down my neck. I moaned when he started to pull my dress aside. But then I remembered how it had felt the last time. Not the amazing sex, but the pain that had followed. How gutted I'd been when he'd acted as if I meant nothing to him.

"Stop," I said, even as my body shook when he slid his hand up my thigh. "I'm not doing this. Not again."

After months of misery, I was finally in a better place. I couldn't go back to where I had been. Piper was right. Jonathan would never change, and I couldn't let him drag me in again with vague promises and unrealistic fantasies.

*I deserve more.*

He removed his hand, and I stepped back, adjusting my dress and then crossing my arms over my chest. "I will not be your dirty little secret. I will not be a mistake. I will *not* be nothing."

# CHAPTER TWENTY-SIX

## Jonathan

N*othing.* The word echoed throughout the room, pounding into my skull. I'd never regretted *anything* more in my life.

I couldn't win. I'd tried to stay away from Sumner out of respect for my friendship with Ian, and it had nearly broken me. But loving her would wreck Ian and destroy a friendship spanning decades. Worse still, though, it was hurting Sumner. *I* was hurting the woman I loved. Even though I thought I'd done what was best for her in letting her go.

I squeezed my eyes shut. I was fucking this up even more than I already had. "You're not nothing, and I'm sorry I *ever* made you believe that. The truth is, I'm nothing without you."

Her lips tilted upward but then quickly reversed course. "It's too late. I've moved on." She turned for the door.

I couldn't let her leave. I *couldn't*. She was mine.

"I sold the Wolfe Group," I blurted.

She paused, turning to me. "You did what?" I nodded, and then she asked, "Why?"

"My heart was no longer in it." I held her gaze. "A raven-haired beauty ran away with it."

"I'm glad you realized you needed a change, and I hope you did it because it was what *you* wanted. Not to prove something to me—or anyone else, for that matter."

"It is what I want, just like *you* are what I want." I stepped closer, taking her hands in mine. "You gave me the courage to make some necessary changes, as well as others I'd long desired."

If only I could've found that same courage in my personal life sooner. But the stakes were different, higher. My relationship with Ian meant more than the money in my bank account. He'd known me before the success, before I was Wolfe, when I was just Jonathan. But Sumner... Sumner was ingrained in me. She understood me, she challenged me, she completed me in a way no woman ever had. I realized that now—I couldn't let her go. I just hoped it wasn't too late.

"Congratulations," she said, but her smile didn't quite reach her eyes.

"I want to find a way for us to be together." I cupped her cheeks. "I *will* find a way," I said with more conviction. I blew out a breath, brushing my thumbs along her jaw. "I love you, Sumner."

Her lids fluttered closed, tears falling down her cheeks. I kissed them away, hoping they were tears of happiness.

"Do you know how long I've waited to hear you say those words?" She shook her head, and I didn't understand her reaction. Why wasn't she happy?

"But I can't keep doing this," she turned for the door, hand poised on the knob. "This—*us*—we're toxic. And..." She released a shuddering breath. "I don't think we should see each other again."

I jerked my head back. *Wait. What?*

"Goodbye, Jonathan."

The door closed behind her with a snick, and I stared at it, wondering where I'd gone wrong. Why couldn't she understand? I'd sold my company. I was prepared to upend my life to be with her. Why wasn't that enough?

I couldn't… I gasped for air, the room spinning. I couldn't do this. I couldn't live without her. I marched out of the bathroom, intent on persuading her to change her mind. But I was stopped by a guy in a suit.

"Excuse me," I said, pushing past him. "I need—"

"Are you Jonathan Wolfe?" he asked.

I hesitated, glancing around for Sumner, then said, "Yeah." *Where is she?*

"Oh, thank god." His shoulders relaxed, and he pressed a button on his headset. "Found him."

I furrowed my brow. "I'm sorry, but do I know you?"

He shook his head and held out his hand to shake. "I'm Landon, and I'm with Juliana Wright Events. Let's get you onstage."

"Onstage?" I felt as if I were in a daze, allowing this stranger to lead me back to the ballroom.

"Yes. I'm with the event planner for Ian's birthday weekend. We're about to do the slideshow and speeches. Ian's daughter's up first, then it's your turn."

He spoke quickly into his headset, but my mind was on Sumner. On her parting words, which kept playing on a loop in my mind. *Toxic. Shouldn't see each other again.*

I was going to have to toast Ian and pretend I hadn't just kissed his daughter. Hadn't told her I loved her and would do anything to be with her. And then watched her walk out on me, walk out of my life. I needed to find her. To talk to her. I'd never felt so torn—between my loyalty to my best friend and my love for his daughter.

"I don't think I can do this," I said, my stomach lurching. "I—"

"It's okay if you didn't prepare," Landon said, misinterpreting my anxiety as he guided me toward the ballroom. "You can wing it." He leaned in and lowered his voice. "Most people do."

"Right." I smoothed my hand down my shirt, following him to the front of the room. I grabbed a glass of champagne from a passing waiter, taking a large gulp.

Ian turned to smile at me but frowned. "What's wrong?"

I shook my head. "Nothing."

"No birthday party would be complete without some toasts," Juliana spoke from the stage, microphone in hand. She then introduced Sumner.

Sumner assumed her position on the stage, full of grace and poise. She spoke with such eloquence and love, and it was clear that Ian was proud of her. Was I really prepared to destroy their bond as well as my own friendship? I'd moved heaven and earth to make sure she wouldn't sacrifice her dreams for me, but what about her relationship with her dad?

Ian leaned over to me at one point. "You did a great job with her this summer. She really blossomed during her internship."

How the hell was I supposed to respond to that? I couldn't. So, I didn't say anything, keeping my attention on the stage.

All the while, I kept wondering how I could ever tell him that I was in love with his daughter. I'd lose his friendship for sure. But how could I *not* tell him if it meant losing Sumner? It was a no-win situation. Either way, I lost someone I loved. And their relationship would be forever changed.

Ian and Lea peered up at the stage, warm smiles on their faces. They were happy, buzzed, and they had no fucking clue. *No one does*, I thought when the room burst into applause.

Sumner returned to her date's side, and he whispered something in her ear before handing her a drink. She smiled, and I nearly growled at him.

*Look at me,* I pleaded in my head. *Sumner. Baby, please just give me a sign. Something.* But she continued to stare straight ahead, shoulders back, just as I heard my name called. This was all my fault. I'd pushed her away so many times that she'd finally moved on.

I climbed the stairs to the raised platform and accepted the microphone.

"Ian." I cleared my throat. *Fuck.*

"You can be an annoying ass at times," I said, and he chuckled, flipping me off on the side of his glass. I took that as a good sign. "But you're also one of the most loyal, persistent, smartest people I know."

I inhaled a deep breath. I'd intended to keep this short and sweet, but my thoughts were all over the place. My attention kept drifting to Sumner, to what she'd said. Ian was my oldest friend, but she was the love of my life. I couldn't live without her.

Just the thought of it—the reminder of what the past few months had been like without her—had the band around my chest tightening. The room spun, and I gripped the microphone as I struggled to remain upright. I was a bastard. The worst kind of friend.

But Ian—he'd been there for me through everything. So, for once, I didn't hold back. By the time I was done with my speech, the crowd had laughed and cried, and I'd even wiped away a tear. So many incredible years of friendship.

"That was a really nice speech, Jonathan," Lea said, pulling me into a hug.

"Thanks."

Ian slapped my back. "Must be the girl," he teased, but I

could tell he was just as affected as me. Though I stiffened at his words.

"What girl?" Lea asked, her ears perking up. She was always trying to set everyone up. She said it was because she was so happy with Ian that she wanted everyone to experience that type of love. I'd never understood until now, until Sumner.

"He was seeing someone this summer, and he's been such a mopey bastard lately. Does this mean you fixed things with her?"

*Fuck.* This was so fucking messed up.

I shook my head, watching Sumner as she headed for the dance floor with her date.

Ian took another sip of his drink, draping his arm over Lea's shoulder. He was well past buzzed by this point. "It's good to see her happy again."

"Right?" Lea peered up at him with a dazed smile. "I knew she and Damien would hit it off."

"What do you mean hit it off?" I asked. "I thought they'd been dating a while."

"No." Lea laughed. "I set them up. This is their first date."

*Moved on, my ass.* She'd lied to me.

"Excuse me," I said, relieved when Ian and Lea were pulled into another conversation. I'd had enough.

I didn't even wait for the song to change before cutting in. Sumner's date glared at me but quickly backed off when I bared my teeth.

"What are you doing?" Sumner hissed as I lifted her hands, draping her arms around my neck. She looked everywhere but at me.

When she attempted to pull away, I tightened my grip on her hip, bringing her into me. Exactly where she belonged. The music continued to play, but everything faded to a dull roar.

"Moved on, huh?"

She rolled her eyes. "Don't start."

"It's your first date."

Ian's sister and her husband danced closer, too close for comfort. So I said nothing more for the moment, steering Sumner farther away from the crowd.

"I have a good feeling about him."

"Bullshit. Who's the one playing games now?"

"Is there a point to this conversation, or are you just trying to be a dick?"

I nearly barked out a laugh. Fuck, I loved this woman. "If I tell Ian about us, I need to know you're with me—one hundred percent."

"What?" she gasped, searching my eyes before finally saying, "You're serious?"

I nodded. "I love you, and I want to be with you. Say yes."

"I..." She hesitated, and my heart caught before feeling as if it had tumbled down a flight of stairs. "That all sounds great, but how can you expect me to trust you when you've burned me so many times before?"

Everything and everyone around us stilled, my vision tunneling in on the woman I loved. It was just Sumner and me, and I knew I had to lay it all on the line or risk losing her for good. And even if I did pour my heart out, it still might not be enough. But I had to try.

I took a deep breath. "I finally took your advice. I defined what success means to me, and it doesn't include the Wolfe Group, my house, the cars...any of it. Those *things* don't give me a sense of contentment—they never have. Our relationship, loving you, that's what gives my life meaning. And, if you give me a chance, I vow to spend the rest of my life showing you just how important you are to me."

She gaped at me, and I held my breath, waiting for her to shut me down once and for all. I'd deserve it after the way I'd treated her, but...damn. I needed her. I'd do anything to be with her, even beg.

"Please, Sumner. Please give me another chance. If you're ready to tell Ian, then so am I." Despite my previous mistakes, surely that proved how much I loved her. That I was serious.

I could see the battle raging within, but I sensed she was close. It was in the way she leaned into me, her posture relaxing ever so softly. Her eyes pooling with something that looked a lot like forgiveness. "When?"

I wanted to keep dancing with her and forget all about Ian. He seemed so happy; I didn't want to ruin tonight for him. Plus, he was already too far gone at this point. I could find excuses for the rest of our lives, but she deserved more than vague promises.

"Tomorrow." I swallowed down the words and the anxiety that idea produced. "I'll tell him tomorrow at breakfast."

"No." She shook her head, and a pit opened in my stomach, until she added, "We'll tell him together."

*Together?* She couldn't be serious. "I'm not sure that's—"

She pressed a finger to my lips, her expression unyielding even as she quickly removed it and glanced around to make sure no one was watching. "We'll tell him together or not at all."

She was right. This was something we needed to do together. And I sensed this was something she needed to do for herself. It wouldn't be easy, but I respected her even more for it.

I let out a deep sigh and muttered, "Okay. Yes."

"Okay." She smiled, a sort of tense excitement bouncing between us like a pinball in a machine.

"Okay?" I grinned, so fucking close to pulling her into my arms and kissing her.

Instead, we stood there, arms wrapped around each

other, safe in our embrace. Tomorrow, I was going to destroy one of the most important friendships in my life. But this moment—this woman—left no doubt in my mind. I would walk through fire for her.

I pulled her closer, grateful for the slower song which allowed me to do so. I wanted to kiss her so fucking bad, but I paused, taking a moment to just inhale her, enjoy her. Love her.

"I love you," I whispered, wishing I could shout it instead. I couldn't believe I'd ever thought it possible to deny my feelings for her.

"Is it too early to make our escape?" She grinned.

"Um, no." I wanted nothing more than to be with Sumner. Alone. Where I could worship her body and savor every drop of pleasure.

"Good, but I need to talk to Damien first."

"I'll do it." I moved, but she pulled me back to her.

"I've got it covered, caveman. Okay?" She peered up at me with the sweetest smile, the first real one she'd given me in months. It felt as if my lungs expanded fully for the first time, my heart able to soar. As if I could say no to her.

"What room are you in?" I asked as the song ended.

"Uh…440." Her fingertips glided against my palm before she made her way across the ballroom. When she reached the door, she glanced over her shoulder and grinned at me.

I stayed at the party a while longer before slipping out. It felt like an eternity, when really no more than twenty minutes had passed. After a quick stop by my room to grab my bag, I headed for Room 440 and Sumner. By the time I finally made it, I was fucking drained. And she was just as quiet, undressing before the mirror with a contemplative expression that spoke of sadness. For me, at least—and I assumed for Sumner as well—the reality of what we were doing was sinking in. The possibility that, come tomorrow, my best friend would hate me and her father likely wouldn't speak to her. We climbed into bed, and I pulled her to me, tucking her into my side. There would be time to worship her body later. Right now, I just wanted to hold her.

"My dad seemed so happy tonight." Her voice was wistful and tinged with regret.

"Are you having second thoughts?" I asked.

She spun to face me. "Are you?"

"About us?" I brushed her hair over her shoulder. "Never. But I think we both know things will change tomorrow."

She nodded, burying her head in my chest. "I just... I hope he can accept us."

*I hope he can forgive us.*

I didn't want to promise anything I couldn't guarantee. Instead of answering, I slanted my mouth over hers, losing myself in her touch. And when we made love that time, it was slower, more deliberate. It felt even more amazing than I remembered, even better now that I'd stopped fighting this, us.

*Us.* I'd never really been part of an "us," apart from a failed engagement. Rachel and I hadn't belonged together; we never should've let it get that far. But Sumner... Wrong as we were in many ways, we were right in so many others. In the ones that really mattered. Hell, I was about to risk the single most important relationship in my life to be with her.

She fell asleep on my chest, and I lay awake for a long time, staring at the ceiling and thinking about life. About friendship. And about what tomorrow would bring.

With time, Ian would forgive Sumner, love her. But he'd be looking for someone to blame, and that blame would fall squarely on my shoulders. Rightfully so. Regardless of what happened, come tomorrow, our friendship would never be the same.

# CHAPTER TWENTY-SEVEN

*Sumner*

"Sumner? I can barely hear you," Piper said at my hushed whisper.

I sighed and sent a request for her to FaceTime, not even sure why I thought I'd be able to whisper. Though at least I'd had the foresight to grab my headphones.

"Hey." I kept my voice low and glanced at the door, making sure it was closed. It was two in the morning, and I was currently holed up in the bathroom.

"Why are you whispering? And are you—" she held the phone closer to her face "—in a bathroom?"

"Because Jonathan's in my hotel room."

"He what?" she shrieked, and I squeezed my eyes shut.

"Shh." I placed my finger to my lips, bracing for what would come next.

"I knew I should've gone as your date."

"Listen," I said to stop the stream of profanities she was currently spewing. "He wants to be with me."

"Right." I could feel her eye roll from across town. "How many times has he told you that before?"

"No." I shook my head. "He's ready to tell my dad."

"What? Seriously?"

I tucked my legs beneath me, giddiness and nerves making me sick to my stomach. "And he sold his company, sold his house, and plans to move to Palo Alto."

"Wow. What brought on this change?"

"He..." My cheeks pinched, just remembering those words from his lips. "Loves me."

"Wow," she said again, and I nearly laughed. "Never saw this one coming. And you're sure he's going to go through with it—telling your dad, I mean?"

"Yes," I said with more conviction than I felt. I knew I wouldn't be able to relax until after we'd delivered the news.

"I sense some hesitation."

"We agreed to tell him tomorrow. Or, I guess, today," I said, remembering what time it was. "At breakfast."

"Are you sure?"

I nodded. "Yes," I whispered.

"Like really, really sure? One-million-percent sure? Because once you tell your dad, you can't go back."

"I know." I swallowed. "I *know.*"

"That's...a lot. How do you feel about everything?"

"Excited. Anxious. Like I might throw up," I admitted, standing from the counter, Jonathan's shirt skimming my thighs.

"I sure as hell hope he follows through. Because if he doesn't, I will cut off his balls myself."

I laughed nervously. I wouldn't put it past Piper. "That won't be necessary."

"Okay, but if it is, you know where I am." She used her fingers to mime cutting with a pair of scissors.

"Thanks, Piper."

"Call me if you need me."

"I will," I said and added "Thanks," before disconnecting the call.

I waited a few minutes before finally tiptoeing back to bed. Jonathan was snoring softly. I climbed beneath the covers, and I tossed and turned, my thoughts even more restless than my body. I'd waited for this for so long, pushed so hard, and now it was finally here. We were going to tell my dad and be a real couple. It was everything I'd wanted, but were we doing the right thing?

I must have drifted off at some point, but when my alarm chimed, I didn't feel rested. Far from it—I'd barely slept, and I didn't think Jonathan had fared much better. But we got up and pretended as if everything was fine. We showered and got ready, neither of us speaking much.

I stood before the bathroom mirror, and I turned to face him, smoothing down his collar. "You ready for this?"

He nodded. "Are you?"

I pressed my lips to his, hoping it would calm me. "I'd be lying if I said I wasn't worried."

"About how your dad will react?"

"That and...us."

He pulled back, lifting my chin so I was forced to meet his gaze. "What about us?"

"I don't know. Never mind." I glanced away, thinking it was silly. Despite my resolve to speak my mind, despite all my progress, I still struggled at times. "We should go."

"Fuck no." He caged me against the sink. "Answer me, Sumner."

I drew in a shuddering breath, knowing this needed to be said. I needed to say it, especially if I wanted to have a real relationship with Jonathan, a lasting relationship. "I guess I never really stopped to think about what life would be like if we were actually together. We've been lying and hiding for so long. Hurting each other for so long... What if that's all we know?"

INEVITABLE

"Baby." He kissed me. "Think about all the times we were together—the two of us. Were you happy?"

I nodded emphatically. "So happy."

"See?" He smiled, kissing me again. "We're going to be happy. I promise. It may not seem like it now, but we will."

I wanted so badly to believe him, but I wasn't sure how it could possibly be true. We were good at sex. We were good at secrets. We were good at lies and destruction. But could we actually build a life together?

"We don't have to do this if you aren't ready," he said, rubbing my arms.

I remembered what the past few months had been like. What life was like without him. I'd told him we were toxic, but that was only because he'd poisoned me for anyone else. My heart had always belonged to him, and it always would.

"No." I shook my head, knowing this wouldn't get any easier. "It's time."

"Okay." He cupped my cheeks. "Okay." He drew a deep breath. "I love you, and we will get through this—together."

I nodded. "I know. I love you too." He slanted his mouth over mine in a brief but bittersweet kiss that belied our hopes and our fears.

We rode down in the elevator in silence, and I wondered if Jonathan was preparing his arguments like I was. I had no idea what to expect. This wasn't like a client I could court or persuade. This was my dad. No matter what I said, I was afraid he wouldn't approve.

Jonathan and I were the first to arrive at the restaurant. I kept turning my bracelets on my wrists, fidgeting with the napkin, anything. He placed his hand over mine but quickly removed it when we spotted my dad and Lea making their way over from the hostess stand.

"Good morning." My dad pressed a kiss to my forehead

265

and said, "Morning, kiddo," before taking the seat across from Jonathan.

"Hello." Lea smiled, her voice cheery as she took a seat.

The waiter came by for our drink order, and then we were alone again. Lea and Dad busied themselves with the menu, but I was too preoccupied to even consider eating.

"So…how did things go with you and Damien?" Lea asked, finally setting her menu aside. "He didn't want to join us for breakfast?"

"He was nice, but, um…"

"But what?" Lea prodded, and I turned to Jonathan. This was it. This was the moment. Before I could open my mouth, he spoke.

"You know how important your friendship is to me, Ian" Jonathan said, and Dad nodded. "And you know I would never want to do anything to hurt you, right?"

He leaned back in his chair. "Why are you being so dramatic? It's my birthday weekend. Let's get some mimosas."

"Because there's something I need to tell you," Jonathan said, and I gripped his hand beneath the table. "I—" He took a deep breath, and I braced myself for the bomb he was about to drop. "I'm in love with Sumner."

He'd done it. Oh my god. He'd said the words. He'd just claimed me, consequences be damned.

For a moment, it seemed as if everything and everyone froze. All I could hear was the beating of my heart. Feel was Jonathan's hand clasping mine beneath the table. See was my dad's expression as he tried to decipher the words.

Dad narrowed his eyes at us and then threw back his head and started laughing. When he finally caught his breath, he said, "You really had me going there for a second." He swiped at his eyes, but Lea was smiling nervously. "Good one, guys." He laughed some more, but no one joined him.

"Dad," I said, unable to hide the hurt and hesitation in my tone. "It's not a joke. Jonathan and I are together."

Dad immediately sobered, blinking a few times. "What do you mean...*together*?"

"Honey." Lea's tone was gentle as she placed her hand on his forearm. "They're a couple, right?" She turned to us.

We nodded.

"No." Dad let out an unintelligible sound, his complexion paling. "No. That's impossible. You were dating Jack." He glanced at me before careening toward Jonathan. "And you," he panted, eyes widening as if something had just dawned on him. "Someone..." He turned his attention back to me. "Younger. Someone you worked with."

I shook my head, allowing it to drop between my shoulders. "There was no Jack."

Dad slumped back against the chair. "Oh my god. Oh my god."

"So..." Lea glanced between Jonathan and me with a puzzled expression. "Every time 'Jack' called or texted. Every time you were staying over at 'Jack's place,' you were actually referring to Jonathan?"

I'd been so focused on my dad's feelings all this time, I hadn't considered how Lea would react when she found out. We'd always been close, and I could sense her confusion, her disappointment.

I nodded. "I'm so sorry. I didn't want to lie. I just didn't know what else to do."

Lea's face crumpled, and something in my chest twisted. "I'm so sorry, Lea. And I'm sorry, Dad. I know—"

"How long?" Dad's face was red. I wasn't sure I'd ever seen him this angry. Not even when he'd fought with my mom over the classic Mustang he'd restored. She didn't actually want it, but she knew he did. He'd loved that car.

"Does it really matter?" Jonathan asked, perhaps the only person at the table with any remaining composure.

"Well, I-I forbid it," Dad sputtered.

"Dad," I sighed. "I'm a grown woman, fully capable of making my own decisions."

"He's twice your age. He's *literally* old enough to be your father. How could you be so fucking stupid? I thought you'd learned your lesson after what happened with the professor. And you—" He turned to Jonathan, his skin practically steaming with anger, ready to erupt. "How could you? She's my daughter! You're fucking my daughter."

His words sliced through me like shards of glass.

"Ian," Lea hissed, probably noticing that others around us had stopped to stare. Jonathan gripped my hand tighter.

Dad pinched the bridge of his nose, clearly reeling from this revelation. I tried to imagine how I'd feel if I were him. I tried to understand the betrayal and hurt he must be feeling. I tried to excuse the harsh words and the hurled accusations. But it was difficult.

"I can't believe you'd do this," he said to Jonathan. "I thought you were my friend. I thought I could trust you."

"You can."

"Oh yeah. I can trust you to 'take care of' my daughter. Is that why you agreed to bring her on as an intern? So you could sneak around behind my back?"

"Stop putting all the blame on Jonathan," I said, finally finding my voice again. "I wanted this just as much as he did, if not more."

Dad ignored me, banging his fist against the table as he glared at Jonathan. "You could have any woman you want. Why her? *Why?* She's... No," He shook his head, his face turning redder and redder. "She's too young. She... We agreed. *You* agreed that grad school was the best plan."

"Agreed?" My attention snapped between them. What was

I missing? And was that what Dad really thought of me? My mind couldn't seem to keep up. It was like I was a wiener dog trying to run the Iditarod with the huskies.

"Why do I feel like you guys are talking in code?" Dad looked away, and I glanced to Jonathan for an answer. "Will one of you just tell me what's going on?"

Jonathan sighed. "I wanted to offer you a permanent job. I was going to ask you to stay."

"You…*what?*" It came out garbled, much like my thoughts. "Then why did you tell me it was time to move on? Why did you…"

"Because I asked him to. Because you were getting too attached to Jack. Who was apparently *Jonathan*." Dad spat out his name with an accompanying glare.

Lea narrowed her eyes at the two of them, and I felt a pit open up in my stomach and swallow every important relationship along with it.

"Wait." I shook my head. "So, you both—what? Got together and thought… Hmm. Sumner's so stupid, we need to decide this for her?"

Their matching guilty expressions were answer enough.

I stood, throwing my napkin down on the table. I was done. Done with this pissing contest. Done with their lies. Done with everyone else thinking they knew what was best for me. "I may be young, but I'm not the incapable little girl you both seem to think I am."

Jonathan scrambled out of his chair. "Baby, wait."

"No," Dad cried out, a keening sound, and stood. "She's *my* baby. *My* daughter."

I glanced up, wiping away tears as I tried to ignore the fact that everyone in the restaurant was gawking at us. I'd trusted Jonathan, my dad, and they'd lied to me. They were no better than Nico.

But I wouldn't continue to be the naïve fool they believed

me to be. I would no longer stay silent. I would assert myself. I would stand up for myself, even in the face of the two men who were supposed to love and protect me.

I held up my hand. "Dad, I know you're upset, but you have no right to speak to me the way you did."

His lips were drawn in a line as if his mouth were zipped shut. I turned to Lea. "Lea, I'm really sorry." She nodded but also said nothing.

"And, you." I turned to Jonathan, yanking my purse from the chair. "I can't even…" My breath was shaky. "After all the times I built you up. After all the things you said to me about choosing my future and speaking up for myself. And you didn't even believe in me."

I was numb as I ducked my head and darted through the restaurant. I walked quickly, but it wasn't fast enough for me to avoid the curious and judgmental stares. I knew what they were all thinking.

*How could you?*

*Whore.*

*Terrible daughter.*

It was written on their faces, even if they hadn't spoken the words aloud. Or maybe it was my dad's words in my head, the insults he'd lobbed at me. He'd always promised to love me—no matter what.

*He also probably never expected that you'd fall in love with his best friend.*

God. I felt like an idiot. To think we could tell my dad and he wouldn't react the way he had. To hope that…I didn't know. That he'd accept us.

And while that hurt, knowing Jonathan was hurting too only made it worse.

But that wasn't even the worst part. The worst part was that they'd both lied to me. That they really thought so little of me.

"Sumner." Jonathan jogged up behind me. "Sumner, wait."

I spun on him. "Do you not trust me to know my own mind? All those times we worked together and you told me how brilliant I was, were you just being nice?"

"Sumner." He grabbed my elbow, pulling me down an empty hallway. "Listen to me. Of course, I believe in you. But I couldn't be the one to hold you back."

"Can you see how limiting my decisions, not trusting my ability to decide for myself might be holding me back?"

"Yes."

"Yes?" I yanked my gaze up to his, noticing that his eye was pinched shut, the skin turning a bluish hue.

"Yes, baby. I'm sorry. I was an idiot. About so many things."

"Why didn't you tell me? Why didn't you at least give me the chance to decide for myself?"

"Because I want the best for you, and I didn't think that was me."

His honesty sucked the air from my lungs, my heart softening. I thought back on all the times he'd encouraged me to pursue my dreams—from suggesting I work with Isla, to seeking my advice himself. And ultimately, I believed him. He didn't want me to limit myself, and it was why he'd pushed me to leave. Even though he nearly broke me.

I cupped his cheek, dropping my hand when he winced. "Did my dad punch you?"

He nodded. "I deserved it."

"I'm not sure I agree with that. But I do understand why you did what you did, even if I don't like it."

"And the reason I didn't tell you was because I didn't want to come between you and your dad any more than I already have."

I nodded, considering everything he'd said. He was

271

always putting me first, even if it was misguided at times. But apparently, he wasn't done.

"And, at the time, I couldn't own up to what I really wanted." He reached into his pocket, pulling out a slip of paper before unfolding it. "I was going to show it to you last night, but—"

I accepted the piece of paper from him. In his neat scrawl were a few lines, but the words were so impactful.

I'VE BEEN CHASING THE WRONG THINGS, FILLING MY DAYS, MY *years, with stuff. With obligations and expectations. But now I know the true meaning of success isn't to be found in things. It's to be found in people. In relationships.*

AND THEN HE WENT ON TO LAY OUT HIS VISION FOR SUCCESS, including a house for us that he'd remodel, a life together, a plan for his days.

"This is... Wow," I whispered, emotions bubbling up inside me, threatening to spill out through my tears. "It's beautiful. I can see you've really given it a lot of thought."

"Yes, but it's just an initial draft. I left space for you to add your goals, your dreams, your definition of success. You have a voice," he added. "You always have. And I'm listening. I promise I won't make decisions for you or us without talking to you first."

I folded the paper and handed it back to him.

"Please. Give me a chance. Give *us* a chance," he pleaded, his blue eyes filled with conflicting emotions—hope, fear, love, sincerity.

"I have a few conditions."

"I wouldn't expect anything less." He smiled, then winced.

"What have we done?" I said, mostly to myself, reality

sinking in. Even as upset as I was with my dad, I knew I'd hurt him too. "That was a disaster."

My dad's shock had registered first, followed quickly by disgust, betrayal, disappointment.

"Hopefully, he'll come around."

"And if he doesn't?" Jonathan didn't have an answer for that. Neither of us did. I sighed. "I'm worried that you'll come to resent me. That you'll regret this."

"Baby, look at me."

I shook my head, fighting back tears. He lifted my chin, forcing me to meet his gaze. "I could never regret being with you. I love you, Sumner."

"I love you too," I said, though it didn't come with the sense of joy I'd hoped it would. It was tinged with sadness and fear, regret and longing. And I worried that neither Jonathan's nor my relationship with my dad would ever be the same.

# CHAPTER TWENTY-EIGHT

## Jonathan

*Two Months Later*

Sumner sat at the kitchen table, books littering the surface. Her eyes were glued to her laptop, and when she let out a deep sigh, dragging her hands through her hair, I knew I'd let her be long enough.

"Maybe it's time to take a break from studying," I suggested, grabbing a drink from the fridge. She jolted, quickly typing something on her keyboard.

"There's that new Thai place down the street," I said, dropping a kiss on her head. "We could grab some dinner."

"I don't have time to take a break." Her eyes never left the computer. Her hair was piled on top of her head in a loose bun, strands falling around her face. She'd never looked more beautiful. "Everyone knows this professor is evil, and I need a good grade in his class."

"Come on." I placed my hands on her shoulders, hoping the massage would soften her, relax her. "Just a little break. I want to show you something. *Please*," I added.

"Mm. That feels good," she moaned, body going limp.

I grinned but kept kneading her shoulders, smoothing away the knots beneath the surface, wishing I could just as easily relieve all her cares. As happy as we were together in our new life, there was a sense of loss over what had happened with Ian and Lea. It was this ever-present shadow that hung over us. Whether we talked about them or we didn't, I knew they were often on Sumner's mind.

She let her head drop forward, and I leaned down to kiss her neck. She shivered when I ran my nose along the column of skin. I stilled, my eyes catching on one of the browser windows.

"What's that?" I asked, pointing at the tab.

"Oh, um. Nothing." She slammed the laptop shut and stood quickly.

"Ooh. Was it porn?" I teased, though I already suspected the answer was no.

"What would you do if I said yes?"

I lifted a shoulder. "Ask if we could watch it together?"

She rolled her eyes, though she couldn't hide the way her pupils darkened, breath quickening. *Interesting.* I stored that little tidbit away in my memory bank.

"What did you want to show me?" she asked.

"Nuh-uh." I shook my head. "You're not getting off so easily. I want to know why you were looking at an article on the Electra complex?"

"It's, um, for class," she answered, avoiding my gaze.

"Really? Which class?" I asked in a nonchalant tone. The fluttering of her eyelashes told me to keep pressing. I had a feeling she was lying.

"Finance."

"Interesting."

"Yeah. It is a pretty fascinating concept that relates to world markets and the—"

"Sumner." I placed my hands on her shoulders. "I think we both know it has nothing to do with world markets."

She hung her head. "Yeah. You're right."

"Are you worried you have Daddy issues?" I asked, half joking.

I was vaguely familiar with the Electra complex—enough to know it was the female equivalent of the more commonly known Oedipus complex. The theory that children sought partners of the opposite sex who most closely resembled their parent. We'd never discussed it, mostly because she and Ian had always had a great relationship—loving and support-ive. At least until I'd come between them.

"No." She huffed, her cheeks blossoming with color.

"I'm not judging you," I soothed. "Merely trying to understand."

"I was looking for articles on situations like ours. I was trying to find out if anyone's parent had forgiven them or found a way to accept their relationship. And I came across the Electra complex and was curious."

"Curiosity is a good thing," I said, wanting her to feel nothing but my love and support.

"You're not mad?" she asked, seeming nothing like the confident, assertive woman I knew her to be.

"Mad?" I asked. "Of course not. Baby, I would do anything to make this better for you. I'm just not sure the internet is the best place to look for answers."

She let out a heavy exhale. "I know. But he still refuses to talk to either of us, and it's been nearly two months since…"

*His birthday.*

*The blowup.*

"And I'm trying." Her voice was strained, and it pained me to hear it. I knew she'd sent emails. Texts. Calls. All of which had gone unanswered. "I'm not sure what more I can do," she sighed.

Despite how hurt she'd been by his words, she still wanted a relationship with her dad. She was his only child. They'd always been close. And I'd come between them. He'd lost his best friend and his daughter in one fell swoop, and I knew it had to be eating him up inside.

I'd tried reaching out to him a few times myself, but Ian wouldn't budge. He continued to act as if neither of us existed. Ian's words from all those months ago still reverberated in my mind. "I don't ever want to speak to you again."

But it was the way he'd spoken to Sumner that had pushed me over the edge. The fact that Thanksgiving was approaching and he seemed intent on pursuing this course. Even now, I was still angry with him for hurting the woman I loved. I deserved his rage; she didn't. And I'd vowed to find a way to make it right.

So far, it wasn't going so well.

I pulled her into my chest, my shirt muffling her sniffles. "We'll figure this out together." I smoothed my hand over her back. "I promise."

"Can I have my surprise now?" she asked.

I chuckled. "Will that make you feel better?" She nodded, and I wiped away her tears with my thumbs. "Okay. Close your eyes."

She did as I said, and I moved behind her, steering her down the hall.

"What did you do?" she chided, though we both knew she was teasing.

I squeezed her shoulders. "No peeking."

Framed pictures lined the wall, and I still couldn't get over the fact that this was our home.

After Ian's birthday, we'd returned to Palo Alto, and I moved into her apartment. I'd already been scoping out houses with a realtor. Alexis had connected me with someone more local, someone with more of an eye for historical homes. I hadn't wanted just any property; I wanted something unique. Something we could make our own.

We'd found a house we loved and closed on it quickly. Keys in hand, I'd immediately started working with a team of contractors. The kitchen had been the first big renovation. Sumner had given some input, but mostly deferred to me.

With that completed—and me sick of driving back and forth between the house and the apartment—we'd moved in to one of the downstairs bedrooms while we updated the master suite. And day by day, a little more of the house was completed. Floors refinished. Hardware installed. Windows cleaned. It was a work in progress and a good outlet.

"Can I look yet?" she asked.

"Almost." I angled her so she had the best view of the room. "And...now."

Her eyes fluttered open, and the moment she took it all in, she smiled. "Oh my god. Is this—"

"Your new office."

She squealed, moving around the room, touching everything. "It's amazing. Did you do this all by yourself?" she asked, skimming her finger along the bookshelves before running a hand over the curtains.

"I had a little assistance with the decorating." Alexis's friend Lauren had helped with the design.

The hardest part had been keeping it a secret. But with Sumner busy with finals, I'd been able to manage it. It meant our master bedroom wouldn't be ready as soon as we'd hoped, but seeing her reaction was worth the delay. Besides, I didn't care where we slept, so long as we were together.

"It's gorgeous," she said, pressing up on her tiptoes to give me a kiss. "Thank you."

"I wanted to give you a space to work, free from distractions. And I thought this would be a great spot to meet with clients, since it has a French door off the side for easy access."

"You are incredible," she said and then faltered. I followed her gaze to a frame on the bookshelves, where an image of her and Ian was displayed. I'd considered removing it, but I thought she'd want it there.

I stepped behind her, wrapping my arms around her. "Do you want to take it down?"

"No." She shook her head. "It's nice. I just—"

"I know, baby. I hope he'll come around too."

"Thanksgiving is next week."

"Do you want to go somewhere? Spend a week on the beach?"

She shook her head. "I just want to be with family."

"You're my family," I said, knowing she'd understand just how much that meant to me. "And I love you."

"And you're mine." She kissed me then nestled into my side. "I knew this wouldn't be easy, but I've always spent it with my dad, even after the divorce. Even Lea won't respond to my texts. And it hurts." She sniffled, and a small piece of me broke. It shouldn't be this way. She shouldn't have to choose between Ian and me.

"Enough about that." She stepped out of my arms, wiping her tears with her sleeve. "I can't change it, and I'd rather focus on all the things I have to be grateful for. Like my amazing boyfriend and this beautiful office he built for me." She grinned.

"I'm grateful for you. Every single day." I kissed her.

She pulled out the desk chair and sank down in it. "How do I look? Professional, right?" she teased, alluding to her yoga pants and long-sleeved off-the-shoulder shirt.

My mouth went dry, some of my earlier concerns forgotten. Sumner had a way of doing that to me. Of making me forget anything but her. "Sexy as fuck."

She grinned, crooking her finger. "Come here. Let me thank you."

"Mm. I like the sound of that," I said, kneeling between her legs.

She wrapped her arms around my neck, slanting her mouth over mine. I could taste the saltiness of her tears, I could taste her hopes, her dreams, her fears. They were the same as my own.

The kiss turned fevered as it always did. We were explosive, kinetic, communicating without words. She tugged on my shirt, and I took the cue, yanking it off from behind my neck. Her hands were on my skin, blazing a trail, making their mark. I fumbled with her leggings, eager to remove them, desperate to sink inside her.

"Fuck," I hissed when she reached into my pants and wrapped her hand around my cock. "Fuck, baby." I closed my eyes, leaning my head back.

"Feel good?" she asked, a smile in her voice as she stood, pulling me along with her. She knew damn well what she did to me.

"Yes." I placed my hand over hers, but she wouldn't be deterred. "But this wasn't—"

"Shh." She covered my mouth with hers, silencing my protests as she removed my pants. This was supposed to be about her. I was supposed to be making her feel good. But all I could think was how amazing her touch was.

"Sit." She pushed me down on the chair, and I stared up at her, a little dazed. I reached out for her, but she leaned forward, pressing on my forearms gently. "Don't move."

Her voice was stern, and it was a fucking turn-on to see this side of her. To watch her assert her confidence and power. To have her trust me.

I swallowed hard, my attention glued to the way she moved, with such grace. She spun around, revealing her back and taking her time as she removed her shirt then her bra, casting them aside before kneeling in front of me.

My cock jerked in her direction, clearly not one to follow instructions. I gripped the armrests of the chair, but the moment she started touching me, licking me from root to tip, I wound my fingers in the fine black silk of her hair.

She released me with a pop. "What did I tell you?"

"I *need* to touch you."

"Not yet." She smirked. "Not until I say so."

"Someone's awfully bossy," I teased.

She grinned. "This is my office. I'm the boss in here."

I chuckled, pressing my lips to hers. This girl was something else. And I loved her. Loved the strength of her spirit and the beauty of her heart. Cherished that I was a part of her past, reveled in the fact that I was part of her present, and hoped I would be her future.

"Baby..." I tucked a strand of hair behind her ear. "You're the boss of me everywhere." And then I let her take control because this woman owned me, heart, body, and soul.

❦

I STARED UP AT THE HOUSE AND TOOK A DEEP BREATH. I'D returned to LA to wrap up a few things relating to the Wolfe Group, but I'd also hoped to have the chance to talk to Ian. To convince him to reconcile with Sumner, even if he never wanted to speak to me again.

I walked up the path to the house, wiping my palms on my pants. Thanksgiving was a few days away, and I knew how much it would mean to Sumner to hear from her dad.

I rang the doorbell, and then, surprisingly, it opened. Ian glared at me, growling, "Go away," before slamming the door in my face.

"Ian." I banged my fist against it. "Ian. Come on, man. It's been two months. Give me a chance to explain."

It was quiet, so I waited. Hoping. And then I realized he

wasn't coming. So, I banged again. I'd given him time, but I'd had enough. Enough nights of Sumner crying herself to sleep. Enough days when we both avoided mentioning her dad and Lea for fear that we'd break.

"Please," I begged. "For Sumner."

Still nothing.

I sank down on the porch and remained there for a long time. When the sun started to dip lower in the sky, I finally resigned myself to the fact that he wasn't going to budge. I stood with a sigh and left.

The next day, I resolved to force him to see me. He was a creature of habit, and so I headed to a park where he played soccer in a league with some guys. I waited until after the game to get out of the car and approach. When Ian spotted me, he immediately turned and started walking away.

"I know you don't want to see me," I said with his back still turned. He paused, and I took that as a signal to continue. "But please...don't punish Sumner anymore. She's hurting. *We're* hurting her."

He clenched and unclenched his fists, and then he walked off without responding.

I hung my head, overcome with defeat. I didn't know what more I could do. I would give Sumner the world, but I couldn't give her the one thing she really wanted.

# CHAPTER TWENTY-NINE

## Sumner

"So...big plans for Thanksgiving?" I asked Piper, glancing at the phone screen as I placed it on the counter.

"Yeah. Well, the usual—dinner at my parents'."

I leaned my elbows on the counter, flipping through *Casa Beautiful,* a home design magazine Jonathan had left for me. He was obsessed with the house—he put a lot of thought into every detail, every decision. I was glad he seemed to be enjoying himself. And, hey, I wasn't going to complain. His taste was as gorgeous as it was expensive.

I tried to focus on the finishes instead of the fact that I wouldn't be spending the holidays with my parents. My mom was going to be on a yoga retreat—nothing new there. And Dad...well, he still wouldn't talk to me. Nor would Lea.

"But I'm bringing a date," Piper said.

That got my attention.

"A date. *Really?*" I stood, stretching out my arms. "You never bring a date to Thanksgiving. This must be serious."

"Nah." But her nonchalant tone couldn't fool me. They'd

been seeing each other exclusively for months, and I knew she liked him more than she let on.

"Mm-hmm. So, when do I get to meet this guy?"

"Soon. At least, if he survives my family."

I laughed. "Of course he'll survive your family. You guys are fun," I said, thinking back on holidays I'd spent with them. The drinking games, the laughter, the love.

"Sumner?" Piper asked, and I realized I'd zoned out on the conversation, my mind drifting to memories of Thanksgivings past. Of holidays spent with my family.

"Yeah?" I shook my head as if to clear it.

"I asked what you and Jonathan ended up deciding to do for the holiday."

"He's been in LA the past few days on business. But we're going to keep it low-key, grill some filet mignon and bake some pies."

"That sounds nice," she said.

"Yeah." Even I could hear the wistful note to my voice. "Yeah. I'm sure it will be."

"Tell me why you didn't take him up on the trip to the Caribbean again?"

I sighed. "I'm beginning to wonder myself. I guess I was just holding out hope that maybe my dad would magically change his mind or something."

"Still nothing?"

"Nope." I popped the "p."

I carried the phone with me as I grabbed some ingredients to start preparing dinner. My phone buzzed with an incoming call, and I glanced at the screen, expecting it to be Jonathan, not...

"Oh my god," I gasped, nearly dropping my phone and the onions and potatoes with it.

"What's wrong?" Piper asked.

"I, um—" I stared at the screen, wondering if I was imagining things. "I've got to go. It's Lea."

"Yes. Go. *Go!*"

I dropped the produce on the counter, an onion toppling onto the floor as I rushed to connect the call. "Hello?"

"Sumner?"

I felt as if I might jump out of my skin. Why was she calling? Was it just to say hello, or… *Oh god.*

"Lea? Is everything okay?" It came out with a whoosh of breath.

"Yes. Yeah. Do you have a minute?"

I exhaled, though my body remained coiled with tension. "Of course. I, um, did you get my messages?" After the blowup, I'd tried to call Lea several times to apologize. I rolled my eyes. Of course she'd gotten my messages. She'd obviously been avoiding me, and I couldn't blame her after what I'd done.

"Yes. Thank you. I wanted to call." She paused, then said, "I've wanted to call for a while."

*Why didn't you?* I nearly whispered but figured I already knew the answer. "I'm glad you did."

"I'm not going to lie—I was upset. I always thought we were so close, and I needed time to process everything that happened."

I nodded. "That's fair. And, again, I'm sorry for lying. Truly."

"Thanks. And I'm sorry too—for not being more supportive. I was blindsided, though I can't say I'm all that surprised."

I jerked my head back. "No?"

She laughed, and something eased in my chest. "You've always looked at Jonathan as if he hung the moon."

And here I thought I'd done a good job hiding my feelings for him.

"And now I've seen the way he looks at you too."

I nodded, my eyes filling with tears. "Thanks, Lea. Thank you for calling. I can't tell you how much this means to me."

"I love you, Sumner. You know that you've always been like a daughter to me. I know we aren't spending Thanksgiving together this year, but I'll be thinking about you."

"I'll be thinking about you too. I love you, Lea. And I'm so very grateful for you."

"Well, um, I have to get going. But I'll check in again soon. If that's okay," she added, a rare note of hesitancy in her tone.

"Yes, of course. I'd really like that."

"Good."

We were both silent, and I strained my ears, hoping my dad would ask to cut in on the conversation like he often did. Finally, I said, "Have a happy Thanksgiving, and tell Dad I love him."

"Bye, Sumner," she said without committing to anything.

Even so, I was still trying to wrap my head around the fact that she'd called. For the first time in months, I was hopeful.

After that, Lea and I settled into a routine of sorts. We'd spoken on the phone a number of times, mostly sticking to "safe" topics like school or fashion. She mentioned my dad, but he still hadn't spoken to Jonathan or me. I'd expected it would take him time, but I hadn't realized how painful waiting would be.

Still, communicating with Lea felt like progress. Like we were rebuilding a bridge. Since that first call, our relationship had mostly returned to normal. Well, a new normal where we dodged the topic of my dad or Jonathan.

"How were finals?" she asked.

"Good." I smiled, tucking the phone between my shoulder and my ear as I stirred the soup on the stove. "I worked my butt off, and I'm more than ready for a break."

"I bet. I'm sure you aced them, like always."

"Thanks. I hope so." I tapped the spoon against the pot before setting it on a dish next to the stove. "So...I'm hoping you're calling to tell me that you and Dad are coming for Christmas."

We'd invited my dad and Lea to celebrate Christmas with us in Palo Alto, and she'd been cagey for weeks.

She let out a sigh, and my shoulders slumped as I prepared myself for the bad news. "You aren't coming," I said, finally accepting that was the likely outcome.

"I'm sorry, Sum. I just don't know if it's a good time."

"I guess I really hoped if Dad saw us together, saw how happy we were—then maybe..."

"I'm trying. But you know how stubborn he can be."

I switched the phone to my other ear and wiped down the counter. Maybe love really didn't conquer all. I'd been naïve to think my dad would accept my relationship with Jonathan.

"Well, I appreciate it," I said, tossing the sponge in the sink. "And I'm sorry if you feel caught in the middle."

"Thanks. Look..." She was quiet a moment, and then her voice was softer. "Don't give up yet. I have a few more tricks up my sleeve."

I wasn't sure I wanted to know what her tricks involved, so I left it at, "Thanks, Lea. You're the best."

"I have to run, but I'll see you on the twenty-second, even if it's just a girls' trip."

I nodded before remembering she couldn't see me. "I'd like that."

We ended the call, and while I was grateful to have Lea in our corner, that didn't change the fact that my dad still hadn't called, hadn't texted or emailed since his birthday. Despite numerous attempts on my part—and Jonathan's—to reach out, my dad wouldn't respond. I was beginning to wonder if he ever would.

I knew he was hurt. But why couldn't he just give Jonathan and me a chance, especially since I was willing to forgive him for what he'd done?

As disappointed as I was, I reminded myself of all the things I had to be grateful for. I was pursuing my MBA and excited about the future. And I was building a house, a life, with the man of my dreams. A man who supported my dreams.

When I heard the hum of the air compressor from upstairs, I decided to go investigate. I pushed open the door to the future master bedroom and found Jonathan adjusting his safety glasses. I'd thought he was sexiest in a suit, but I'd been wrong. Watching his forearms flex as he built something for our home was so much hotter. I leaned against the doorframe and observed him for a minute before he realized I was standing there.

He removed his safety glasses and stepped over some boards to kiss my cheek. "Hey. I'm almost done in here."

"It's looking really good," I said, admiring the built-in shelves he was working on.

He rested his hands on his hips, surveying his hard work. "It feels good."

I grinned, filled with pride for this man. He'd seemed much happier, much lighter since selling the Wolfe Group. And while I knew the situation with my dad pained him, renovating our house helped.

"I just talked to Lea," I said. "She doesn't think they're going to make it for Christmas."

Jonathan ran a hand through his hair, which was damp with sweat. "I figured as much."

"I just hoped—" I started to tear up, and he pulled me into a hug.

"I know, baby."

"Ew. Gross," I teased, pushing him away. I didn't want to cry. Didn't want to dwell on this.

"Oh, come on." He stalked toward me, reaching out for me. "I don't smell that bad."

I laughed, backing my way toward the door. "Um. Yeah, you do. Go shower. Dinner's almost ready."

He grabbed me, pulling me against him with my back to his front. "I'd rather eat you."

My core quivered with anticipation. "Mm. I like the sound of that. How about we eat dinner, then you can have me for dessert?"

"Or…" He tugged on the hem of my shirt, lifting it over my head. "You could join me in the shower."

"I guess dinner can wait," I teased, knowing the soup could simmer a while longer.

We undressed each other slowly, and when I stepped into the shower, I was reminded of our time in New York. Water sprayed over my body, and he tracked my every move. And yet, this was nothing like that morning—when his touch was punishing and his eyes swirled with regret. He was tender now as he worshiped my body, whispering words of love as I fell apart in his arms.

A few days later, I was putting the finishing touches on one of Jonathan's presents when the doorbell rang. I furrowed my brow and headed to answer the door, figuring it was just another delivery. I peered through the peephole and shook my head, positive I was hallucinating.

I looked again. Shook my head. Then I opened the door. "Dad?"

There was no way he was just "in the area." Palo Alto was a five-hour-plus drive from LA in good conditions.

"Hey." He kept his eyes focused on the doormat, which was red with the word "Merry" printed in a cursive font.

I stood and gawked at him a moment before finally asking, "Do you want to come in?"

"Is he…" He glanced around, as if looking for someone. "Are you home alone?"

I nodded. "Jonathan had to run some errands." He winced when I said Jonathan's name. "Come in. I have coffee, tea, cookies, chips…" I rattled off the items, not sure what to do or say.

"Thanks." He stepped inside but didn't move to take off his jacket. "I won't stay long. But I was in the area for business, and I…" He cleared his throat, toed at the floor. "Nice floors."

"Dad," I sighed, laughing. Leave it to him to comment on the floors when we hadn't spoken in months. But it broke some of the tension, and I was so overcome with emotion that I leaped at him, giving him a tight squeeze around the middle. "I missed you."

He tensed briefly then sighed almost as if with relief and returned my embrace. "I missed you too, Sum."

When I pulled away, I had tears in my eyes and hope in my heart. "Come on," I said, linking my arm with his. "I'll give you a tour."

"I—" He hesitated. "I don't know."

I frowned. "Why not?"

He swallowed, glancing toward the ceiling. "I'm trying here, *really*. But I can't…" He shook his head and blew out a breath. "I'm not ready to see him," he ground out. "Or the bedroom you share."

I nodded. "Of course. Sorry. Um, well, what are you ready for?"

"I'm ready to talk to my daughter again."

I smiled, so incredibly happy and pleased by his words. It was a start. It was a new beginning, and that was all I needed.

"And I want to apologize for making decisions for you. As

well as for how I spoke to you the morning after my birthday," he continued. "I was shocked and hurt, and…I'm sorry."

I nodded. "I'm sorry too. I'm sorry that you feel betrayed. I'm sorry my decisions caused you pain and disappointment."

He shoved his hands in his pockets and rocked on his heels. "I should've been more understanding. You never judged me for my relationship with Lea, and I never thanked you for being supportive. Even when you had every right to be angry or disappointed with me for ending my marriage to your mom."

I nodded, appreciating his words. "Thank you."

We were quiet a moment, then he said, "You look good, Sum. Happy."

I smiled. "I am."

He turned for the door. "I should probably get going."

I frowned, wishing he'd stay. He'd only just arrived, and I wasn't ready to say goodbye. "I know you said you need to take it slow, but we'd love for you to stay for dinner. I know Jonathan misses you too."

He hesitated a moment, some emotion passing through his eyes before he said, "Maybe another time."

My shoulders slumped, but I reminded myself that this was a good thing. It was a start. My dad had opened the door to communicating, and I only hoped it would get better from here. We hugged, and then he said, "I'm proud of you, Sumner. I'm proud of you for having the guts to go after what you want. To seize happiness and love even in the most unexpected places."

My eyes stung as he released me. "Thank you."

"Merry Christmas, kiddo."

"Thanks, Dad. Merry Christmas to you too."

I closed the door behind him and watched as he backed out of the driveway in a rental car. I stared after him, still reeling from the exchange. I was so distracted I didn't hear the door from the garage open or footsteps approach. When Jonathan placed a hand on my shoulder, I startled.

"Hey." He frowned. "Everything okay?"

I shook my head and turned away from the street. "Yeah." I smiled. "Everything is going to be okay."

He tilted his head. "You seem really...I don't know. Calm."

I laughed. "My dad stopped by."

He jerked his head back. "What? When?"

I nodded, fighting a smile. I gave him a quick rundown of our conversation, and with every word, I could see the tension drain from him. I felt it too. It was as if a huge weight had been lifted.

"That's great news." He smiled, picking me up and spinning me around the living room. He set me down slowly, cupping my cheeks. "I love you, Sumner."

"I love you." I leaned up and pressed my lips to his, knowing with every beat of my heart that we belonged together. No matter the obstacles. No matter the pain. We were inevitable.

# CHAPTER THIRTY

*Jonathan*

*A Year Later*

"Jonathan," Sumner giggled, batting away my hands as I attempted to untie her robe. "We're going to be late."

"So what?" I kissed her neck, the marble of the hotel bathroom floor cool beneath my feet. "They'll give our table to someone else. And then I'll slip them a tip, and it'll be fine."

"No." She shook her head. "I've been looking forward to trying this place for months."

We were spending a few days in LA to attend Piper's engagement party and catch up with some friends before the holidays. Tonight, we were headed to dinner with Lea, and I was looking forward to brunch tomorrow with Alexis and her family.

"Can't I have one little taste? Please?"

She narrowed her eyes at me, and I knew she meant business. But I could be *very* persuasive when I wanted to be.

"I'm serious, Jonathan." She wagged her finger at me,

backing away. "Besides, Lea's meeting us. And what if my dad decides to show?"

I scoffed. "Right. How many times have we invited him to join us as a group, and how many times has he taken us up on it?"

We both knew the answer—none. He still wouldn't speak to or acknowledge me, though Sumner claimed he didn't shy away from my name as much in conversation. I tried not to read too much into that. I knew Ian well enough to know the man could hold a grudge.

She dropped her head down between her shoulders. "I know, but I keep hoping."

"There's nothing wrong with that," I said, lifting her chin so her eyes met mine. "I just don't want you to be disappointed."

She nodded. "I hate this. It's been over a year, and he still won't speak to you. Shouldn't he realize by now that we're together and that's not going to change?"

"Baby, I hate to say this, but Ian may never accept us."

"No." She shook her head. "No." Her tone was more adamant. "I refuse to accept that. If he can't even speak to you, well then, maybe I...*I* won't speak to him anymore."

"We're not going down that road again," I said, smoothing my hands over her shoulders. Ian and Sumner had rebuilt their relationship. But she was his daughter. I was... "Let's just be happy with the progress we've made."

She let out a deep sigh, and I wondered what it would take for Ian to forgive me, to move past this. Even though things had improved, I knew it still weighed on Sumner. Hell, it weighed on me. There were many times I'd pick up my phone to text him something or call with a question, but then I'd put it down, knowing he'd never answer.

We finished getting ready and headed for the restaurant. Sumner filled the silence with talk of her latest coaching client. She was one semester away from graduating, and I was so fucking proud of her. Not only was she going to graduate with honors, she didn't even need the degree. Her coaching business was killing it, and she'd already had to bring on an extra pair of hands to help with the workload. My old assistant, Cody, had been only too happy to join her team as her virtual assistant.

When we arrived at the restaurant, I handed the keys to the valet and then placed my hand on Sumner's lower back. The hostess led us to the table, and I faltered when I saw Ian sitting there with Lea, his arm resting on the back of her chair. My mouth went slack, and I felt a sudden need to sit down.

Sumner gasped, turning to glance at me. "Oh my god. He actually came."

"You didn't know?" I asked.

"No." She shook her head. "I... Wow. Hi, Dad." Her smile was brilliant.

He stood and gave her a hug, and I watched as if in a daze. Was I imagining things?

Lea snapped me out of it, giving me a hug in greeting before saying hello to Sumner. While they embraced, Lea whispered something in Sumner's ear. Ian and I stared at each other, and I didn't know what to do or how to approach him. After all this time, after all these years of friendship, it felt as if I were looking into the eyes of a stranger.

And yet, it was as if no time had passed at all. As if we were both fifteen again, young and dumb, and the best of friends. I felt it all in that moment—the joy of the past, the pain of the present, and uncertainty for the future. Suddenly, it seemed as if a lot hinged on tonight. On this moment.

"Jonathan," Ian said, finally extending his hand.

"Ian." I shook his hand, a silent tension settling over the

group like a blanket. Lea and Sumner watching, holding their breath.

"I'm so glad you could join us, Dad," Sumner said, turning to him. "And I see you've met my date."

I couldn't help myself; I laughed. *A date?* Was that how she was going to play this? When she glanced back at me with an encouraging smile, I figured she'd given me an opening. I could work with that. Even Ian seemed amused.

Ian and I were mostly silent throughout the meal, and I was grateful that Lea and Sumner seemed more than willing to make conversation for the table. Occasionally, one of them would address Ian or me, but otherwise, we kept to ourselves. Even so, I could feel his eyes on me, on us, watching, assessing, judging Sumner and me.

I barely ate, gulping down some wine in the hopes that it would calm my nerves. It was odd—sitting across from him, years of history behind us. Yet the gulf between us had never seemed so wide.

"So…" He leaned back in his chair. Sumner and Lea had excused themselves to the restroom, and I assumed it was mostly a pretense to force Ian and me to talk.

I took a deep breath. "So…"

He sucked in a breath then blew it out, his cheeks puffing. It was good to know I wasn't the only one struggling here. "How have you been?"

I debated my response but ultimately settled on honesty. "Good. Better than good."

"That's what Lea tells me. Still happy you sold your company?"

"No regrets."

He tilted his head to the side, mouth drawn. "None?"

"Well, I do regret what happened between us," I said. "You've been my best friend, my brother, for years. This past year without you…" I shook my head. "Well, I've missed you."

"And Sumner?" he asked, giving away no clue as to his own feelings.

"She missed you too. I'm glad you guys were able to put your issues aside."

"Our issues?" He chuckled, though it was without humor. "I think you mean 'issue.' *You're* the issue," he ground out.

I gripped my thighs, trying to keep my temper in check. I'd braced myself for this all evening, and I should've known he was playing nice until we were alone. But he'd come to dinner—that had to count for something. And I wasn't going to waste this opportunity.

"I know you don't want to hear this, but I love Sumner. And she loves me. We've built an incredible life together, and I know she'd love for you to be a part of it. So would I."

"So this is serious—the two of you? It's not just a midlife crisis?"

I laughed. *How did he not realize that by now?*

"One day, I'm going to ask her to marry me. Not now," I added, when Ian pulled a face. "But I'm not going to wait forever either. I want your support. She'll want your blessing."

"You're really laying all your cards on the table, aren't you?"

"You know me. When I want something, I go after it."

"True." He leaned back in his chair, a smile on his face. "God, I remember that time you wanted Jimmy Bishop's Discman CD player. You were so determined."

I laughed, remembering it well. "That was a big deal back then. You know why I really wanted it, right?"

"So Crystal would think you were cool enough to date?"

I shook my head. "For you."

"For me?" He furrowed his brow.

"Yeah. I knew how much you loved music, even then. A guy like Jimmy didn't appreciate it. He was a spoiled little shit who wanted to flaunt his parents' wealth. But you...you were obsessed with bands and music."

His expression softened. "But then my parents gave me a portable CD player for my birthday." I nodded. We both knew I'd given Jimmy's to Crystal, though Ian never knew the true reason. "I never realized. You did that for me? Why?"

"Because you're my best friend. I would've given you anything I had."

His eyes clouded, his expression hardening. "And yet you took my daughter."

"I didn't..." I sighed, pinching the bridge of my nose. "I'm sorry that loving her cost me your friendship. I am. But I do love her. Against all the odds, despite all the reasons we shouldn't be together, I'm crazy about her. And that will never change."

I didn't know what more I could say. I'd apologized. I'd made my position clear. It was up to Ian now—either he accepted us and moved on, or he didn't.

"I can see that," he finally said. "And despite my reservations, you're good for her. You're good for each other." I blinked a few times, certain I'd misheard. He chuckled. "Doesn't mean it's not still weird for me to see you two together. But..." He sighed. "I'll try—for Sumner."

"For Sumner." I nodded, swallowing down the lump that had suddenly formed in my throat at his words and her approach.

"So," Lea said, joining us with a smile. "Did we miss anything?"

Sumner placed her hand on my shoulder, and I placed mine over hers, smiling up at her. She seemed to relax, as did I. And when she took her place at the table, I felt a sense of peace, of rightness that I hadn't felt in a long time.

"I was just going to ask Jonathan if he wanted to play a

game of basketball tomorrow," Ian said, shocking the hell out of me.

Sumner flashed me a watery smile, squeezing my thigh beneath the table. "Success?" she mouthed.

I nodded. The evening had definitely been a success, and the reminder of that word brought a smile to my lips, the memory of our first coaching session coming to mind. At the time, I'd had no clue what success meant to me. I just knew how unhappy I was. So much had changed since then—and all because of this woman. Because she made me want to be a better man, not just for myself, but for her.

I leaned over to whisper in her ear. "I love you."

She turned to me, cupping my cheek in her hand. "I love you too." She pressed her lips to mine, and I lost myself for a moment.

When she pulled away, Lea was smiling, and Ian—well, at least he wasn't frowning. I took it as a good sign that he hadn't walked out or tried to punch me.

As conversation resumed, I settled back, my arm resting on the back of Sumner's chair. If Sumner had asked me to define success again today, I wouldn't have listed the millions in my bank account or even the home I'd rebuilt using my own two hands. No, true happiness and fulfillment could only be found in the love of a good woman. Like the one at my side. And success had never tasted so sweet.

# CHAPTER THIRTY-ONE

*Summer*

*Six Months Later*

"I'm so proud of you," Dad said, pulling me in for a hug.

A gust of wind nearly took my mortarboard off, and I grabbed it, holding it to my head as my cardinal-red graduation gown fluttered about my legs. Students and their families congregated nearby, everyone laughing and congratulating each other in a sea of red.

I'd skipped my graduation ceremony at MIT, so it hadn't taken much for Jonathan to convince me to attend this one. I'd worked too long and too hard not to celebrate. But it wasn't just the classes I'd taken or the exams I'd passed; it was the thought work I'd done.

I no longer hesitated to speak my mind, to stand my ground. And I'd discovered something interesting—the more I enforced my boundaries, the more people respected both them and me. All along, I'd been afraid of alienating the people I loved. But by being honest about who I was and what I needed, it encouraged them to do the same. To be vulnerable. And my relationships—with family and friends—had never been stronger.

Jonathan stood off to the side, hands in his pockets. I hadn't seen him since this morning, when he'd left to play basketball with my dad and Piper's fiancé, Mason. His gray pinstripe suit hearkened back to his days at the Wolfe Group, when I'd been his intern. It seemed like so long ago, even though it had only been two years. But so much had changed since then.

"I got some great pictures," Piper said, Mason next to her. "Thanks."

"Hey, baby." Jonathan pulled me into his side, less reticent about showing affection in front of my dad. "You ready to go?"

I nodded. "I'm hungry."

"Me too," Piper said.

"Good." Lea smiled. "Because we have tons of food back at the house."

"Uh oh." I laughed. "What did you do?"

"You said we could celebrate."

"I said we could have a *small* celebration."

"Come on," Jonathan said, wrapping his arm around me as we walked toward the parking lot.

Dad and Lea waved and climbed into their rental car with Piper and Mason, while Jonathan opened the passenger door of his truck for me. I removed my cap and tossed it in the back seat before unzipping my gown and doing the same.

"Fuuuck," he all but moaned, sending a bolt of desire straight to my core. He gripped my hips, and I could feel the heat emanating from him.

I bit back a smile and slowly spun to face him. Piper had given me the dress as a graduation gift. When I'd pulled it out of the box, I'd been hesitant. I mean, a white bodycon dress?

But I should've known better than to doubt her. It looked amazing on, and it was surprisingly comfortable for such a formfitting dress. I loved the neckline—notched just enough so it gave a peek of my cleavage without revealing too much. And the same for the slit up the front—sexy yet sophisticated.

We'd spent the morning getting ready together, and it had been nice to catch up and talk about her wedding plans while she did my hair and makeup. In a few months, she'd be the one getting ready for her big day.

Jonathan backed me against the truck, his eyes pooling with desire. "Baby. Are you trying to kill me?"

"No." I laughed, resting my hands on his lapels. "Is it too much?"

"Too much?" he choked. "Can we skip the party?"

I rolled my eyes. "No, we cannot skip the party. I'm the guest of honor, and it's at our house."

"Okay, then…" He ran his nose along my cheek until his lips were resting beside my ear. "Back of my truck."

I shivered from his words and his hard-on pressing into me. It was tempting. We hadn't had much alone time the past few days between all our guests.

"It wouldn't be the first time."

He inhaled deeply and let it out slowly. "No." He released me. "No. This is your big day, and we're going to celebrate."

I was impressed by his restraint but couldn't help laughing when he adjusted himself. "Okay," I said with mock-seriousness.

"Climb in." He gestured toward the passenger seat. "Before I change my mind."

I shook my head and placed a foot on the step before I felt his hand sliding up my inner thigh. My core clenched, and I let out a little gasp. "Jonathan."

"Yes. Right." He removed his hand, and my body ached for his touch. "But damn, baby."

"Later." I patted his chest and climbed into my seat. "You can do whatever you want to me later."

He swallowed hard, eyes darkening. "Promise?"

"Yes," I said and pulled the door shut before he could change his mind.

He was quiet on the ride home, oddly so. "You okay?" I asked, a country song playing in the background.

It was about a dad and a daughter, and I tried not to pay too much attention to the words for fear I'd cry. It was so sweet, and it made me think of my relationship with my dad. Despite all that we'd been through, we were stronger than ever. I got the feeling it was still weird for him to see Jonathan and me together, but I hoped with time that would continue to lessen.

"I'm great." He grabbed my hand and pulled it to his mouth for a kiss. "This is a big day."

I nodded. "I'm so glad everyone could come to celebrate."

"Me too," he said and pulled into the driveway of our home. A "Sold" sign was in the yard, and we'd be packing up and moving back to LA in a few weeks.

He'd done an amazing job renovating the house, but we'd always known it was temporary. I was looking forward to being able to hang out with Piper more often. And to resume weekly family meals with my dad and Lea.

I didn't see Dad's rental car, and I assumed maybe he'd parked it down the street. But when we walked into the house, it was empty. A big "Congrats" banner hung over the fireplace, and balloons were scattered throughout, fresh flowers on nearly every surface.

"Where is everyone?" I asked, glancing around.

"Maybe they got caught in traffic," Jonathan said, though he didn't seem surprised.

I grabbed a few crackers from the plate, careful to rearrange the remaining ones. When I turned around,

Jonathan was right behind me. And I jumped, holding a hand to my chest as if to calm my racing heart.

"Holy shit. You startled me."

He chuckled, but then took a deep breath. "Sumner." His tone was serious when he spoke, ominously so.

"Jonathan," I said, attempting to mimic him.

He smiled, seeming to relax some, though his shoulders remained tight. "All my happiest memories involve you."

I cupped his cheek, smiling. "Mine too."

"You once asked me if I believed in soul mates. In the idea that there's one person for each of us."

I nodded, wondering where he was going with this.

"At the time, you teased me for being a cautious romantic. But since then, since we've been together, I've realized that there's no one else I want to be with. You are *it* for me. You're my one and only."

He knelt to the ground, and I stared at him, mouth agape. "What are you…"

He produced a box from his pocket and opened it, the diamond sparkling against the red velvet. "Sumner, I love you, and I want to spend the rest of my life making memories with you. Will you marry me?"

"Are you kidding?" I could barely wait for him to put the ring on my finger before I jumped into his arms and covered him in kisses. "Yes. Yes, of course, I'll marry you. I love you so much."

He chuckled, holding me tight. "I love you."

When he buried his head in the crook of my neck, I whispered, "Is this a dream?"

"No, baby. We're getting married." He set me down gently, and I righted my dress.

I peered up at him with tears in my eyes and so much love in my heart. "I can't wait to spend the rest of my life making memories with you."

"Congratulations," Dad said, and I whipped my head around to find him walking into the living room along with Lea, Piper, and Mason. My eyes were focused on Dad, trying to gauge his reaction. Had he known about this?

Piper gave me a huge hug. "I'm so happy for you!" She held my hands, evaluating me. "And that dress looks killer. Your hair and makeup photographed beautifully."

"Wait," I paused. "Did you know he was going to propose?"

"Maybe." She bit back a grin, looping her arm over my shoulder as Lea popped the cork on some champagne.

"Did everyone know?" I glanced around at their faces, and they nodded.

"Any other surprises I should know about?" I teased, accepting a flute of champagne from Lea.

She butted my shoulder with hers. "Not that I'm aware of. Though I did talk to Juliana Wright—the event planner from your dad's forty-fifth birthday. She'd be honored to help you plan your wedding."

I laughed. "Wow, Lea. You're on the ball."

"Just excited for you, honey." She gave me a hug, and warmth spread through my limbs. I couldn't believe it. I was going to be Jonathan's wife. And my dad...my dad actually seemed happy about it.

Jonathan placed his hand on my lower back and spoke in a low voice. "At least we already have our song for the first dance."

I furrowed my brow. "We do?"

"'WAP,'" he whispered.

I laughed but shook my head. "We are *not* using that as the song for our first dance. I'd rather have a country song than that."

"Okay."

I groaned. "I was joking."

"Nope. You said it. I'm going to hold you to it," he teased.

Dad came over and shook Jonathan's hand. "Welcome to the family, officially."

I glanced between them, relieved that their friendship seemed stronger than ever.

"Is it weird that I'm going to be your son-in-law?" Jonathan asked, a smile curling his lips.

Dad chuckled. "Maybe a little, but I'm happy about it. You have my blessing, not that you need it."

My shoulders relaxed. Even though I knew he'd accepted our relationship long ago, it wasn't until this moment that I realized how much I still wanted his approval.

"So, you'll walk me down the aisle?" I asked.

Before Dad could answer, Jonathan asked, "How are you going to be my best man if you're walking Sumner down the aisle?"

We all laughed, but Dad said, "It's okay. I'm sure I can do both. I'm just glad to be a part of your special day."

Dad raised his glass to toast, and everyone followed suit. "To Jonathan and Sumner. Cheers to love, laughter, and happily ever after."

I smiled and took a sip of my champagne. It was a happily ever after, indeed.

# Acknowledgments

This couple...gah. Wolfe was little more than a footnote of a character, mentioned briefly in *Unexpected* and *Unpredictable*. But in my mind he was so much bigger than that—so much more consuming.

I wanted to write him. I *needed* to write him. And I finally got the chance with the *I Have Lived and I Have Loved* charity anthology. I was honored to collaborate with so many incredible authors to raise funds for the Thousand Lives charity by Willow Winters. If you haven't checked out the charity, please do!

Anyway...the more time I spent with Sumner and Wolfe, the more I wanted to. And so, unable to let them go, I turned their short teaser of a story into full-length one.

I loved their push and pull, and I loved getting to explore the angst and ache that came with falling for someone you aren't supposed to. Maybe because it's so similar to my own real-life love story. More on that someday!

Thank you for reading *Inevitable.* I love writing for the pleasure of it, but seeing reader's reactions is definitely a highlight. To all the bloggers, bookstagrammers, and readers who get excited, who post about my stories, and who have shown me a sense of genuine community and support —thank you!

To all the authors who have been so kind and generous. Who have welcomed me into this community and answered so many questions. Not to mention all the authors who have joined me for Writer Wednesdays on IGTV. Talking to each and every one of you has been both fun and inspiring!

A big thank you to the Hartley's Hustlers and my Girl Gang (not just for girls!). You guys rock! I cannot possibly tell you how much your support means to me! I appreciate everything you do to promote my books and to encourage me throughout my writing journey.

To my editor, Lisa with Silently Correcting Your Grammar. I so appreciate your attention to detail, and your patience with my questions. You always go above and beyond and this time was no exception. Whew. This story was a bit of a doozy, but we got there in the end. Thank you for putting up with me and the major changes. For listening when I was struggling. For being a friend.

Thank you to LJ for designing such a gorgeous cover that really captures the feel of the story and characters.

Thank you Kirsten Kiki for being honest about, well, everything. You have helped me so much, and I'm so grateful for your advice and friendship.

Thank you to Ellen, as always. Thank you for being so supportive and positive, for being a friend. And thank you for sharing your incredible eye for detail. Your comments are always priceless, and this book was no exception!

A huge thank you to Kristen for being such an amazing friend. I value your judgment and honesty, and I so appreciate your support. We've been through so much together, and I treasure your friendship and advice. Seriously, I cannot thank you enough for all that you do. You're always willing to read "just one more time," and I so appreciate it.

Thank you, Jade. You make me a stronger writer, and you challenge me on pacing. You are so clever and always provide great insight. I'm so grateful for your friendship, and our long chats!

Thank you to Brit! I love writing strong, badass female main characters, and you help ensure that they live up to their potential. And that the men who dare to love them do too.

A huge thank you to all my beta readers. Thank you for

making me a stronger writer, for offering your unique insight and advice. You each bring something different to the table, and I'm always amazed and impressed by your suggestions. I'm so incredibly honored to have you on my team!

Thank you to my husband for always encouraging me. For always supporting my dreams. You are better than any book boyfriend I could ever imagine. And to my daughter, for always putting a smile on my face. You are spirited and independent, and I wouldn't have it any other way. Dream big, my darling.

Thank you to my parents for always being so encouraging. For reading my books. For being my biggest fans!

Dear reader, if this list of people shows you anything, it's that dreams are often the effort of many. I'm grateful to have such an awesome team. And I'm honored that you've taken the time to read my words.

# About the Author

Jenna Hartley writes romance about strong women and the men who dare to love them. Her stories feature sexy, sweet, and laughable moments that reflect real love.

When she's not reading or writing, Jenna is chasing after her daughter or enjoying another episode of the Great British Bake Off with her husband. She lives in Texas with her family and loves nothing more than a good book and good chocolate.

www.authorjennahartley.com

## ALSO BY JENNA HARTLEY